D1168566

Mesozoic Murder

Mesozoic Murder

Christine Gentry

Poisoned Pen Press

Poisoned Pen Press

Poisoned Pen Press
6962 E. First Ave., Ste. 103
Scottsdale, AZ 85251
www.poisonedpenpress.com
info@poisonedpenpress.com

Printed in the United States of America

This one is for my mother,
Mary Jeanette Upcraft-Gentry

Acknowledgment

Thanks to the Bloody Pens Writing Group
from West Palm Beach, Florida. Tapping
a literary vein with all of you has been
the experience of a lifetime.

Chapter 1

"There is no death. Only a change of worlds."

Seattle, Squamish Chief

Ansel sinks into the water, far down near the bottom of the pond where the black mud and darkness pull at her with deadly fingers. Light from the ice hole above funnels down like a spotlight. She thrashes harder. Murky water, peppered with rotting debris, swirls around her. So cold. The pain of not breathing hurts. She can't hold her breath.

When she screams, a moaning sound and huge gurgling bubbles pour from her mouth. She inhales. The first swallow of frigid, foul-tasting water rushes over her tongue and into the back of her throat. Panic overwhelms her. She gulps madly for air that will never reach her tiny lungs. Then she begins to die. Slowly.

Ansel Phoenix jolted back to reality, gasping for breath. The crushing black water didn't exist. She was sitting on a metal stool in front of her drawing table, safe and sound in her office. Except that her heart pounded in her chest like a galloping horse.

Ansel's fingers clutched the edges of the drafting board, pressing crescent marks into the soft wood. Just a flashback, she reasoned. She could handle this. She'd been through these chronic anxiety attacks a hundred times.

Instinctively, Ansel reached her sweaty right hand toward the blue stone hanging from a leather cord around her neck. The cool, solid feel of the azurite pendant quelled her sense of panic. She caressed the natural star-shaped design on the sea urchin fossil with her fingertips. It had been her grandmother's childhood Iniskim.

Her mother, Mary Two Spots, had given her the lucky stone when she was five. After the accident. That's what they called the events of that winter day so long ago when she'd been clinically dead. But it wasn't an accident. Eight-year-old Rusty Flynn had taunted her, and then pushed her through an ice hole on the pond behind her house.

Ansel stared down at the large, colorful pen and ink drawing taped to the tabletop. A snaking thread of water was about to soak into the paper's upper edge.

"Damn."

She grabbed an old rag and quickly blotted up the liquid. A paper cup filled with rinse water for her brushes was leaking, and light reflecting off the liquid-silver trickle had set off an alarm in her head. The telephone on the bookcase rang. Ansel's arm jerked, nearly toppling the cup with her elbow.

"Double damn." Who would call her business line at six in the morning? She yanked up the receiver. "Phoenix Studios."

"Where is my Stegosaurus?"

Ansel flicked a strand of waist-long, black hair away from her still flushed face. "Dr. Andreasson?"

"Of course. I'm supposed to have your drawings by today."

Ansel swallowed. The editor of *Science Quest Magazine* had commissioned her to do five black and white renderings and one full-color cover spread for the December issue. Andreasson, a world-renowned paleontology scholar, needed to approve her drawings before they accompanied his dinosaur article.

"I'm finishing up the final color work. I'll mail the port-folio by Express Mail. It should arrive by noon tomorrow."

"I can't wait much longer. I have deadlines, my dear. You came highly recommended by Rodgers at Folsom Publishing. Don't disappoint me."

"I won't."

"I'll call after I look them over. Good-bye, Ms. Phoenix."

Ansel dropped the remote into its stand and groaned. She glanced at her wristwatch. She was running out of time. She was teaching a field seminar at ten.

She spent another hour on the finishing touches and gazed at the cover art with satisfaction. A green-brown Steggie stood munching on the succulent shoots of a Cycad palm and eyed a large Jurassic butterfly perched on a frond above. Nearby, a puddle of rainwater mirrored the images of the reptile and the butterfly.

The Steggie drawings incorporated three months of research and multitudes of rough anatomical sketches of Stego-saurus bones, ligaments, and skin into vibrant, three-dimensional creations. She had achieved a national reputation as an innovative paleoartist because of her ruthless attention to scientific detail coupled with dashes of artistic flair that filled in gaps of paleontological knowledge.

Ansel sealed the mailing package, addressed it, and left the renovated airplane hangar which now provided a roomy space for her commercial art business. She walked toward the trailer porch through an Alpine-like meadow burgeoning with colorful Indian paintbrush, beargrass, astors, colum-bines, and dogtooth violets. At one time the area had been a grass runway where the former owner, Marlin Valentine, had taxied his Bonanza six-seater.

"Okay. Everybody out."

Ansel balanced Andreasson's package on one arm and shooed two honeybees out the screen door. The Langstroth hive in the field adjacent to the hangar was a legacy from Valentine that vexed her to no end. All year long she tried to avoid confrontations with the fifty thousand insects that buzzed and dive-bombed across forty acres of property.

By eight thirty Ansel was driving along Highway 13 toward town and savoring her view of the slightly rolling terrain. This time of the year, the land ran riot with perennial plants, shelterbelt trees, and fragrant flowering bushes. Willows and cottonwoods towered over dense strands of service berries, Oregon grape, and kinnikinnick. The sky overhead was brilliant blue without a cloud in sight. Northeastern Montana was called the Big Open for a very good reason.

Grinning, Ansel drove past the huge billboard proclaiming "Welcome to Big Toe. The Dinosaur Capital of the World." The sign sported the cartoon caricature of an overweight, brown and green, three-horned dinosaur wearing a cowboy hat and six guns. Seeing the town mascot, Tilly the Torosaur, always made her day.

The town of Big Toe owed its existence to this little oasis growing amidst the monotony of the prairie. During the early eighteen hundreds, Sioux Indians had traveled here in search of curing plants and discovered the large, three-toed tracks etched into rocks along the Missouri River waterways.

The Indians had called the area *Sipa Tanka*, which meant "Big Toe," and so the town had acquired its name from a Mesozoic dinosaur wandering through the flood plains in search of aquatic plants. Today Big Toe was a tiny, but relatively prosperous community with a population of more than eight hundred merchants, cattle ranchers, wheat farmers, and a few native peoples.

Ansel parked the truck in a spot next to Dino-Mite Drugs and lugged Andreasson's package up to the pharmacy counter that doubled as a postal station.

"Hi, Mr. Tudor." Ever since she remembered, Wilson Tudor, a tall and distinguished-looking gentleman with gray hair and liquid-brown eyes, had manned this counter.

"I see you've been drawing again." Tudor smiled warmly as he grabbed label stampers and postal stickers from a counter also cluttered with prescription bottles and insurance printouts.

Ansel slid the box and prepared forms toward him. "This has to go Express Mail." She reached for her wallet.

Tudor worked quickly at tagging the box. "Your mother would be very proud of you, Ansel." She smiled her thanks as she paid. As he made change, Tudor asked, "Your family getting ready for the buffet?"

"Yes. It's going to be bigger and better then ever."

"That Road Kill Chili last year was the best I've ever eaten." He winked. "Don't tell Mrs. Tudor I said that."

"She won't hear it from me. See you there."

Relieved to be finished with the drawings, Ansel hoped Andreasson would be satisfied, and she'd get paid the second half of her contractual advance. She glanced at her watch. Nine thirty already.

Ansel jumped into the pickup and sped out of the parking lot, heading south on State Highway 200. If she pushed it, she could talk to Pitt and still reach the seminar site on time. When she finally gunned the pickup off the main highway and onto an eroded, gravel road leading to the farmhouse, she feared the axles would never survive the trip.

This land was radically different from Big Toe. Treeless, rolling shortgrass prairie mottled with green mudstone and red sandstone, underlaid with shale, surrounded her. Pockets of prickly pear, range grass, and honeysuckle eked out an existence in temporary dirt pockets accumulated by the wind. An intermittent breeze carried a pungent odor through the pickup's air conditioning vents and her nose wrinkled. Pitt operated a pig farm, and the air reeked of dung and urine.

Ansel passed through another barbed-wire fence and parked the truck. As she hopped from the cab, the sun beat down on her head with griddle-hot ultraviolet rays. On either side of her, huge pens filled with obese, black Montana pigs snorted and sprayed muck in all directions. A few porkers farted. The smell was horrendous, a methane factory on the hoof.

"Hey, Ma'am," called Feltus Pitt from beneath the visor of a dirt-laden cap brim that read *Pro-Plan*.

Ansel smiled as the welcome scent of spicy aftershave filled the air. "Hi, Mr. Pitt. I stopped by to tell you I'll be teaching a seminar near Cottonwood Creek this morning. Thanks for letting my field class explore for fossils. We don't often meet private landowners like you who will let freelance diggers excavate on their land. The Pangaea Society really appreciates your generosity."

Feltus let loose with a phlegm-popping chuckle and grinned from ear to ear. "No problem, Ma'am. Any old bones in my fields would just dry up and blow away if you don't take 'em. Can't see the sense of that. It's just hard for me to believe that one of those dinosaur critters could eat a pig whole. Now that would be something to see."

"Most of the bones we find come from vegetarian dinosaurs."

"You don't say." Feltus' sunburned face turned pensive, skin shifting into a wrinkled likeness of the eastern Badlands. "Hey, Ma'am. Have you done the spring inspection of your hive?"

Ansel moved toward the pickup. "Not yet."

"Not good to let the hive overwinter and go sour in the spring. Those bees will swarm. I'll check your hive any time."

"I'll think about it, Mr. Pitt. I've got to meet the kids. Talk to you later."

A short drive beyond the house, Ansel spotted Cottonwood Creek. The tools in the flatbed shifted forward with a scraping thump when she halted the truck near a rocky knoll. Outside the cab, she reached in and grabbed her black Stetson just as something fell across her right arm with a sinewy tickle. Her necklace cord lay in the dirt. How odd that the leather string had unknotted itself. The second she grabbed it, Ansel realized that the Iniskim was missing.

Alarmed, she frantically searched the ground for several minutes. When that yielded nothing, she looked inside the cab in case the amulet had fallen there. The charm was nowhere to be found. Tears of frustration flooded Ansel's eyes. She couldn't bear to lose it. A cold shiver skittered up her spine despite the prairie heat. Losing her lucky rock was a very bad omen.

The sound of grinding gears yanked Ansel's attention away. No time to fret over it. A van, a station wagon, and a compact car headed her way.

"I can't wait to begin," said Lydia Hodges. She was padded in khakis from head to foot and looked ready to single-handedly bag a live dinosaur while on safari. "I've wanted to hunt fossils ever since our last seminar."

Biology student Shane Roco looked down at his shirt, shorts, and white leather running shoes and scowled. "Well, nobody told me that we were going to be out in a rocky pig field. Why do they call this place Cottonwood Creek? There's no creek. And there aren't any trees."

"The creek dried up in the eighties," said Tim Shanks, pulling off his straw cowboy hat with feathered hatband and running one hand through his shaggy blond hair. "The cottonwoods just died." He replaced the headgear and flashed Ansel a smile, green eyes accenting the neon colors of his Hawaiian shirt. An expensive-looking 35mm camera hung from a strap around his neck.

Ansel watched the three familiar graduate students before her, silently assessing their behaviors in terms of dinosaurian characteristics. This mind game had amused her since her college days. As she studied toward her geology degree, she'd taken some elective classes in the Department of Fine Arts just for fun. She could always draw well, even as a child, and had spent many adolescent years sitting in her room doing pen and ink landscapes, nature studies, or portraits.

During the art classes she had realized that she liked to draw humongous, snaggle-toothed reptiles with attitude rather than petite human models with great orthodontia and stunted personalities. From that moment on her desire to be a paleoartist had bloomed into a full-blown passion.

In her mind's eye, Lydia was like a Panoplosaurus dinosaur: stout, non-threatening, social. Ansel likened Shane to Ornitholestes: a bird-like loner and hunter with a tendency to snap. She smiled as she gazed at Tim. He was the Deinonychus of the group: attractive-looking and social, quick, strong, and very good with his hands.

"We're standing at the southeast tip of a geological area known as the Hell Creek Formation, one of two Montana sites containing Cretaceous Period dinosaur fossils," Ansel began. "At one time all of Montana was an inland sea. Over millions of years, this sea retreated eastward, allowing sediments to accumulate in the shallow sea basins offshore. The bedrock here is mostly shale with a sandstone or mudstone covering, and it's perfect for finding fossilized dinosaur bones."

Ansel pointed behind her. "During the late Cretaceous, this field looked almost the same except there were streams running through it. These stream banks existed as heavily forested woodlands, but huge herds of Hadrosaurs roamed the open areas just like the buffalo herds of the eighteen hundreds. Carnivorous dinosaurs such as Allosaurus also hunted here."

Ansel pulled a pen and a battered red notebook from her rear pants pocket. "Today I want you to take your field notebooks and picks and survey the area looking for fossils. Remember, fossil hunting requires a keen power of observation. Focus your senses on detecting unnatural symmetries or characteristic fossil shapes and noticing differences in ground color and texture."

Shane sighed. "How are we supposed to do that?"

"Look in a systematic manner. Work the base of slopes and study the natural exposures. Examine the side light striking them. Turn over rock fragments. Get on your hands and knees if you have to. Use back lighting to prevent fossils from becoming translucent so you don't miss them altogether. And if you find something, let me know. All of us should see the fossil as you first found it."

Ansel glanced at each student. "Before I let you go, I want to tell you about the Beastly Buffet at my father's ranch. It's next Saturday. You're all invited."

"Isn't that where everyone brings a food dish made from a weird animal?" Lydia asked.

"That's right. The food is made from exotic animals, birds, fish, or other creatures. The weirder the better as long as it's not made from an endangered species."

"How do we get there?" asked Tim.

Ansel pulled small paper sheets from the back of her field book. "The driving directions are on these." She handed a flier to each student. "Now let's go fossil hunting."

Lydia and Shane wandered off in different directions, but Tim remained. "Miss Phoenix, I was wondering if I could talk to you sometime about the Montana State University. I know you went there. I just got my Master's in zoology, and I want to go there for my doctorate."

"That's wonderful, Tim. Sure, I'd be glad to discuss the university with you. We could meet at my art studio. I'm free Monday afternoon."

"Great. What time?"

"How about two o'clock?"

"Perfect."

"Give me your flier, and I'll write my address."

Tim passed the paper, and Ansel scribbled across it. "I'll see you then. You'd better get hunting or those two will find something first," she said with a grin.

Tim nodded and walked off. Ansel took a moment to write site information in her battered field notebook. Thoughts of her missing Iniskim invaded her mind. She'd have to go back to Pitt's homestead and search the ground.

Moments later Ansel closed the notebook and looked around. Lydia was staring into a gully. Shane probed the edge of an interesting rock outcropping, kicking at shale chips littering the prairie. Tim halted on the open grassland and snapped pictures of the terrain and of his fellow searchers.

Ansel loved fieldwork despite its demands as an exacting science, and she really wanted to convey the same sense of excitement and adventure to her students. It appeared that Shane and Tim didn't quite grasp the concept of making fascinating paleontological discoveries. Only Lydia was enjoying this excursion. The geology student had hopped into the gully and was examining the ground with fierce concentration.

As she walked toward Lydia, Ansel slid the journal into her pocket and pulled out a fossil hammer hanging from the tool belt around her waist. She reached the gully's edge and looked down. "Find anything interesting?"

Lydia brushed a curly lock of brown hair away from her perspiring brow. "I see something in this hole. I think it's a piece of gold, Ms. Phoenix."

"Let me take a look."

Ansel jumped into the three-foot-wide wash, then kneeled beside the opening. Natural erosion had loosened the dirt beneath a six-inch-long shale overhang. She could see the flash of gold metal a foot away. An unpleasantly sweet odor wafted outward.

"I see it, Lydia. Stand back." Ansel got to her feet.

"What are you going to do?"

"I'm going to open up the hole with my pick. This is wild prairie. I know people who've been bitten by poisonous snakes, badgers, and even black widow spiders because they weren't careful."

Ansel excavated the cavity, loose dirt falling easily away. She took several strikes at the rock overhang. Working the pick deeper into the gully wall, she finally exposed the mysterious object.

Lydia grimaced. "Shoot. It's just a pair of dirty, old glasses."

Ansel picked them up. The plastic lenses were scratched and dirt-smeared. The left lens had a spiderweb crack radiating from its center. Shane and Tim appeared above them.

"What's going on?" Shane demanded.

Ansel glanced up. "Nothing much. We've uncovered some eyeglasses."

Shane's face twisted into a smirk. "Great going, Lydia. Which dinosaur wore those?"

"Let's get back to fossil hunting," Ansel said, trying to avoid any conflict.

Tim started to walk away and then stopped. "Geesh. What's that smell?"

"Pigs," Shane shot back. "What do you think?"

The rancid odor Ansel smelled earlier had returned full bore. She noticed Lydia's straining effort to walk up the gully side. Her feet kept sinking deep into the loose soil. Curious, Ansel thought.

The wash had been dry since the March thaws, and it hadn't rained in months. The rest of the gully was bone dry and hard-packed. Despite the arid conditions, the flora around the gully flourished in the late June weather. A verdant growth of range grass and prickly pear had claimed most of the wash. Except for the area surrounding the hole. It formed a dead patch.

Ansel stared at the broken glasses. New glasses. And that foul odor of decay. Her head snapped upward.

"Lydia, get off that wall right now."

Lydia stopped abruptly. Loose dirt shifted beneath her. She began to slide as chert and rock debris gave way in an avalanche of loose ground. Ansel loped to her aid, reaching up a hand so the girl could grab it. She hauled Lydia onto firmer ground at the bottom of the gully.

"You all right?"

"Yeah, Ms. Phoenix."

"Well, he's not," said Shane. He stared down at the new depression above Ansel and Lydia.

The dust-laden head of a man had emerged in the center of the collapsed gully wall. His swollen, pitted, and hideously mottled blue-green face protruded through the sandstone grit and gave the disconcerting illusion of being cut from marbled stone. Two angry, feasting sand scorpions scuttled out from the dirt around his chin. The three-inch-long, yellow and black arachnids snapped their pincers and twirled in a disjointed dance of death.

"Oh, my God." Lydia threw her hands up to her face, shielding her senses from the sight and smell of the corpse.

Tim Shanks lifted his camera and clicked off a rapid succession of shots.

Ansel was too shocked to berate him. Her lungs sucked in rancid air while her mind tried to make sense of the hideous scene. The gold wire glasses. That face. Despite the disfiguring ravages of decay, she knew the man.

The glasses slipped from her fingers and fell with a thud next to the grave of her ex-lover.

Chapter 2

"Everything on the earth has a purpose.
Every disease an herb to cure it,
And every person a mission."

Mourning Dove, Salish

Lieutenant Reid Dorbandt stared at the male victim decomposing in the gully. He reached to scratch an itch on his nose with a latex-gloved hand. No use. He kept forgetting that he was wearing a painter's half-mask because it did very little to keep foul fumes from entering his nose and mouth.

Bacteria had ballooned and pitted the corpse's flesh inside the jeans and long-sleeved shirt. Resourceful sand scorpions had also done a bang-up job of cutting skin off the exposed parts of the victim's face, neck, and hands, while burrowing beetles had gone for the soft parts. The eyes and lips were almost completely gone.

Dorbandt shook his head. The last thing he needed this morning was a murder that had *America's Most Wanted* potential. His heartburn shot acid up into his throat like a .38 Special loaded with dum-dum bullets, and he was certain that his gray, three-piece suit would never lose the downwind stench of pig feces and rotting man-meat even after drycleaning. He sighed and focused his eyes on the suited Doc Tweedy.

As the witnesses had been escorted to the farm house, the firefighters had cleared the dirt and territorial scorpions away from the corpse so the associate medical examiner could move in. The silver-haired Tweedy was on his knees in the gully, carefully palpating the victim's head. He resembled a giant, bug-eyed fruit fly inspecting a melon at the grocery store. At least he got to wear a full-faced floater's mask, Dorbandt thought with envy.

A small Crime Scene Unit and one other detective had moved into action, too, collecting evidence samples, taking photographs or site measurements, and sketching everything. Later they would collect more forensic clues from the corpse with forceps and vacuums. Yellow crime scene tape isolated a fifty-foot square running parallel to the wash and across the bottom. EMTs waited to bag the body and transport it to the coroner's office.

Murders weren't common in Lacrosse County, and Dorbandt felt like the site had become a freaking petting zoo. The only element missing was the predatory howl of circling reporters. Upon his arrival, he had assigned two uniforms to contain the scene. So far the rookies had done a good job, but with news like this traveling over police bands, it wouldn't last long.

At last Doc Tweedy left the body, stepped over the tape, and tossed his mask onto the ground before gazing at Dorbandt. "He's dead."

"So my suspicions are confirmed." It never failed to irk Dorbandt that MEs appeared at homicides to proclaim the obvious so that the real investigative work could begin. What a cushy job. "What killed him?"

Tweedy snapped off his fluid-stained rubber gloves. Then he pushed them into a plastic bag for disposal in a bio-hazard container carried by the CSU. "You're not going to like it."

"I rarely do."

"I don't know for sure."

Dorbandt's eyebrows rose. "No kidding?"

"No kidding." Tweedy picked up his bag, floater's mask, and clipboard. "Let's move upwind. He stinks worse than sheep shit in July."

Tweedy walked toward his unmarked car, positioning the clipboard so he could sign the top sheet with a flourish, officially authorizing a post-mortem exam. They stopped twenty yards from the makeshift grave.

"Now where was I?"

Dorbandt pulled off his mask, snapping one ear painfully with the elastic strap. Except for the reek of pig, the air smelled better. "You don't know what killed him."

Tweedy nodded. "That's right, but I found an ante-mortem puncture on the back of his neck. Looks like a needle hole."

"Somebody gave him a shot?"

"Yeah. Might have been a sedative or a narcotic to get him out here without a fuss. Might have been something else altogether." Tweedy gazed back at the victim.

Dorbandt grimaced. "Shit. When you get that faraway stare, I know two and two won't add up to four. What's eating you?"

"He's got anterior and posterior post-mortem insect bites, but he's also got an inordinate number of ante-mortem lacerations and bruises on the head, shoulder blades, back, buttocks, and calves. His fingernails are badly torn, and the palms and elbows took a pummeling. These aren't defensive wounds, and they aren't the result of being beaten or dragged. They came from a sustained trauma. I think they're self-inflicted."

"You think the drug caused him to thrash around?"

"I can't be that specific. However, given this rocky terrain and his wounds, I do believe he suffered from convulsions or seizures. The toxicology screen will identify the drug."

"Not much to work with."

"Well, I know that he didn't have an easy death. Who is he?"

"According to one of the witnesses, his name is Nicholas Capos. He was a botanist from Glasgow. Married. No children."

"What a waste. Anything else you want to know?"

"How long has he been dead?"

"Hard to tell." Tweedy spoke with consideration. "More than a couple weeks. The weather's been cool so decomposition has slowed down, and there aren't a lot of bugs. Howdun will have to give you an approximate time of death after his autopsy."

Howdun was the deputy coroner. Since Sheriff Bucky Combs was also the elected county coroner and on a fishing vacation along the Kootenai River, Howdun had to fill in on this one. Dorbandt suspected Bucky would spit metal sutures when he learned how he'd missed doing the autopsy on one of the most gruesome homicides to pop up in years.

"Hokay. Thanks. One more thing, Doc. Have you got anything in your little black bag that cures heartburn? My stomach is killing me."

"Sorry. You been eating a lot of chocolate?"

"Yeah. I'm a chocoholic," Dorbandt admitted, thinking of the malted breakfast drink he had chugged down that morning.

Tweedy chuckled. "Chocolate's the worst thing for a weak esophageal sphincter. It has a chemical in it that relaxes the stomach valve. I've seen plenty of stiffs with a one-way valve that swings like a doggy door. Take it easy, Reid." The ME hobbled away.

"See you."

An acid burp propelled past Dorbandt's tonsils with nuclear intensity. That would teach him to share his gastrointestinal ills with a slice-and-dice man. Too much information. He slapped his notebook shut. He'd peruse the area and then get to the next pressing issue: interviewing witnesses.

From his shirt pocket, Dorbandt pulled a slip of paper which a deputy had handed him earlier. It contained preliminary information about the people who found Capos.

His eyes immediately locked on the first name. Anselette Phoenix.

No. It couldn't be. He had hoped his luck would change sometime today. Sure, Dorbandt ruminated, and black pigs could fly.

Ansel shifted uncomfortably in the wooden chair at Pitt's kitchen table and tried not to look overly nervous. After all, the detective introducing himself in a deep voice as Lieutenant Reid Dorbandt had to ask questions. The suited cop had nothing to do with the fact that her seat bore an unnerving likeness to a wooden electric chair. Lydia, Shane, and Tim had already been questioned and dismissed.

Three hours after finding the body it was her turn, and she felt sick to her stomach. Pitt's kitchen, though clean and orderly for a widower, smelled of greasy pork sausage. She was totally drained by disbelief, sadness, and worry. Losing her lucky stone had heralded more than just bad luck for herself. Who in the world would want Nick dead?

Dorbandt stared at her from his seat across the table. Ansel had seen that speculative gaze a hundred times. Her mixed Blackfoot heritage, evident in her high cheekbones, caramel skin, and raven hair, often evoked curiosity. Dorbandt was sizing her up, and she met his blue eyes without hesitation.

Ansel gave Dorbandt the once over, too. When standing, he looked over six feet. Early thirties with brown hair clipped into a short, squeaky-clean professional cut. He looked hot and tired. A brown holster strapped beneath his right shoulder told Ansel that he was a lefty. It was also a grim reminder of the seriousness of the situation.

Dorbandt fixed her with an unblinking stare. "Are you related to Chase Phoenix?"

Ansel tensed, surprised by Dorbandt's first question. "I'm his daughter. Do you know my father?"

"I've never met the guy. Just heard of him. He owns a big cattle ranch, doesn't he?"

"Yes. The Arrowhead. Who mentioned his name?"

"My supervisor. Captain Ed McKenzie."

"McKenzie is my father's friend?"

"I don't think so." A strange smile softened the edges of Dorbandt's square jaw line. "I didn't know he had a daughter."

"I went to college and worked out of state, but I've been back in Big Toe for two years."

Dorbandt pulled out a pen and leather pad. "I need to verify information. You don't mind if I make notes, do you?"

"No."

"You're Anselette Sarcee Phoenix. Home address is 77 Platte Road. Born December 14th, 1973?"

"Yes."

"What's your occupation?"

"I'm a freelance paleoartist doing fossil artwork for magazines, books, and museums."

"I'm curious. Where'd you go to school to learn all this?"

"Montana State University in Bozeman."

Dorbandt scribbled in his notebook. "Bozeman. Isn't that where that famous fossil hunter works? The guy who dug up all those dinosaur nests."

"Jack Horner?"

"Yeah. You ever meet him?"

"Yes. He's the curator of paleontology at the Museum of the Rockies. It's affiliated with the university."

"Hokay. What were you doing in Pitt's field this morning, Miss Phoenix?"

"I was conducting a field seminar in fossil hunting for the Pangaea Society. I'm the president."

"What does this society do?"

"We're a non-profit, community-based organization devoted to the study of fossils. We try to advance the state of the science, educate the public, and collect and identify fossil specimens."

"Can anyone join this society?"

"Yes. It's open to any interested amateurs or professionals. Even children."

Ansel continued to answer as Dorbandt's questions led her up to Lydia's discovery of the hole in the gully, and she began to shiver inside the stuffy little room. "Lydia saw something gold inside the hole. I saw it, too, but couldn't tell what it was so I used my pick hammer to open the entrance. There was an unpleasant smell."

Dorbandt looked at her with new intensity. "Go on."

"I found a pair of broken glasses."

"Then what happened?"

"Lydia walked up the side of the wash. The dirt kept moving under her. That's when I knew something was wrong."

"Why?"

"The smell got worse, and I noticed that the rest of the gully was hard-packed and choked with vegetation. I wondered about this barren patch above the hole. On my father's ranch we called circular, dead spots like that beef cakes."

"Why is that?"

"Because it's the spot where a cow dies and decomposes for a couple weeks. The body fat liquefies and leaches into the ground. This causes the soil to become so acid that nothing will grow there. The same happens if you bury a cow close to the surface. I realized it was a grave."

"How did you discover the body?"

"The dirt wall collapsed, and we saw Nick's face. I couldn't believe it. I still don't."

"You called 911?"

Ansel nodded. "I went back to my truck and used the cell phone. A sheriff's officer arrived twenty minutes later."

Changing tracks efficiently, Dorbandt asked, "You told this officer that Capos was a botanist. Do you know where he worked?"

" Yes. He worked at the Montana Monitoring Cooperative in Glasgow."

Dorbandt scribbled. "Did Capos belong to your society?"

"Yes. He was the vice president."

"How long was he a member?"

"About four years."

"And what was your relationship with Capos, Miss Phoenix?"

Ansel's mouth went dry. Now what she going to say? She'd only slept with Nick one night. He had simply caught her at a weak moment, and she'd been drinking. After that one lapse of good sense, they had returned to being just friends.

"I was a friend and colleague."

"When did you last see or talk to him?"

"About three weeks ago. At the last board meeting for society officers held at my workshop. June second. Eight to ten in the evening."

"How did Capos act?"

"What do you mean?"

"Was he unusually sad, excited, or angry about anything?"

"Perfectly normal as far as I can remember," Ansel said honestly.

"Did Capos have any problems with other members?"

Ansel tensed again. Police interview or not, she didn't like spreading gossip. She wanted to go home. Her stomach felt better, but a dull ache pounded in her left temple.

"Nick didn't get along with Dr. Cameron Bieselmore, but Cam isn't an easy person to deal with."

"Spell that last name for me, please." When she did, he asked, "What was the problem between them?"

"Cameron is the director of the Big Toe Natural History Museum. He hired Nick to design the plant displays surrounding some dinosaur models. Nick wanted to include some ideas in the dioramas Cameron didn't like. They argued, and Nick walked off the project. The delay cost a lot of extra time and money."

"When did this happen?"

"June of last year."

"Who else did Capos have a problem with?"

"I don't know. He rarely discussed his problems with me."

"And his wife's name is Karen?"

Karen. She hadn't thought much about her. What would she do now that Nick was dead? "That's right."

"How did he get along with her?"

"Not well. Nick left Karen about six months ago. He moved to Wolf Point."

"Capos' license says his home is in Glasgow. Is that where Karen still lives?"

Ansel suddenly felt a million miles away from the tiny kitchen. Talking about Nick made the reality of what happened begin to sink in. She wouldn't see him again. She'd never see his boyish, lopsided smile or hear him say her name. They would never again discuss the latest fossil finds or go hiking together. Damn it. Some monster worse than any prehistoric nightmare she could imagine had killed Nick. Ansel felt a deep, dark rage building inside her. Whoever killed Nick deserved to pay.

"Miss Phoenix?"

Ansel jerked to attention. "Yes?"

"Does his wife live in Glasgow?"

"Yes."

"Do you know Capos' Wolf Point address?"

"No. I've never been there."

Dorbandt pursed his lips before speaking again. "All right. I need you to give me a list with the names, addresses, and phone numbers of the society members as soon as possible."

"Sure. Give me your email address."

"My card." Dorbandt pulled a white rectangle from his notebook and pushed it across the table. "If you think of anything important regarding Capos, call me."

"I will." Her head was coming off at the shoulders. She really needed to eat something.

"I'll write up your statement and have you sign it. Then we'll get your fingerprints."

Ansel swallowed the lump in her throat. "Why?"

"Because you picked up those glasses. I want you to understand that this is an active homicide investigation. You are not to discuss anything you've seen or heard. Is that clear?" He fixed her with a stern gaze.

"Yes," Ansel replied, feeling swept helplessly along in a procedural eddy.

Dorbandt shut his notebook and pulled a white paper from a file folder on the table. He took several minutes quietly writing before looking up. "Please read this and make sure everything is correct. If you agree with it, sign at the bottom." He slid the paper toward her.

Ansel took the form and looked it over. It was riddled with police jargon. She signed anyway and pushed the sheet back.

The detective scribbled his name below hers. "Thank you." He got up and walked to the kitchen doorway. "Odie, I need you to get some prints from Miss Phoenix."

As Dorbandt withdrew into the kitchen, a huge, suited detective appeared. "Come this way, please."

He led Ansel through the living room. She passed Feltus Pitt and nodded a quick farewell in his direction. Feltus didn't look happy as he sat on a swayback sofa drinking a can of orange soda, his eyes as wide as a swine in a slaughterhouse. She felt awful for the pig farmer. What a horrible thing to happen on his property. There went the society's fossil hunting privileges.

After her fingerprints were taken, Ansel departed through the front door. She walked across the rickety farmhouse porch and down the wooden steps feeling shell-shocked. Only the smell and sound of thousands of keening pigs pierced her dazed senses. The odor didn't seem to affect anyone else.

Crime scene personnel used the house as their headquarters and milled around on the porch or ate lunch in the shade cast by larger vehicles. Drinks and deli sandwiches flowed like manna from heaven among the lethargic county employees.

Despite the stink swirling around her, Ansel's mouth watered. She watched with unabated lust as a short, balding fireman in tan overalls passed her taking large bites of a salami and cheese sub. Her stomach growled.

Ansel finally hopped into the scalding truck cab and surveyed the trampled yard. If her Iniskim had fallen off here, the chances of finding it in one piece looked hopeless. The blue stone had been mounted on a silver backing with a four-pronged clasp arrangement. Most likely it had been destroyed under the boot of some Lacrosse County drone. She whispered a foul curse beneath her breath.

Just as she started the Ford's engine, Lydia tapped on her driver's window, motioning wildly for her to roll it down. "Lydia, I thought you'd left. Are you all right?"

"Ms. Phoenix, I've got to talk to you."

"What about?"

"About this dead guy."

"Nick Capos? What about him?"

"I can't talk here."

"My email address is on the seminar outline." Ansel's head pounded. She felt gray cells dying with every passing second.

"I know. I need to talk to you by phone. What's your number?"

"Just a second." Ansel scrabbled through the junk thrown on the dash with black-smudged fingertips. Damn that ink. At last she found a beat-up business card and passed the sun-faded paper to Lydia.

"Thanks. Bye."

"Lydia," she called, but the student had spun away, disappearing within a mire of vehicles. What was that all about?

Ansel rolled up the window, set the air conditioning to arctic freeze, and began the spine-jarring trek down the washboard drive toward the main highway. A minute later she saw a ribbon of asphalt. She also spied a squad car, two deputies, and a white WBTV news van with a satellite dish on the roof. Her wildly thumping heart leaped into her stomach.

The press. Radio. Newspapers. Television.

What would happen to the Pangaea Society's plans to construct the Preston Opel Paleohistory Center when the media bombshell about Nick's murder hit the airwaves? The Pangaea Society was supposed to receive three hundred thousand dollars next week that would make the construction of the public visitor center possible. Three years of planning, community support, and financial finagling could be obliterated in an instant.

Ansel punched the accelerator, and the truck skimmed past the police and reporters. Once on the main road, she headed at warp speed toward Big Toe. She also reached for her trusty cell phone stashed in a cup holder on the center console. Her plans to eat lunch, take a quick shower, and grab a nap dissolved.

She had to call an emergency meeting of the society officers right away. Before the cow chip hit the fan.

Chapter 3

"Anger is something we can share, like food."

Lame Deer, Sioux

"Who would kill Nick?" asked Evelyn Benchley.

A moment of silence followed as every society officer in the art studio considered Nick Capos' untimely passing. Normally Ansel looked forward to these hangar meetings. This Sunday morning made an exception.

Ansel stared at the pit sofa partially hidden beneath an assortment of splayed newspapers bearing black and white photos of a fallen comrade. The images didn't do justice to Nick's patrician face. It was his ruddy Greek features that had attracted her from the moment she saw him.

"I don't know," Ansel replied, her voice echoing off the twenty-foot-high ceiling struts, "but no one deserves to die like that."

Leaning wearily against the microwave counter, she sipped a second cup of black coffee. She had yet to rebound from a horrible, sleepless night, spent swinging between sentimental reminiscences about Nick's life and shedding angry tears over his death.

Finally Ansel tore her gaze from the couch, bloodshot eyes glancing at the colorful, framed magazine covers, oil paintings, and limited edition prints which covered the walls. They represented her artistic milestones but provided no pleasure to her now. No comfort.

Dr. Cameron Bieselmore's surly voice fractured the uneasy silence. "Well, we can rule out the possibility that Nick read Leslie's new book and decided to end it all. Guilt by association."

Dr. Leslie Maze, editor of the monthly *Pangaean Times*, bolted upright from a recliner, his face twisted with indignation. The sudden forward movement from the scarecrow-like figure almost sent his horn-rimmed glasses flying.

"That's not funny. It's petty and vulgar. You've always been jealous of my success in the literary field. For your information, fifteen thousand copies of my new book have been sold, it's received rave reviews, and it's also being considered for a Newbery Award Medal nomination this year."

Ansel exhaled a long breath. Maze and Bieselmore sparred at every meeting, but the skirmishes had escalated along with Leslie's rising fame as author in residence. Leslie held a geology doctorate from Yale and an honorary doctorate in literature from Harvard. He was spending his retirement years writing children's books.

In an appropriately reptilian fashion, his latest hardcover, *Walk Your Dinosaur*, had leapfrogged up the young adult bookseller lists. The story about a lonely boy who photographed imaginary dinosaurs appealed to adults and kids alike. The factual prose about dinosaurs, computer-doctored photos of the boy's gigantic pets, and Leslie's witty humor had parlayed the book into a mega-winning jackpot.

"A Newbery? Why that's wonderful news," Evelyn said. "Congratulations, Leslie."

Leslie smiled. "Thank you, Evelyn. At least not everybody in this room is lacking civility."

"That was a nasty thing to say," Ansel agreed. "Show some respect, Cam."

Annoyed, Evelyn pushed a strand of platinum hair from her face, which made her flushed, blotchy-red complexion more evident as she stared sharply at Bieselmore.

"Ansel didn't call this meeting so you could hone your acerbic barbs on us. What happened is dreadful. Nick was held in high esteem by this society. He deserves our unconditional respect."

Ansel stared as well. She admired Evelyn for her distinguished work as a fossil preparator and for her ravishing good looks at the age of fifty-two. Time, geological or temporal, rarely affected Evelyn's appearance, and she could easily pass for a woman in her thirties. Except today.

The disheveled secretary slumped against the deep sofa cushions looking as if a Precambrian rock slab had fallen on her. Her aquamarine silk dress was wrinkled and her matching low-heel pumps badly scuffed. Ansel watched, fascinated, as Evelyn systematically chewed at her professionally manicured nails.

"First, I don't think a child's book is the meter by which I'd want to measure my life accomplishments," Cameron said. "Second, we all know that Nick didn't fit in with this society."

"What do you mean?" Ansel asked.

Cameron gave a wave of dismissal. "Come now. I think I speak for all of us when I say that we have devoted our lives to the study of ancient life forms because we want to increase our knowledge. We also hope to contribute something to the general pool of geohistorical data. Nick was a fair to middling botanist who wanted fame, fortune, and a free ride."

Leslie jumped to his feet. "You pompous ass. I bet you won't be so cocky when the police come knocking on your door. You hated Nick ever since you two fought over that museum diorama."

Cameron's face contorted. "Piss off, Leslie. My objection was valid. That diorama was a scientific re-creation of extinction scenarios. Nick wanted to incorporate ridiculous, pseudo-scientific theories that reduced the display into a sideshow exhibition. I had every right to fire him."

"Well, I think it's suspicious that you admit to being such the expert on how to make things extinct," Leslie parried.

Evelyn gasped. Cameron's mouth drooped. Ansel swallowed coffee and nearly choked.

"Are you suggesting I had something to do with Nick's murder?"

Leslie's smirk was wicked. "The police should know the details of your dispute."

"And maybe the authorities would like to know that you loaned Nick money. Maybe you got tired of waiting for your cold, hard cash, Leslie."

"Shut up, Cameron," Leslie said ominously. "For once in your life just shut up."

Ansel's eyebrows rose. She'd never heard that Nick borrowed money from Leslie. She set her coffee cup down next to the microwave. This had to stop.

"Enough arguing. Leslie, sit down. Cam, cool it. We're all upset, but that's no reason to take it out on each other."

Cameron capitulated first. He leaned back and set his lips into a grimace as rigid as plaster. When ashen-faced Leslie tottered to his seat, Ansel prayed he wouldn't have a stroke right on the spot.

"Let's get down to business," Ansel ordered. "We've got a major problem. The final funding for the paleohistory center is about to come through any day. It's essential that we forestall any negative publicity. We've gone through a lot in the last few years. First, purchasing the property near Elk Ridge. Second, having a former society member bequeath us the money so we could build on it."

The group was silent again. The National Park Service had sold them five acres of distressed land on the edge of a reserve which had once been used as a work/storage area for rangers. The twelve-by-sixty-foot metal Quonset had been abandoned for years and was badly deteriorated. Selling the land and the structure to the Pangaea Society as the building site for a proposed educational and visitor's center had been a relief to them.

When avid geologist and fossil hunter Preston Opel had died the year before, he had left a memorial gift of three hundred thousand dollars to the Pangaea Society for the building of a eight-thousand-square-foot building on the parcel. As president of the Lacrosse County Historical Society as well, Opel's concerns were for the proper storage of geohistorical archives and records, library collections, and curatorial work.

The only stipulations in his will were that the building be called the Preston Opel Paleohistory Center and that its initial organizational structure would be a partnership between the society and the Montana Museums Association. After its construction, the center would become an independent institution solely operated and managed by the Pangaea Society.

"My Lord," sputtered Bieselmore. "You don't think that the MMA board could get a retraction of the POP Center funds, do you?"

Ansel blew breath through her mouth. "No, I don't think they can do that, but they could refuse to fulfill Preston's requirements to be our endowment partners. If they back out on us because of bad publicity, it could take months or years sorting through the legal ramifications. We've got to decide what to tell the media. Since last night I've been plagued with calls from reporters trying to get a statement. Nick's death could create negative feedback for the society."

"I don't think that we should make any statements to the press," Evelyn insisted. "It doesn't matter what you say, Ansel. They blow your words out of proportion and, if they're not juicy enough, they dig around until they find something really rotten hidden away."

Ansel shook her head. "I don't think the ostrich technique will work. I think we should express our shock and grief over Nick's death and remain neutral on all other subjects. Stonewalling will cause the press to chase us even harder."

"Ansel's right," Cameron agreed."If the press can't reach you by phone, they'll show up on your doorstep. Before I drove over, Mary Kilpatrick from Channel Three was at the museum entrance, minicam crew in tow."

"You didn't tell her anything, did you?" Evelyn's anxiety made her snap.

"I never saw her. The landscaper told me she was there, and I stayed out of sight until she left. Luckily the area is fenced so she couldn't ambush me before opening hours. Like it or not, Nick's murder has made a sensational splash. We could all get cornered by Kilpatrick or somebody like her. Better to downplay the society's role in Nick's shenanigans than duck speculative potshots about our involvement with him."

"What shenanigans?" Leslie demanded.

All heads turned toward Bieselmore. Cameron calmly picked lint off his black, long-sleeved shirt. Ansel wondered if anybody had ever told the treasurer that his standard Stygian apparel made his bald head glow pinker and did nothing to hide his middle-aged paunch.

He sneered, "I'm not going to be called a pack-hauling equine with delusions of grandeur again, am I?"

"If you know something we don't, spit it out," Leslie challenged.

"All right. We all know Nick had trouble with his wife. I heard Karen is living with another man. Who knows what bad blood brewed there."

Leslie snorted. "That's gossip."

"On the contrary. It's a fact."

"Did Nick tell you this?"

"In a roundabout way. Obviously someone went to a lot of trouble to kill him and dump him in a pig field. Nick ticked somebody off. Don't you agree, Ansel?"

Caught off guard, Ansel stared into Cameron's squinty brown eyes, thinking it was no wonder people called him "Biesel the Weasel" behind his back. The first time she met Cameron, she'd pegged him as a Pachycephalosaurus: a dinosaur with a skinless and bony dome-like head studded with knobs and spines. The Latin translated into "thick-headed reptile."

"I don't know what to think."

Cameron frowned. "How can you not have an opinion? You found him. Which reminds me. You still haven't told us what happened at Pitt's farm."

"There's a police investigation so I can't talk about it. I can tell you that I emailed a membership roster to a detective yesterday afternoon."

Evelyn sat forward. "You're not serious?"

"Unfortunately I am. Detective Dorbandt requested the list. Now what about the press?"

"We must keep the society's reputation buffered from any association with Nick's personal life," Cameron implored.

Evelyn nodded in resignation. "I guess you're right, Ansel. We've got to tell the media something and, as president, you should do it. Make it short."

Ansel's blood pressure spiked. Evelyn had just pulled a slick transfer-of-responsibility maneuver. "I appreciate the vote of confidence, but I'd like a more equitable team effort."

"Nonsense," announced Leslie. "I concur with Evelyn. You have the most experience with the public and lay media."

How in the world did he figure that? Ansel looked at Cameron.

"I second that," the treasurer said heartily.

Ansel got the message. The fact that she had been elected by the membership for the two-year term as president automatically made her the fall guy when the ground gave way beneath the organization's feet. Another year and they couldn't look to her for instant answers or instant guilt.

"There's another matter," she added. "I think we should contact Karen and express the society's condolences. We should send a flower spray as soon as the funeral arrangements are announced, too. Everyone agree?" There were grunts of approval. "All right. I'll be in touch. Thanks for coming."

Evelyn slapped on a pair of sunglasses, said her farewells, and left in a flash. Leslie followed on her heels without saying another word. Only Cameron remained. Ansel moaned silently and walked to the coffee machine for a refill. She stalled as much as possible, quietly filling the cup and adding cream and sugar before speaking.

"What's up, Cam?"

"Do you know if Nick had a will?"

The unexpected topic caused her to gulp coffee and burn her tongue. So much for trying to evade his interrogation. "I have no idea. Why would you ask me?"

"You two spent a lot of time together. I wondered if he ever mentioned it."

She ignored his reference about being with Nick. "We never discussed inheritances. Where are you going with this?"

"I'd simply hate to see Nick's fossil collection go to that harpy Karen."

Ansel tried not to smile. According to Nick, Karen had never approved of his hobby and considered paleobotany an expensive, boring preoccupation with dirty, dead things. On the flip side, Nick's expertise about ancient plants and trees was legendary. She wondered if someone might have killed Nick for a fossil artifact in his possession. Then she had another thought.

"You're hoping Nick willed his collection to the society, aren't you?"

A dreamy look enveloped Cameron's face. "One can only wish. Even if Nick didn't have a will, maybe the society could purchase his collection inventory from Karen. I'd be more than willing to display it at the Big Toe Museum until the POP Center is built. We could use it to promote the Pangaea Society, too."

"First, we'll have to wait and see what happens with the murder investigation."

Bieselmore stood up. "I suppose so. Who do you think did it?"

"I have no idea."

Ansel walked toward the office door. Cameron stared at her, and she had the distinct impression he'd been hinting at something, but she couldn't figure out what the devil it was. Did Nick say something to Cameron about her? She decided to throw him a well-deserved curve.

"Speaking of ideas, where did you get the notion that Nick borrowed money from Leslie?"

Cameron's expression morphed into a cagey smile. "Leslie owed his annual dues. When I called him, he said he was short of cash because Nick borrowed money from him. It simply slipped out before he realized it."

"Listen," Ansel said, herding him toward the hangar exit, "let me handle the media and the museum association board. This will blow over. Until then, I expect us to stand united regarding Nick's positive contribution within the society."

Cameron smiled thinly. "In other words, keep my feelings to myself. Don't worry about me, Ansel. I have no intention of besmirching this organization for the likes of Nicholas Capos."

With those endearing words, he left the hangar. Ansel followed, hurrying toward the trailer. A quick check of her living room answering machine revealed five messages. Too early for Dr. Andreasson to call. The messages most likely had come from society members and the press. Or Lydia.

As Ansel stood there hesitating to play them, the phone rang. More reporters? Time to buckle down and make her first official statement. Ansel grabbed the receiver on the second ring.

"Hello?"

"Ansel Phoenix? This is Karen Capos."

Ansel hitched in a breath. Karen had always been Nick's invisible spouse. She'd never attended a weekend field party for members and family or attended a posh society fund raiser. And she certainly had never deigned to communicate with an Indian woman from Big Toe.

"Karen, I was just going to call you about—"

"I need to see you. Come to my house, and we'll talk."

Ansel sifted through her feelings before replying. Karen didn't seem the least distraught over her husband's murder. Disgust tempted her to deny Karen's demand on the spot, yet the possibility of finding out what she knew about Nick's activities during the last few months intrigued her more.

"How about tomorrow morning?"

"Fine. That's 1501 Aberdeen Avenue in Glasgow. Be here at nine."

"Karen, what's this about?"

The dial tone buzzed in Ansel's ear like an angry bee.

Chapter 4

"Women can help to turn the world right side up."

Wilma Mankiller, Cherokee

Ansel was preparing a lunch of tuna fish on rye with potato chips when the phone rang again. She abandoned the plate next to some kitchen counter bowls containing fossils percolating in cleaning fluids and bolted into the living room. Maybe it was Andreasson.

She'd already made statements to three newspaper journalists, dodging bullets concerning Nick's personal activities by playing dumb, and she fully expected Nancy Kilpatrick from WBTV to appear on her doorstep any minute. It was Pearl, her stepmother.

"Ansel, how are you?" she asked, concern lacing her voice. "Your father and I read about the Capos murder. You found him?"

Ansel's tense shoulder muscles relaxed a bit. "Hi, Pearl. Yes, I did, but I'm doing okay."

"Well, you don't sound too chipper. I can't imagine this happening near Big Toe. Is there anything we can do?"

"No. I would have called. I've just been busy with reporters. They're asking questions about Nick and the Pangaea Society."

"I'm sure the whole thing has been horrible for you. Your father is very worried about your well-being."

"It is horrible. One moment my students and I are looking for dinosaur bones, and the next minute we find a human grave. I recognized Nick even though he was in bad shape. It was quite a shock."

"You should have called us."

"I didn't feel like talking, Pearl. Especially after my round with the homicide detective."

"You were interrogated? Don't tell me the police think you had something to do with it."

"It's standard procedure. Do you know a sheriff's detective named Lieutenant Reid Dorbandt?"

"No. Why?"

"He asked about dad."

"What exactly?"

"He wanted to know if I was Chase Phoenix's daughter. He gave me a strange look. It was weird."

Pearl remained quiet for a moment. "Your father had a run-in with the sheriff's department a few years ago. You were in college."

"Did it involve Captain Ed McKenzie?"

"How did you know about him?"

"Dorbandt said McKenzie knew dad."

Pearl laughed. "That's an understatement. Your father looked into a murder case and stepped on some law enforcement feet. McKenzie was a toe. He'd roughed up Indians trying to get a confession. When Chase stepped in, McKenzie almost lost his job. The county cops still get prickly when the name Phoenix is mentioned."

"Really? Dad never said anything."

"It's ancient history, but you know how volatile tribal issues can be. Just don't let the bastards intimidate you."

"I won't. Something else happened. I lost my Iniskim."

Pearl clucked. "Oh, Ansel, you must be devastated. How did it happen?"

"I don't know, but when I got to the seminar site the cord fell off, and the pendant was gone. I've looked everywhere for it."

"It's a special stone. It'll turn up," Pearl insisted.

"I hope so. It came from Grandma's medicine bundle."

"I think you should spend a few nights at the ranch."

Ansel paced the living room, considering the offer. "I can't leave. Today I'm expecting a call from a client that I can't miss, and tomorrow I have an appointment in Glasgow. I'll see you at the buffet. We can talk then."

"I guess you know best. I met Nick Capos at last year's Beastly Buffet, remember?" Pearl spoke in a pleasant sing-song voice which her husband often joked was as smooth as a silkworm's rump. "Nick told me about his grandparents coming to the United States from Greece right before the Nazis invaded. He mentioned that his grandfather and his father, Isidoro, were glass blowers."

Ansel had totally forgotten about Nick's immigrant grandparents and how they had come to America in the 1940s, but Pearl had a mind like a bear trap. The woman could read or hear something and reiterate explicit details at any given moment. Pearl's comment also reminded her about Nick's small glass-art collection which he inherited upon his parents' death a few years before. Nick had learned some of the family glass blowing skills before going to college.

"Nick showed me his glass collection once," Ansel said. "His grandfather made vases and his father created large hand-blown spheres and paperweights. They were beautiful." Peeved, she wondered if Karen Capos would get all of that priceless art glass as well as Nick's fossils.

"Nick seemed like a very nice person. And so devilishly handsome. What a tragedy."

Tears stung the corners of Ansel's brown eyes. "It's all so unreal."

"I wish your father could talk to you, but he's out rounding up bulls in the east pasture. I just had to call. I'm so happy you're coming to the party."

Ansel brightened. "Absolutely."

"Are you still going to bring a dish?"

"Of course. I've made arrangements to have it delivered it to the ranch that morning. It's called crow gut."

"Sounds interesting. How many crows does the recipe take?"

Ansel laughed. "Crow gut isn't made from crows. It's an old Blackfoot delicacy made with the large intestine of an elk or moose turned inside out and filled with meat and vegetables. Then the whole thing is roasted, cut up, and served."

"Marvelous. None of the other guests will have that recipe."

"How are your party preparations coming?"

Pearl sighed. "Slow. Which reminds me, I've got to trot. A man from the party store is coming to tell me how many tents I need."

"Tell Dad I love him."

"I will. If you need anything don't hesitate to call."

"I won't. Bye, Pearl."

As soon as the remote hit the stand, the phone chirped again. Ansel looked with longing at her sandwich and chips, but the phone trilled insistently.

"Hello?"

"Doctor Andreasson, Ansel."

"Yes. Hello. Did you get my drawings?"

"That's why I'm calling. I've looked them over, and they're wonderful."

His evident excitement was infectious and Ansel's spirits lifted. "I'm glad you're pleased. You're sure that you don't want any corrections?" She hated asking, but the last thing she needed was Andreasson finding something wrong after the deadline to go to press had passed.

"I'm sure. The four black and white anatomical drawings are quite accurate and well rendered, but the full color cover art is exceptional. You've caught the spirit of a thirty-foot-long Stegosaurus magnificently. You've certainly breathed new life into the old 'roof lizard.'"

"Thank you." She was elated to have pleased the fussy paleontologist.

"I'm going to call Rodgers and tell him the news. I'm also recommending your talents to my colleagues. I'll send these on to Folsom Publishing. Talk to you later."

"Good-bye, Dr. Andreasson."

A knock reverberated on the front door and Ansel jumped. Her nerves *were* on edge. "Coming," she called. The pounding got louder. Did they have to break the door down, for Pete's sake?

Wide-eyed and disheveled, Lydia Hodges stood on the concrete stoop. Frizzled, brown ponytail hairs had escaped around her ears and damp forehead.

"Lydia, what are you doing here?"

"I just had to see you, Ms. Phoenix."

"No problem. Come in."

Lydia rushed into the mobile home. Before Ansel could close the door, Lydia started chattering. "I just can't believe we found that man. It's like a bad dream. I wish I could relive that day and not go to the seminar at all. You know, oversleep or feel sick so I can't show up? All this stress is making my zits absolutely explode."

"Lydia, you're rambling. Calm down. Have a seat. Want something to eat or drink?"

Lydia's face relaxed as she flopped into a rocking chair positioned in front of the bay window. "Sure. Thank you. I'll have a rum and coke."

Ansel's eyebrows lifted. She had a sandwich and soda in mind when she'd made the offer, but what did it matter? The girl was over twenty-one.

Ansel walked into the kitchen. She found an ancient bottle of rum and pulled it out. Did rum go bad or just get better with age? She fixed the mixed drink and grabbed herself a beer from the fridge. She also wrangled up a bag of pretzel sticks and her orphaned lunch plate.

"Here, Lydia. This should help." She placed the foodstuffs on a round glass coffee table, then passed over the drink. "What did you want to tell me yesterday?"

Lydia chugged a third of her drink, and then gave a deep, heaving sigh to steady herself. "I know something about that dead guy Capos."

Ansel stopped in mid-chomp. This was the last thing she expected. "What?"

"First, I have to explain some things," Lydia began with determination. "You know I take classes at Bowie College, but I also work part-time at the campus bookstore. I work Monday, Wednesday, and Friday nights. Three to nine. Last month when I was on break, I went outside to use a pay phone. I called my mother. She was expecting me home after work, but I'd promised to stop by my girlfriend's house to help her work on a term paper. Do you know Cindy Lansing?"

"Nope," Ansel answered, nipping a quick bite of sandwich.

"Oh. Well, Cindy's working on her master's in psychology. She has to do this dissertation on abnormal behavior, but she can't write well. You'd think somebody who's gone through twenty years of schooling could make reports, wouldn't you?" Lydia stared at Ansel.

"You'd think so. Did Cindy know Nick Capos?"

"Cindy? No."

"Did your mother know him?"

Lydia swallowed another third of her mixed drink. "Of course not."

"Well, I'm lost," Ansel said in frustration. "Just tell me about Nick."

"Okay. When we found that body, I didn't recognize Capos because he was all puffed up and gross, but after that cop showed me his driver's license, I nearly blew my cool. Capos used another pay phone while I talked to my mother that night. I didn't tell the police about it."

"Why not?"

"Because I was too scared. Capos was yelling on the phone. I heard some of it." Lydia's hand dove with gusto into the pretzel bowl.

"What did he say?"

"He ordered the other person to listen to him. Then he got mad. He spoke the name Griffin right before he slammed the phone and walked away."

"Griffin," Ansel repeated.

She couldn't think of anyone named Griffin. And what was Nick doing at Bowie? The private school had a good academic reputation but, as far as she knew, Nick didn't attend classes, teach, or serve on any of the college alumni or trustee boards.

"It makes me sick to my stomach, Ms. Phoenix. I actually stood next to a man who got murdered."

"Can you remember the date of that phone call?"

Lydia chewed more pretzels and finished her drink. "Uh huh. Friday, May twenty-fifth, right before the end of spring term."

"You've got to tell Lieutenant Dorbandt. He could track this Griffin person down."

Lydia's eyes grew wide. "I'm not going to tell him anything. One official statement will be enough for the rest of my life. He'll think I'm guilty, too."

"Why?"

"Because I didn't tell the truth from the beginning. I lied, and he'll wonder why."

"Lydia, it's your duty to help," Ansel replied. She buried the thought that she was a hypocrite. It was also her duty to tell Dorbandt about her one-night stand with Nick.

Lydia set her glass on the coffee table and stood up. "I don't want anything to do with this murder. I don't want crazy killers coming after me because they think I know something." She grabbed her purse and started for the door.

Ansel jumped up. "Lydia, where are you going?"

"Do what you want with the information, Ms. Phoenix, but leave me out of it."

Lydia rushed down the steps toward her Hyundai on the gravel drive. Ansel watched the blue car as it was swallowed by a cloud of dust which evaporated by a stand of pine trees near the end of her property.

Ansel reached for her Iniskim, but grabbed air. She'd forgotten it was gone, the leather cord now balled up and pushed into her fanny pack.

Well, she thought despondently, at least her trip to see Karen Capos wouldn't be a total waste. She couldn't wait to ask Nick's wife if she knew anyone named Griffin.

Chapter 5

*"It matters not where we pass the remnant
of our days. They will not be many."*

Chief Seattle, Squamish

Goosebumps spiked on Dorbandt's arms as he reviewed the last page of Nicholas Demetrius Capos' autopsy report. He'd seen some gruesome murders in his job, but few had been carried out with such calculated malice.

Opinion: *It is my opinion that Nicholas Capos, a thirty-two-year-old male, died as a result of a subcutaneous injection into the neck of 200 mg of strychnine poison in aqueous solution. The poison entered the circulatory system causing respiratory paralysis of the lungs and secondary pulmonary arrest of the heart due to lack of oxygen. The cause of death was strychnine poisoning. The mechanism of death was asphyxia. The manner of death was homicide.*

Dorbandt probed his memory. What he recalled about strychnine had been learned from academy training. Strychnine was most often used to control varmint populations. In Montana, a lot of farmers and ranchers used strychnine-based pesticides, but poison-dusted seeds or grains were effective only when ingested. Somebody had used a hypo on Capos. Very unusual.

He also knew that strychnine was a slow-acting poison. Once injected, within the hour a series of tetanic-like convulsions contracted the body muscles into a locked, arched-back position. Only the head and feet touched the floor. A muscular facial grimace, *risus sardonicus*, pulled the lips back in a contorted grin. The deadly seizures, often triggered by the slightest sound, could go on for hours.

Dorbandt noted the coroner's opinion on the date of death. Dr. Dickerson Howdun stated that due to the moderate 50- to 70-degree Fahrenheit temperatures, the lack of rain, the burial, and the small number of larval insects, pinning down Capos' date of death was impossible. However, going by the post-mortem swelling, leaking fluids, and advanced bacterial decomposition, he guessed that Capos had expired approximately three weeks prior to discovery.

Dorbandt looked at his desk calendar. Capos probably died between June first and June eighth. Canvassing witnesses and determining who last saw him alive might closer pinpoint the day.

"God damn it." His heartburn fired up again and he rubbed his chest.

"How's it going, Reid?"

Captain Ed McKenzie materialized by his desk. The division chief had perfected his cat-footed approaches into a bureaucratic art during his many years in the Homicide Division.

"Capos was murdered with strychnine."

"Somebody used rat bait?"

Dorbandt tossed the folder on his desk. "Something like it, but as a concentrated liquid. I saw the autopsy yesterday. Messy. A lot of self-inflicted damage because of the convulsions. Never seen a corpse munched on by sand scorpions either. No defensive wounds. Capos probably knew the perp."

"You think you've seen it all, then a case makes your hair stand on end. Remember that lady in Fort Peck growing poison Panther mushrooms in her garage, grinding them up, and feeding them to neighborhood kiddies in heart-shaped cookies? She thought she was providing a community service. A miracle nobody died. Just made them sick as hell."

Dorbandt nodded. "This perp is better at covering tracks. Maybe I can trace the injectable poison."

"Got anything solid?"

Dorbandt shrugged. "Wasn't a robbery. Capos had his valuables on him. According to DMV, he owned a 1997 silver Subaru Outback. I talked to his landlord this morning. Adam Knapp owns the Sky View Apartments in Wolf Point and says the Outback is parked in the garage: unlocked, keys in the ignition. I'm leaving to check it out."

"So the killer rode with Capos to the farm and returned the car, or transported Capos in his car," McKenzie figured.

"Ground's dry so I couldn't find treads worth casting. Access to the property was gained via a utility road on the south side. Fencing was pulled down. The owner, Feltus Pitt, didn't see or hear a thing. What nags me is why Capos was buried at the pig farm. Killer went out of his way to put the body there. I'm checking into Pitt's background."

McKenzie rubbed his jaw. "Maybe Forensics will find something on the Outback."

"Maybe."

"Suspects?"

Dorbandt's esophagus filled with acid. "I'm drinking from a mud puddle, but it's early. Capos' background check was tame. No criminal records or court judgements. Graduated with a master's degree in botany. He worked as a research assistant for five years until a year and a half ago. Then he quit and didn't get another job. Married to Karen Davis Capos since 1997 and recently separated. Bank account records, credit history, and utility bills come in today or tomorrow. His employment records are being faxed. Since Capos didn't have an income, I'm wondering how he paid his living expenses."

"Talk to the wife?"

"Last night. She's indifferent. I didn't get any bad vibes. She's got a new boyfriend living with her, though. Alexander King. Owns a pet store called Bird Haven. He's on my short list."

McKenzie nodded. "He sounds promising."

Dorbandt grinned. "Hey, you'll never believe who found the body."

"Who?"

"Anselette Phoenix."

McKenzie's face darkened. "Phoenix? You're shitting me."

Dorbandt yanked McKenzie's chain again. "Scout's honor. She's cute."

"Cute like a pygmy rattler," McKenzie complained. "Chase Phoenix is nothing but a troublemaker. She probably is, too."

"She looks Indian."

"Half-breed."

Dorbandt noted the racial slam, and it justified his opinion that McKenzie was a certifiable idiot. "I've seen Phoenix's wife in the paper. She doesn't look Indian."

"Pearl Phoenix is his second wife. The Injun died. So where did Anselette meet Capos?"

"A fossil club."

"Any chance she's involved?" His piercing, hazel eyes gleamed.

"She's been cooperative. Right now everybody's got potential."

"Check her out. Maybe it's no coincidence she found the body. If they belonged to the same club, maybe they practiced extracurricular hobbies together. Maybe she lost it because he didn't divorce his wife, and she decided to fossilize him. Poison is a woman's weapon of choice."

Dorbandt remembered how Phoenix had avoided his gaze when he asked about her relationship with Capos. There was something she wasn't telling. She was pretty cool under pressure but was she icy enough to watch a person die a slow, agonizing death?

"If Phoenix is hiding something, I'll find it."

"I need you to work fast, Reid. The media is hounding me. I'm short on manpower so this is your baby. I'll reassign your cases. When you need a buddy, take Fiskar. Reporters want a statement soon, and Sheriff Combs needs the department to look good while he's away. Don't let me down."

McKenzie marched away. Dorbandt resisted the urge to shoot him the finger. The department, hell. McKenzie wanted to look squeaky clean, especially if Chase Phoenix got dumped into the mix. McKenzie couldn't afford to look bad a second time.

Now he'd been strapped into the hot seat. If he didn't have something bigger on tap in forty-eight hours, the trickle of clues would go dry fast. If that happened, McKenzie would have tons of fuel to dump on him when Bucky Combs and the newsies needed a public execution. That's when they'd torch the kindling around his feet.

Dorbandt surveyed his desk. None of the crime scene reports or photos were back. He'd completed the tedious task of writing his initial and supplemental crime reports. Time for him to hoof it out to Wolf Point.

Wolf Point was a nice town, and he'd often attended the Wild Horse Stampede, a large rodeo and Indian celebration known throughout the state. The city started out as a trading post where frozen wolf carcasses were thrown in a pile near the river until they thawed. When Indians captured the landing one spring, the decaying meat stack became a landmark for Missouri steamboat captains. This trip wouldn't be enjoyable.

Dorbandt left his desk. Odie Fiskar was a bear of a man who rivaled Grizzly Adams in stature and girth. The neatly dressed, dark haired, and bearded detective barely fit into his puny rolling chair, even with the arms removed to accommodate his dimensions.

Fiskar wasn't overweight. He was toned muscle and tight skin. Better yet, his powerhouse body housed a megawatt brain. Dorbandt had seen Fiskar bench press three hundred pounds in twenty minutes and complete a *New York Times* crossword puzzle in under fifteen.

"Odie, we're going to check out an apartment and car."

Fiskar turned a huge, buzz-cut head. "Now?"

"Right now. Capos case. Manager's letting us in."

Fiskar's eyes expanded. "The pig farm?"

Dorbandt flashed a cheery smile. "That's it. Rise and shine."

"All right." Fiskar put down his pen and stood a full six inches over Dorbandt. "Can we get something to eat?"

That was the kicker with Fiskar. He was also an eating machine. Dorbandt looked at his watch. The station was located in Mission City, the county seat. There were plenty of places to grab a bite before heading for Wolf Point.

"Hokay. What did you have in mind?" he asked while they walked toward a sign-out board.

"The Chicken Barn. A bucket of chicken costs eight bucks. They're open twenty-four hours."

The thought of all that grease made Dorbandt queasy. "You want to eat a bucket of chicken at nine in the morning?"

"No way. I'm gonna need at least two buckets to make it through to lunch."

Dorbandt burped.

Chapter 6

"The soul would have no rainbow if the eyes had no tears."

Sequichie Comingdeer

Ansel moved her head and winced. A headache hitchhiked a ride inside her skull. Last night she had drunk a glass of wine with her spaghetti dinner. That had led to another glass. Soon she had downed the jug of Carlo Rossi, then passed out on the sofa.

She groaned, pulling the black lizard boot over her left foot. Afterward, Ansel put both hands on her skull, checking to make sure it wouldn't blow off her neck. The knocking inside her brain was unbearably loud, and her stomach started doing a nasty trick. It twisted like a pretzel, then pulled as taut as a Gordian knot.

At least she was clean and dressed. Stripping off yesterday's clothes and taking a shower had been an incredible feat of willpower and coordination. Looking in the mirror, she realized her hair was uncombed. She reached for the brush on the bureau with a trembling hand. One stroke down her waist-length tresses and she groaned. Her scalp hurt. Was that possible?

Since she couldn't make a French braid, Ansel used her fingers to smooth down her wild-woman hair. She took a barrette and tenderly clipped the locks back in a ponytail. Good enough. She looked civilized even though lightning bolts of pain seared through her right temple.

Her mother's father had been an alcoholic. He spent most of his life on the Browning reservation lost in a nonstop haze fueled by Thunderbird whiskey. Once as a little girl, her mother had taken her to meet Grandpa Two Spots. Her only memory of the encounter was of a nice old man who smelled bad.

Drinking got Ansel into trouble. She'd been drinking burgundy the night Nick visited her and ended up in bed with him. It was still hard to believe she'd been so stupid. That's it, she vowed. Washing her problems away with booze didn't work. When she was human again, she'd throw out every bottle of whiskey, beer, and wine in the trailer.

But first, she had to get to Glasgow. The trip worried her. She had no idea what Karen wanted. Could Karen know about her one night with Nick? The last thing she wanted was a confrontation with an embittered wife.

Ansel slowly walked from the bedroom to the kitchen. She spotted her sunglasses on the sofa and slipped them on. Light hurt. Once she made it to the kitchen alive, she decided to try a few swallows of milk, drinking the cold liquid from the container. Bad idea.

As she spewed milk and acid bile into the sink, Ansel felt like her head was melting from the inside out. After she stopped vomiting, she felt better. She straightened up and adjusted her shades. What a mess. A quick clean-up and a couple spurts of lavender air freshener, and she headed for the door. The phone rang just as she grabbed her Stetson, leather jacket, fanny pack, and camera case. She ignored it. Those news jackals could find somebody else to pester.

Glasgow was in the next county sixty miles away. Originally called Siding 45, the town began in 1887 as a wide spot alongside the Great Northern rails. Homesteaders and ranchers had turned Glasgow into a satellite town for nearby

Fort Peck. The creation of the Fort Peck Dam and reservoir in the 1930s had invigorated the locale as anglers and holiday-makers flowed in to vacation and to fish.

The summer season was in full swing, and Monday rush hour traffic was heavy on Highway 2. Ansel made a hectic drive across the Missouri River and through pancake-flat prairie listening to rock music on Glasgow's KLTZ. She reached Karen's house on Aberdeen Avenue ninety minutes later.

Ansel had been here once before when she had picked Nick up for a fossil-hunting trek along the Missouri River. He had lived in the one-story house with a deck, two-car garage, and basement until his separation. Pine trees abounded, and a large lava garden decorated the ground near the front door. Ansel rapped a brass fleur-de-lis knocker.

She surveyed the flat, suburban topography while she waited. This regional shale bed had been caught in a mountain-making vise and folded so tightly that the strata had metamorphosed into a slate bed. During the Paleozoic era, a small mud and clay inlet existed here. It had been home to marine trilobites, brachiopods, and corals.

A woman opened the door and did a noticeable double take. Had she never seen an Indian before? As an invisible wave of Giorgio perfume enveloped Ansel, she smiled despite her still churning stomach.

"Hello, Karen. I'm Ansel Phoenix."

"Ansel. Come in."

Karen stared once more out of wide, brown eyes haloed by sienna mascara and copper eyeshadow before turning abruptly. As Ansel stepped inside, she pulled the door shut with a resounding bang. Numerous limited edition bird prints rattled on their wall hooks. She winced as her head registered a stabbing complaint.

Tall and sinewy, Karen looked like she'd stepped out of an Outfitters of the West catalog with a red plaid shirt, jeans, and black leather bullet belt. Observing Karen sashay through the foyer from behind was watching estrogen in motion.

God, she's stunning, Ansel concluded with a pang of
jealousy. Even in that cowgirl getup, Karen moved like a
graceful panther. There was no way Ansel could duplicate
that long-legged, sexy stride. Her own body was short and
thin, but any added weight went straight to her hips, which
was great for straddling a loping horse or bearing broods of
babies, but didn't make her model material. She had the same
narrow waistline, but her bust would never reach such fruitful
proportions.

Ansel followed her past a large verdigris bird cage standing
on iron legs in the hallway. Inside two white birds cooed
contentedly.

"Alex gave me those," Karen said. Her full lips were
unsmiling beneath a glaze of beige lipstick and chocolate lip
liner. "He's such a romantic. Doves are supposed to be the
messengers for Venus and good luck omens to lovers. They
mate for life."

Annoyed at such a disloyal pronouncement to Nick's
memory, Ansel went on the offensive. "Who's Alex?"

"My boyfriend." Karen smiled, then made a point of
studying her manicured nails.

So Cameron's quip about Karen playing house was true.
How did Nick feel about that? He'd never mentioned Karen's
lover. Ansel wondered what the deep red, iridescent nail polish
coating Karen's talons was called. Cardinal Sin? Bloody
Murder?

Ansel yanked off her sunglasses and side-stepped the issue
of Karen's boy-toy by walking into the living room. The area
was redecorated in pink and black art deco hues. Compared
to the functional Sears furnishings of Karen's married life,
this was a quantum leap.

"Nice house." Ansel paced across a Berber carpet the color
of Kaopectate.

"You can sit anywhere."

Ansel selected a love seat upholstered in black crushed
velvet. "I'd like to offer you my condolences and those of the

Pangaea Society. If there's anything we can do, please let me know."

Karen took a matching sofa. "I've put most of that fossil crap behind me. It ruined my marriage."

Despite Karen's confrontational tone, Ansel smiled. "I know you and Nick had your differences but…"

"We had more than differences. It's one thing to have an obsession with old plants but Nicky quitting his job was the last straw. My work at the bank couldn't keep a roof over our heads or food on the table."

Ansel's mouth dropped like the operculum of a Paleozoic snail. She snapped it shut. Nick had talked about his job at the last society meeting. He had told her he enjoyed it. Realizing that he had lied through his teeth was a jolt. Just stick to the subject, Ansel coached herself. Karen was spilling everything, a perfect time to pump her for more information.

"When did Nick quit?"

"January. A year and a half ago." Karen pulled a cigarette from a pack sitting on a chromed end table. The gold head of an eagle-shaped lighter flipped back to reveal hot blue flame. Acrid smoke curled around her head like Medusa snakes.

"Why did he quit?"

Karen shrugged. "Said he was tired of the job. Claimed he was looking for another. He did that museum gig around April last year, but it only lasted for a few months."

"What was he doing with all his free time?"

"Sitting around the house. Working on his computer. We fought a lot. Nicky finally left last June. When he split, Alex moved in. I told that snoopy detective the same thing when he showed up. I have nothing to hide."

Ansel considered this wealth of information, staunchly enduring the secondhand smoke irritating her sensitive stomach. "What was he doing on the computer?"

"I don't know, and I don't care."

"Do you know anyone named Griffin?"

Karen ran a free hand through her shoulder-length blonde mane. "Can't say that I do. Why?"

"Nick mentioned the name. It's not someone in the society and, if it's a relative, I'd like to make contact and offer my sympathies."

"All of Nicky's American family are dead. His relatives in Greece haven't bothered to speak to him since he was a boy. I don't see how anyone could miss hearing about the murder. Nicky's finally getting his fifteen minutes of fame, isn't he?"

The heartless comment reminded Ansel of Cameron's complaints that Nick had wanted worldly shortcuts to success. "Do you have any idea who would harm Nick?"

"What about me? I could be in danger. Not to mention how this makes me look. I'll be a pariah. Don't get me wrong. Nicky and I were madly in love at one time. He changed. I changed. I didn't hate him. I accepted things and moved on. We both agreed to start the divorce process in a few weeks. Dead or alive, I want Nicky out of my life."

Ansel stiffened. "Karen, Nick didn't just die. He was murdered. He must have been involved in something very dangerous."

"I have no idea what he was up to. The last time I heard from him was the end of May. We talked about the divorce. Nicky never shared the details of his new life."

"Something happened. Aren't you curious?"

"Not at all." She flicked ash into a pink marble ashtray. "I don't need details."

The jangle of keys in the front door interrupted them. A tall man quickly entered and approached the living room. When he realized Karen wasn't alone, he halted. "What's up, babe?" he asked, making a point of staring at Ansel. A bright yellow tag stuck to the man's shirt pocket read, BIRD HAVEN. MANAGER. ALEXANDER KING.

Karen bolted to her feet. "Alex, what are you doing here?"

"I forgot some invoices. Who is this?"

Ansel took in his appearance, comparing it to Nick. He wore a kaleidoscopic pullover sweater, white twill pants, and olive leather loafers. Another model cut-out, she assessed. The rugged outdoors variety.

Karen puffed her cigarette. "This is Ansel Phoenix. You remember. She's the president of that group Nicky belonged to. She came to offer condolences."

The resident Adonis shifted his rapier, green-eyed gaze back toward Ansel. His long, slicked-back blond hair and square face with a fashionable hair-stubbled chin didn't hide his grimace.

"That's all? You could have called."

"I wanted to tell Karen in person that she didn't have to get through this troubling time without support from the Pangaea Society. Since Nick's death is being investigated, there's going to be a lot of red tape along with the burial details. I'd like to help."

"You can rest easy, Miss Phoenix. Karen's got me to run interference. Right, babe?"

"That's right," Karen responded on cue.

"Well, that still leaves the question of why you asked me to come, Karen."

"Oh, yes. I wondered if you'd appraise Nicky's fossil collection for me. I want to sell it."

Ansel wasn't surprised. The idea of Karen cashing in on Nick's beloved fossil artifacts seemed vile, but what could she expect from an estranged wife? Cameron was interested in the collection. Wasn't it better having the fossils go to someone who truly appreciated them?

Ansel grinned. "I'd be glad to."

"That's wonderful."

"I don't like this." Alex glared at Karen.

"Why not, darling? It's expensive getting a professional."

Ansel ignored Karen's slur. "Normally you pay a licensed appraiser twenty percent of the total estimated value of the collection. I'll evaluate it for free. It's the least I can do for Nick."

"I don't think we should rush into this," Alex insisted. "The police won't like people rifling through his things. It might be evidence."

Karen pouted. "That collection belongs to me. Why should I get rooked by a stranger?"

"Absolutely right," Ansel said. "I have connections through the society, Karen. I know I can get you good prices for the specialty pieces."

"Perfect." Karen's face infused with color. "I'll get the duplicate apartment key. Nicky gave me one for emergencies."

Ansel marveled at Karen's transformation. The thought of getting something for nothing invigorated the woman. She also wondered about Karen possessing an apartment key. If she could access it, so could Alex.

As Karen disappeared down the hallway, Alex glowered at Ansel with renewed ferocity. She grinned back. When this staring game became too much, he pulled a burnished silver lighter from his pants pocket. He lighted a filtered, brown cigarette with great concentration before speaking.

"Nick was a genuine son-of-a-bitch, you know?" His scorching stare continued.

"Really?"

"Yeah. But I guess an even bigger bastard stamped his ticket."

Ansel kept her game face on. She wouldn't give him the joy of intimidating her. "Someone like you, Alex?"

Alex tensed, exhaling smoke through his nostrils. "You've got me wrong, Miss Phoenix. Dumping Nick in a hole isn't my style. He waffled about giving Karen a divorce for months. He didn't want her. He wanted to own her like a rock under glass. Nick needed a good bashing so he could feel what it was like to get stepped on. If I'd killed him, he'd have his damn head blown off."

Karen entered the room, oblivious to the exchange. She handed Ansel a piece of paper and a key. "The address. You can start right away."

Ansel took the items, then rose. "Let me know where the funeral is going to be."

"Sure," Karen agreed. "I think they have to wait until the autopsy is finished."

Ansel choked back her disgust and double-stepped it to the front door without a backward glance.

But Karen had already lost interest. "Alex, I don't have anything fashionable to wear to a burial service. We'd better go shopping."

"Sure, babe."

Closing the door firmly, Ansel pushed on her sunglasses and inhaled fresh air in great lungfuls as if she could purge her soul of a black spot. Now she could search Nick's apartment for clues. A spasm of anxiety rocked her stomach.

Alex was right about Dorbandt. The detective wouldn't like her snooping into his case, pawing through potential evidence, and withholding clues under the mantle of performing a good deed for Nick's widow.

And what about the repercussions to the Pangaea Society if she got in trouble with the law? If her behavior brought down the wrath of the museum association, the Opel funds would be history, too. Last but not least, there was the issue of her father's stand-off with the sheriff's department. Did she want to run the risk of causing problems for him with the county cops?

Ansel felt Nick's gold key sandwiched inside her hip pocket. Her eyes glistened with tears. For better or worse, she couldn't turn back now.

Chapter 7

*"Give me the eyes to see and
the strength to understand."*

Black Elk, Oglala Sioux

Ansel's emotions churned her abused stomach as she drove
east toward Nick's apartment. She didn't know the true
Nicholas Capos; the man who quit his job, deserted his wife,
and got murdered. How could she be so naive?

Visceral hurt speared through her. A niggling inner voice
suggested that Nick must have viewed her as less than human.
Usable. Perhaps disposable. This demon of doubt had ridden
on her shoulders since the day she'd been pushed into that
icy pond.

It had been Thanksgiving day. Her father and mother had
given a small party for her parent's closest friends and relatives,
and there were a lot of children at the ranch. She'd been
delighted to have other kids around. As a five-year-old only
child, this was a special treat which made the festive holiday
that much more exciting.

After everyone had finished a meal of turkey with all the
fixings and the adults were clearing the table, she and five
other children had run off to play. It was Rusty, the eight-
year-old son of her father's best friend, who convinced all of

them to put on their jackets and sneak out of the house with a fishing rod he'd taken from her father's study.

At first she hadn't wanted to go. The ground was covered with a light dusting of snow, and she knew it was a bad move following a boy who had taken the fishing tackle without asking permission to use it. Still this was an adventure. She didn't want to be left behind while they headed for the stock pond in the pasture behind the house.

They went through a cattle gate and onto the creaking, iced-over pond, slipping and sliding. Rusty had pulled out a linen napkin with some turkey to use as bait. Then he'd chipped a hole in the ice with his pocket knife while everyone watched. She'd known for sure that this was very, very bad and when she'd said so, Rusty had turned on her in a flash.

He'd pushed her hard, and she'd fallen on her stomach. Then Rusty had grabbed her by her parka hood and called her a red wiggler. Indian bait. He had laughed as he'd jabbed the hook through her coat hood and tossed her into the hole. Everyone had laughed as she slid through the tiny opening like a pebble down a tube. When her weight had snapped the hook from the taunt fishing line, they weren't laughing anymore. She had sunk like a stone, her waterlogged parka a deadly cocoon squeezing her body.

That's when she'd realized for the first time that she was somehow different from other children. Why exactly had mystified her, even as she flailed to reach them for help. She hadn't understood Rusty's violent hate of her, his snarling, ugly face. What had she done to make him so mad? Why had he hurt her?

Only weeks later, after her mother had explained in calm and soothing tones about her heritage and how some people would react to her, did she get an answer to her questions. People saw only her skin, not her soul. Had Nick done the same thing?

No, Ansel decided vehemently. Nick might have been many things, but he wasn't a bigot.

Pushing the thoughts of her near drowning away, Ansel rationalized why digging into Nick's personal life was the right thing to do. First, Dorbandt didn't know anything about paleobotany. He wouldn't know a Philodendron from a phylogenetic tree. She would. If there was anything out of the ordinary with Nick's fossil dealings, she'd sense it right away.

Second, she wanted to know if a society member was involved. It would be disastrous for the organization, and she wanted to be the first to know about it. Nick kept indexed collection acquisition notes and detailed field logs. Cataloging the collection would reveal if anything was missing or off kilter. His records might point toward the killer.

When Ansel reached Wolf Point, she purposely sped past the street on Karen's note and drove another half block before parking at a strip mall. She rearranged her hair into a bun on top of her head and donned her Stetson. She also buttoned up her leather jacket. With this getup and her sunglasses, anyone watching her enter the apartment would think she was a short man wearing cowboy attire.

As Ansel left the cab, she grabbed her Olympus digital camera. The memory disc stored over a hundred photos. She approached the Fourth Street apartment, a boxy, two-story building sticking out among residential homes. A detached two-car garage sat beside it. Though recently painted, the aged dwelling was a big step down from Nick's house in Glasgow.

A chain link fence surrounded the rental and a small house east of it. The A-frame probably belonged to the landlord, she reasoned. There were no cars out front. This was a week-day morning in a working-class neighborhood. She stopped only a second to snap off a picture.

Ansel crossed the street. Stomach in her throat, she opened the gate and stepped up the sidewalk to the front door. The key went into the lock, and the knob twisted open. She hustled inside and shut the door, relocking it.

Her sunglasses went into her fanny pack. While she inhaled the smell of stale air, standing water, and accumulated dust, the realization of what she was doing hit her full force. Sleuthing for fossils was a world away from sleuthing for homicidal killers. She dealt with dead animals, not living people. She should appraise the collection. No more and no less.

"Bullshit," she said, standing in the dim foyer.

A puzzle was a puzzle. She possessed finely tuned talents of critical questioning, perception, and imagination. She could analyze anything with the proper balance between observation and interpretation. Her knowledge of scientific methodology was a gigantic plus, not a minus. *Get on with it.*

A tiny, clean kitchen opened to her right: used appliances, overhead cabinets, narrow counter with fruit going moldy in a cheap glass bowl. She took a picture, lighting the claustrophobic space with a flash nova.

She moved quickly into a small dining area with a window. Jaundiced light filtered through a pair of cheap yellow curtains. The room was sparsely furnished with a Formica table and four padded chrome chairs centered upon a gold, industrial-grade carpet. A six-foot-high, cherry curio cabinet dominated the room. Nick's glass collection.

Vases, huge globes, and paperweights filled the case, each imbedded with colorful ribbon swirls, bubbles, artistic figural shapes, or mosaic beads. Several contained floral inserts of real blossoms, leaves, and berries captured within the ageless grip of transformed, molten sand. Ansel took dozens of pictures, mostly for nostalgia. How long would the collection remain intact if Karen got her hands on it?

But where was Nick's fossil collection?

Ansel continued down the hall. Nick's master bedroom was on the right. As she stuck her head through the open doorway, she was conscious of the barren feel of the place. Generic landscape prints on the white walls. A double bed and a single end table with a lamp. Walk-in closet. Bathroom.

Ansel trekked toward a large living room. Closed curtains again made the area gloomy. The disarray looked common to a place where a man lived alone. Papers, empty fast food containers, and dirty clothes peppered the flat surfaces. The rented furniture looked well worn except for an elaborate entertainment unit. Wrinkling her nose, Ansel sidestepped an open gym bag disgorging sour tennis shoes and dirty sweats. She went toward the second bedroom.

Nick had set up this room like the fossil bays found in a museum. Three eight-foot-long tables with collapsible legs lined separate walls. The fourth wall had a curtained window. A desk and a gun-metal gray file cabinet stood beneath it. Only one fossil tray rested on a table next to the desk, which was conspicuously void of anything except a cordless telephone. There were no magazines, dealer catalogs, or books. Not even a bookcase.

This wasn't the guy she'd known. Nick's Aberdeen office had been stuffed with specimen trays, towering periodical stacks, and hundreds of reference books. A warehouse full of fossil-hunting supplies, paleobotany memorabilia, potted plants, and plain junk congested that room from floor to ceiling. Where had everything gone?

Ansel peered inside the three-foot tray, hoping to understand what Nick had cared about enough to keep. To her surprise, it contained small chunks of amber. Nodules in assorted yellow hues and clarity lay in separate slots, carefully labeled with tiny stickers.

Ansel lifted the glass cover. The two-inch-long amber nugget she picked up felt extremely light and had a warm plastic feel. A dark millipede was entombed inside. The label identified it as Baltic amber from a conifer called *Pinus succinifera*.

She examined other ambers under the weak window light. Every nodule contained inclusions. Some held trapped insects. Others swirled with plant debris. One lump, which Ansel found extremely interesting, encapsulated a miniature oyster shell attached to a strand of seaweed. Little alarms went off in her head. There were many types of amber. They were excavated from places like the Dominican Republic,

Burma, Romania, Sicily, Mexico, Canada, and even the United States.

Why had Nick forsaken his old interests and focused upon Baltic amber? European fossil resins were the oldest in the world, originating from Early Tertiary Period pine trees forty to sixty million years old. Before closing the tray, she snapped pictures.

Ansel walked over to the scarred, cherry desk. Dust outlines indicated where Nick's computer system and fax machine had been. Dorbandt would have taken any electronic machinery, computer disks, and files. He could glean useful information from memory drives, computer bytes, and carbon copy cartridges.

Ansel opened every drawer in the desk and found only office supplies. The larger bottom drawers designed for file folders were empty. She checked the four-drawer file cabinet. Nothing. Dorbandt had been thorough.

Nick's fossil records were gone. Without them she couldn't determine what he'd done with his collection or what he might have been field excavating. She would have to tell Karen there were no fossils to appraise, just a batch of amber with common fauna and flora inclusions.

Ansel spied some boxes pushed beneath a table and bent to examine them. One carton contained year-old newspapers. Another was packed with unopened bags of sawdust, white sand, and plaster of Paris. A third box held two gallons of distilled water. The last carton stored casting supplies: Sil-Mold, Por-A-Kast, and Wonder Putty.

As she returned a box, a metallic clatter echoed through the room. A cylindrical, stainless steel container rested against the baseboard. The seven-inch can had a domed top with a long funnel spout. A small, leather bellows protruded from the opposite side.

Ansel opened the hinged lid. A smoky, burnt wood smell assailed her nose. Soot coated the inside, and a charred mass rolled around the bottom. She took a picture of the can, then tossed it on the newspapers.

A sound outside the room caused her to freeze, blood throbbing in her ears. She listened, hardly breathing. Then she knew. A door lock was opening.

Ansel jumped to her feet and grabbed her camera. The front door closed with a thud. The fear of discovery gave her the presence of mind to swing the workroom door quietly closed. She left a crack between the edge and the doorjamb so she could hear.

Her mind raced to form plausible excuses why she was hiding in the office like a thief should she be found by the landlord. Or Dorbandt. It could also be somebody dangerous, Ansel realized. Nick's killer was at large.

As she concentrated on listening, sweat coursed down her rib cage beneath the leather jacket. She heard footsteps traversing the foyer. Several gut-wrenching seconds of silence passed, followed by squeaking hinges. The curio door.

Ansel listened as objects clinked against the tempered glass shelving. The magnetic door closures snapped loudly. Silence. Then the front door slammed. She bolted out the door and down the hallway into the living room. Breathing hard, she grabbed a drapery panel across the picture window and pulled it back a few inches.

Ansel recognized the plum-colored Eclipse with a rear wing spoiler. It was parked in front of the garage. Slack-jawed, she watched as the driver disappeared inside the car. In seconds the vehicle backed down the carport and sped away.

She went straight to the dining room and re-shot pictures of every curio shelf. Comparing the before-and-after photos at home would be a cinch.

Then she'd pay Evelyn Benchley a visit and ask her why she had a key to Nick's apartment.

The knock on her trailer door surprised her. She was just gathering her fanny pack and sunglasses before heading to the Roosevelt Museum where Evelyn worked as a preparator. For the last hour, she'd been comparing the digital photos downloaded to her computer. Ansel rushed to the door and opened it to a thick vapor of heat. Tim Shanks' lithe form took up most of the doorway, and she stared at him blankly.

"Hello, Miss Phoenix," he said with a winsome smile even warmer than the simmering air around them. In his hands he held a bulky, brown grocery bag crimped at the top.

"Hi, Tim," she managed to say. Why was he here? If she didn't get on the road, she'd never reach Fort Peck before the museum closed.

Tim's grin melted. "You forgot, didn't you?"

"Forgot what?"

"That I had an appointment to come and talk to you about my major." He watched her with his beautiful hazel eyes, irises exactly matching the color of his tee shirt. "Can I come in?"

"You're right, I did forget, Tim. I'm sorry. Have a seat."

Tim stepped into the trailer and waited until she closed the door before handing her the bag. "I brought you some Valencia oranges from California. Sort of a thank you present. My uncle sent them. Taking Vitamin C is a really good stress prevention, too. I figured you'd need it after what happened this weekend. It was pretty wild."

Ansel took the bag and peeked inside. The tangy sweet smell of citrus filled the air. Vibrant orange balls were nestled inside the sack. Since Montana had no citrus groves, this was a rare treat. She set the package on the kitchen pass-through.

"That's really sweet of you, Tim. No pun intended. I'll have some fresh orange juice for breakfast. Unfortunately, we'll have to make this quick. I've got to leave in a few minutes. Another appointment I can't miss." She sat on the rocker.

Tim took a seat on the sofa and brushed a hand through his blond curls. "No problem. Guess nobody's found the person who killed your friend yet, huh?"

"Not yet, but they will. I have a feeling that Detective Dorbandt won't give up until the killer is found."

"Lydia told me that she'd come by to see you, too."

Surprised that Lydia had mentioned the visit to Tim and unsure how much the girl had told him about Nick's phone conversation, if anything, Ansel said, "It's nice to have such supportive students. Now what can I help you with?"

"Oh, I want to get a doctorate in paleozoology. I'll have to leave Bowie College and go to Montana State, but I'm really excited about it. Since you graduated there, I wondered if you'd write me a letter of recommendation to submit with my admission application?"

"I'd be glad to. It's a tough paleontology program, but it's one of the best in the country. When will you need the letter?"

Tim's grin widened even more. "As soon as possible. I want to start the fall session, and I need to have all the academic paperwork sent out within the next few days."

"I'll write the letter when I get back tonight. Since I have your address on your seminar sign-up sheet, I'll mail it to you tomorrow."

"That's really nice of you, Miss Phoenix." Tim stood. "I won't hold you up. Thanks so much. This is really fantastic." He moved toward the door with long strides.

Ansel followed as he opened the metal portal and retreated, cowboy boots pounding down the concrete steps. "Bye, Tim." He half-turned and waved before hopping into his battered station wagon. A thought flitted through Ansel's mind, and she rushed through the door. "Wait, Tim," she called, but it was too late. The brown oil-spewing behemoth pulled away.

"Dammit," she hissed.

She'd wanted to ask him what ever happened to the crime scene film inside his camera. Did he still have it or did Dorbandt confiscate it? If Tim developed the roll, she wanted to see the pictures, as disturbing as they might be. Maybe there was a clue hidden somewhere in the topography around Nick's body. She was willing to try any lead, any farfetched idea that might point a finger to the killer.

Chapter 8

*"The brave man yields to neither fear nor anger,
desire nor agony. He is at all times master of himself."*

Ohiyesa, Santee Sioux

"I can't take this." Dorbandt threw down the paper. It fluttered to his desk and settled on a large pile of documents awaiting his attention.

He was tired. Yesterday afternoon he'd gone to Glasgow to interview Karen Capos and Alexander King again. Then he'd worked late finishing up reports on Capos' apartment and car. Afterward he'd spent the night tossing and turning, his mind replaying the day.

Back at his desk this morning, he'd reviewed the meager forensic reports trickling in from the state crime lab before poring over confiscated bundles of Capos' personal records and finances.

So far the forensic results were discouraging. Capos's old, partially degraded fingerprints were found on his clothes and personal effects. The fresh fingerprints appearing on his glasses only confirmed Anselette Phoenix's story. No other prints were present.

Toxicology had sent the liquid chromatography results. Testing on Capos' brain, lungs, spinal cord, and liver corroborated

Howdun's conclusions that strychnine was the cause of death. No other drugs or alcohol were found in Capos' system.

Since Capos' faxed employment records were brief, Dorbandt had made a follow-up call to his ex-supervisor. He had learned from Dr. Barclay Stoopsen that the Cooperative was an agricultural lab conducting studies on range land degradation caused by grazing livestock. Capos had been well liked by fellow employees. His work had been exemplary until a few months before he quit. Something had happened, and Dorbandt knew he had to dig deeper.

So far, he'd plowed through several years of Capos' financial records: pay stubs, canceled checks, and bill statements. After Capos left the Cooperative, he'd closed his bank accounts and made a point of paying off outstanding debts, including bank loans, credit card bills, and insurance policies.

Capos had received no unemployment benefits, disability payments, retirement pensions, or welfare aid. It was doubtful that Capos had acquired a long-lost inheritance, or hit it big on the Powerball, Dorbandt mused. How did he pay the bills off so quickly, or survive without income for the last year and a half?

Dorbandt's gut told him Capos had been up to something before he died. Pretty Boy smelled dirty. Without a paper trail, it would be harder to learn what the botanist had been up to, but not impossible.

His second interview with Karen and her boyfriend had been interesting. King didn't hide the fact that he had hated Capos because of the way he treated Karen. King was wound tighter than a tick in dog hair. Would he pop if his anger became too much? Did he have access to strychnine?

Adding to his problems, McKenzie had given him another pep-talk. McKenzie wanted leads. McKenzie wanted a suspect. McKenzie wanted his lead butt to shine like Fort Knox gold on television sets across the county. McKenzie's message boiled down to one nugget of advice: produce or vamoose.

Dorbandt eyed his desk with distaste. It looked like a dust devil had passed through it. Papers were strewn in matted clumps. His computer system had disappeared beneath a tower of pulp. Stacked cartons surrounded his desk, box tops pimpled with Styrofoam coffee cups, soda cans, and candy wrappers. Somewhere lay a clue.

He pawed through the paper avalanche and picked up the Pangaea Society roster. Something else to work on. The personal info he'd gleaned about Anselette Phoenix was anemic, and uneventful. He did learn about the new Opel Center that the society was involved with and briefly wondered if that might play a role in the murder.

The background checks on the seminar kids were the same. Lydia Hodges and Tim Shanks lived in Mission. Shane Roco lived in Big Toe. They attended Bowie College and were excellent students. None had a criminal record. Even Feltus Pitt had lived a life that looked as straight as an arrow.

The phone rang. Dorbandt dropped the email sheets on a Montana Electric and Gas bill. The device shrieked again, but he couldn't see it. He grabbed a pile of papers, dumped them on the floor, and scrambled for the receiver.

"Detective Division. Dorbandt."

"Hey, Reid. Dave Jackson."

Dorbandt smiled. He liked Jackson, a diamond in the rough when it came to employees at the Missoula toxicology lab.

"Thanks for returning my call. I have some questions about the Capos case."

"Fire away."

"Where does strychnine come from?"

"The strychnine used on Capos was made from seeds of a tree called Strychnos nux vomica," Jackson replied. "It's processed by the heating and powdering of seeds, then distilled into a concentrated form. Commercially prepared strychnine is the only kind imported into the states. It comes from India."

"What's the poison look like?"

"A potent, transparent crystal or a white, crystalline powder. Both have a very bitter taste."

Dorbandt leaned back in his chair. "How potent?"

"Strychnine is ninety to one hundred percent pure poison in composition. Two raw, ground-up nux vomica seeds are equal to sixty grains that will kill you if ingested. By comparison, only two-thirds of one grain of concentrated strychnine can."

"And strychnine can be eaten or injected?"

"It's more versatile than that. Strychnine can be eaten, injected, absorbed through the skin or eyes, and inhaled. All with varying effects, depending on dosage and mode of introduction into the central nervous system."

Dorbandt saw a light at the end of the tunnel. "Because of the health issues, the EPA must have international regulations regarding its importation. Plus state and federal guidelines, right?"

"You bet," Jackson agreed. "Strychnine products have to conform to proper warning labels and regulatory constraints. According to EPA registration laws, any end-product user of imported strychnine has to keep detailed records of its purchases, sales, and disposal methods."

"That makes it traceable from overseas to here. Connect the dots."

"Yes, we could conceivably match Capos' poison with the manufacturer that formulated it. Strychnine is often mixed with signature compounds that identify the lab. You could trace possession with shipping receipts and sample testing. You might even hit pay dirt and find your killer. It's just going to take time."

Dorbandt rubbed his chest. He didn't have a lot of time. Not with a perp at large and McKenzie hounding him. However, if he found a suspect with access to strychnine, he could match poison samples, creating a link between the lab, the perp, and the victim. It would be nice to have the documentation to link with forensic evidence.

"Dave, can you get me a list of the Indian manufacturers exporting strychnine and their U.S. distributors?"

"I should be able to. There won't be that many."

"Great. Captain McKenzie is hemorrhaging over this case. I owe you one."

Jackson chuckled. "I'll remember that."

"Can you transfer me to Serology?"

"Sure. Just a second."

An ominous series of clicks assailed Dorbandt's ear. Eventually the phone rang. "Serology. This is Dr. Floyd."

Dorbandt hated dealing with Floyd. The scientist was great at his job, but he wasn't a "people" person. "Hello, Arlen. Detective Reid Dorbandt. Lacrosse County. Do you have anything on the Capos strychnine homicide?"

"I'm not a mind reader. What's the number?"

Dorbandt swept papers across his desk in a panic, looking for Howdun's autopsy sheets. "Case 01-06-23-H-0007."

"Hold on."

Dead air encased half of Dorbandt's head. He passed the time waiting on hold by flipping through the autopsy report.

"I've got it," Floyd barked. "The report's not complete."

"Anything interesting?"

"I'm working on other cases, Detective. Let me read for a minute." Five seconds passed. "Doesn't look like much. Blood, saliva, and hair samples belonged to the victim. Only odd thing is the feather."

Dorbandt sat up. "What feather?"

"A feather found on the body. Don't you read your trace evidence inventory sheets?"

"I don't have any sheets. Tell me about it."

Floyd exhaled. "A thirty-five millimeter, white and brown feather was pulled from the right sock band. It was stuck in the cotton weave. I don't know what type of bird it is. DNA testing hasn't been done."

"Capos could have picked up the feather from the ground, or the wind could have blown it onto his body," Dorbandt considered.

"I don't think so. If that were the case, I'd expect to see the feather on the shoe or on a place exposed to the air. Not caught under the pants cuff between cotton and skin. It was protected from the elements and dirt debris. I think it was picked up somewhere else," Floyd stated. "Probably a transfer contact with the killer. Maybe pushed into the sock top by the killer's hand during the dragging of the body."

Dorbandt thought of Alexander King's bird shop. If he could tie King to the Capos crime scene, he'd really have something. "How long will the testing take?"

"Around six weeks."

Acid pummeled Dorbandt's throat. "Six weeks? Can't you push it up?"

"I'm backlogged. I'll try," Floyd said, his tone promising nothing. "Try later."

Dorbandt dropped the receiver into the cradle just as McKenzie's bulky form stormed his way. McKenzie looked upset. His beet-red face was deformed into a goulish mask. In his beefy hand he clutched a folded newspaper.

McKenzie stomped up and glared. "Reid, I just went out to lunch and saw this." Every person in homicide stared as the lieutenant unfolded the semiweekly edition of the *Sky Sentinel* with edge-ripping fury. He tossed it, front page up, on the disheveled desk.

STRYCHNINE KILLER IN BIG TOE!

Dorbandt's burning throat dropped into his stomach. Somebody had leaked the Capos autopsy findings to the media. He glanced up at McKenzie, whose bug-eyes bulged from rage.

"You've fucked up," McKenzie bellowed. "Well, say something."

"Something?" Dorbandt replied, a plaintive, hang-dog look plastered across his face. If he could wag his tail, he would do it.

Chapter 9

"You have to be God and the devil, both of them."

Lame Deer, Sioux

For over a minute Ansel stood silently in the fossil bay doorway and watched Evelyn Benchley. Her eighty-mile ride to the Roosevelt Museum had been no small feat. After Tim left the trailer, she had hightailed it to Fort Peck in a frenzy, dreading the coming confrontation but determined to learn the truth.

Evelyn sat before a large slab of carbonaceous shale. The tablet was boxed into a three-by-six-foot wooden frame supported on an easel. In her right hand Evelyn held a sharpened crochet hook. With her left she fingered the barrel of a free-swinging, binocular microscope lens. She alternated scraping the hook against ancient stone with minute adjustments of the microscope to offset glare on the rock's surface.

Suddenly Evelyn pulled away from the slab, set down her hook, and rolled her chair around to face the door. She started visibly when she noticed someone there.

"Ansel. Why didn't you say something?"

"I was admiring your work. That's quite a project." As Ansel walked into the room, the overpowering scent of Evelyn's Giorgio perfume enveloped her.

"It certainly is." Evelyn half-turned and picked up a large photo from a work table. "*Astreptoscolex anasillosus*," she announced, passing the print to Ansel. "Paleozoic, segmented worms known from Mississippian era sediments of Montana. They lived in lagoonal regions over three hundred and sixty million years ago. Like modern worms, they had a proboscis to dig mud burrows and two conical-shaped jaws to catch live prey. Neat, huh?"

Ansel studied the black and white picture. It was the photographic copy of an X-ray taken by an electronic dodging machine. The image revealed a dozen fossil worms, invisible to the naked eye, trapped between rock layers. The worms looked like leeches with gills, bristled appendages, and short antennae. Using only this photo as her guide, Evelyn slowly chipped off sediment to reveal the invertebrates.

Ansel passed the photo back. "Sorry. I prefer vertebrates. Show me some *Allenypterus montanus* fish in Bear Gulch limestone from the same era, and I'm in heaven."

Evelyn smiled. "To each his own." Her expression turned pensive. "What are you doing here?"

"I have a few questions. About Nick."

Evelyn blinked, though her eyes never wavered. "Nick? Has something happened with the society?"

"No. This is about Nick and you."

"What are you talking about?"

"You have a key to Nick's apartment."

"No, I don't. Whatever gave you that idea?"

"I saw you there, Evelyn."

Evelyn laughed. "Ansel, you're mistaken."

"I was in the apartment this morning. So were you."

Evelyn's airy facade turned to stone. "I would never do such a thing."

"I even smelled your Giorgio perfume. Karen Capos wears it. I bet it was Nick's favorite."

"Just a coincidence." Evelyn dropped her gaze toward her lap.

"I also know you took a paperweight from Nick's curio, one with red hearts inside. A lover's memento? You had an affair with Nick."

Evelyn glanced up and swallowed. "All right, what if I did have a key and took the paperweight? It doesn't mean I slept with Nick. By your reasoning, the fact that you have a key means that you and Nick were..." She hesitated, distressed by the implication.

"No. Karen gave me the key. She wants me to inventory Nick's fossil collection for resale."

Evelyn's cheeks flared pink. "That bitch. She made Nick's life miserable, and now she's going to steal his fossils." She pitched the photo onto the table.

"There's no use denying your involvement with Nick. It's written all over your face. Did Karen know you were sleeping with him?"

Evelyn's rage dissipated. Her shoulders sagged a mile as resignation settled over her. "No," she murmured, "and she wouldn't have cared. She was seeing that creep from the pet shop." A tear slid down her cheek. "I can't believe Nick's dead. It's like a nightmare." She covered her beautiful face with her hands and sobbed openly.

The situation disconcerted Ansel. She was amazed that Evelyn considered Nick a potential suitor. Almost twice as old, Evelyn's tastes ran toward single lawyers and physicians with bulging financial portfolios. Nick had been handsome and charismatic, but nonetheless a married, middle-income technician with a state pension.

Not to mention that she'd never seen calm and controlled Evelyn exhibiting such mercurial displays of emotion. The no-nonsense preparator had always been the perennial Rock of Gibraltar. Ansel's discomfort gave way to disgust. Had Nick been bedding Evelyn while making a play for her?

"When did your affair start?"

"A year ago," Evelyn whispered, swiping her puffy red eyes and smearing the backs of her hands with mascara. "We started talking after a society meeting, and things just progressed. I know you think I'm crazy, but Nick made me feel needed. He'd already left Karen so he wasn't really cheating."

"That's six months after he quit his job."

Evelyn's head snapped up. "Nick quit his job?"

"January of last year. Karen supported them until they separated last June. You didn't know?"

"No." Evelyn stopped crying. A cold, steely look crept into her eyes. "We broke up last December. Six months together. Nick never told me he left his job."

Ansel felt a tad better. Nick had slept with her long after he'd left Evelyn. "Why did you break up?"

"Nick ended it. He never said why, but..." She stopped.

"But what?"

"Sometimes I thought he loved the museum computers more than me."

"Why?"

"Because he spent hours using them. The bastard told me he was doing research for the Cooperative. It's against Roosevelt policies to let non-museum employees use them unless they have permission from Director Irving. I'd pretend to work late, and Nick would sneak in. Why the hell would he lie to me about having a job? What if I got fired?"

Ansel couldn't answer, but it was obvious that Nick hadn't cared about the risks Evelyn took. "Where are the computers?"

Evelyn turned and pointed to a closed door on the right. Ansel walked over and opened it. The rectangular room was small and cold beneath the overhead flourescent. Three computer workstations sat along one long wall. Two eight-foot-long folding tables flanked another.

"I didn't know the museum had a morphometrics lab."

"It's new. We're using it to study rare museum specimens. We can scan items up to three meters in length and digitally reconstruct them for study."

Ansel inspected the hardware. One workstation comprised a computer with a twenty-inch-long laser scanning wand.

Another desk contained a TDZ station utilizing reverse engineering software. The third station contained a Silicon Graphics Infinite Reality system. She had used similar systems in computational paleontology courses and when she studied digital graphics as a paleoartist.

The laser wand scanned fossil bones and exoskeletons and converted surface dimensions into mathematical points of reference. These dimensions were analyzed by the computer and reassembled as lifelike, 3D models, which could be rotated and viewed at any angle. In this way, ancient life forms and ecosystems could come alive. Even badly damaged or incomplete specimens could be digitally reconstructed.

"What was Nick scanning?"

Evelyn shrugged. "I don't know. I did my own projects."

"You never asked?"

"No. Once I opened the door while Nick was online. He turned off the monitor, but I saw a page of his notebook before he could close it. It said 'HMN-1880.' He told me never to barge in on him again, and I made it a point not to disturb him."

Ansel searched her mind for a meaning behind the cryptic series of letters and numbers, drawing a blank. "Does HMN-1880 mean anything to you?"

"Nothing." Evelyn's red eyes widened with apprehension. "You don't think it has to do with Nick's murder, do you?"

"Maybe. Nick had some reason for using these machines. Did he ever mention Baltic amber?"

"No. Why?"

"He was collecting amber specimens. They were in his apartment office."

"I never saw it."

"Did you know about Nick borrowing money from Leslie before Cam told us on Sunday?"

Evelyn pursed her lips. "Afraid not, but it's funny you should mention Leslie and amber at the same time."

"Why?"

"I just remembered something. Inside Nick's apartment last year I noticed a journal paper Leslie had written. It was published in the *Journal of Metamorphic Geology* while he was at Yale. The topic concerned mineral caustobioliths. Isn't amber a caustobiolith?"

Ansel felt her pulse quicken. Caustobioliths included minerals of biogenic origin, which resembled stone and combusted. "Yes. What was Leslie's paper about?"

"Something to do with developing methods for manufacturing caustobioliths by using heat. I wondered why Nick had the article."

"Do you know a person named Griffin?"

"No. I don't like all these questions, Ansel."

"I'm not the only one who's going to ask. Detective Dorbandt will."

Evelyn's face blanched. "The police? You're not going to tell them about Nick and me?"

"Why would you want me to withhold information?"

"Because Karen might find out," Evelyn sputtered.

"A moment ago you doubted Karen would care what Nick had done."

"What about my career? How will it look, me sleeping with a married man who's been murdered?"

"Evelyn, this isn't about you. Nick is dead. Dorbandt should know he was working on some mysterious project before he died."

"I don't see why I should be pulled into it," Evelyn protested.

"You made the decision to have an affair with Nick. You helped him get unauthorized access to these computers. I don't see how you can stay out of it."

Evelyn scowled. "I'd let you use the computers. Just ask."

Evelyn's offer sounded like a bribe. "I'd never ask to do that. I have the Pangaea Society to worry about. We can't risk losing the Opel monies because executive members are committing adultery and conspiring to hide critical information during a homicide investigation. Our actions reflect on the society, too. I know you had your reasons, but you have to face the consequences. It's the right thing to do, and I'll help you in any way I can."

"You have a pretty high opinion of yourself," Evelyn spat. "I don't need some puffed-up drum beater in designer jeans to boss me around. It will still damage the society's precious image if you tell Dorbandt about Nick and me."

The unexpected bigotry and the venom behind its delivery shocked Ansel. She took a step backward, staring at Evelyn's vicious face in stunned silence. Her Amerind blood began to boil.

Ansel forced herself to smile. "I'll come forward and make a public statement discrediting your affiliation with the organization before I go to Dorbandt."

Evelyn frowned. "Involvement with the police could destroy me."

"Scandal could destroy the society."

"Screw the society," Evelyn shrieked. "People will think I killed Nick. My reputation will be destroyed."

Ansel surveyed the desperate woman closely. Now she knew why Evelyn had been so discomposed on Sunday. She'd been worried over what would happen if the police knew about her romance with Nick. Having slept with Nick, she could empathize with Evelyn's plight, but she couldn't forget the woman's nasty personal attack.

"Did you kill him because he left you?"

"Of course not. If you want to know who killed Nick ask Cameron. He threatened Nick. Said he'd kill him if he didn't finish the museum displays. I think he did it. Where will your precious society be if I'm right?"

Without answering, Ansel whirled and headed for the exit.

Evelyn followed her. "Where are you going? I want to know what you're going to do." She grabbed Ansel's arm in a vise-like grip.

Ansel reached the doorway, turned swiftly, and yanked her arm free. Evelyn stopped in her tracks, paralyzed by the undisguised loathing in Ansel's obsidian eyes.

"I won't tell Dorbandt about you and Nick," she said, thinking of her own entanglement with the botanist, "but I have two conditions."

Evelyn gave a small gasp of relief, then nodded. "What are they?"

"I want you to return the paperweight to the apartment. You stole it. I'll make sure it's been returned, so don't disappoint me."

"All right. What else?"

"I want your email letter of resignation as society secretary on my home computer by the time I reach Big Toe. I want all of the society records returned to me within the week, too. If you don't comply, I'll tell Cameron and Leslie what you said about us and the society. You'll be voted off the board."

Evelyn's grin of relief faltered. She opened her mouth to protest, but said nothing.

"Good-bye, Evelyn."

Ansel left the museum as fast as her legs would carry her. She made it to the truck before her hot temper cooled. Then the treachery of Evelyn's false friendship chilled her to the core. Salty teardrops streaked her face, more bitter medicine to swallow. All because she was Indian.

Chapter 10

*"The coyotes go about at night to rob and
kill. I cannot see them. I am not God."*

Cochise, Apache

Ansel hated coming back to a dark house. The drive from
Fort Peck had taken longer than she'd expected. Rush hour
traffic had been terrible, an ordeal she didn't often experience
with a work-at-home business. She unlocked the trailer door
and stepped inside. The porch halogens cast brilliant white
beams across the front yard after she flipped a wall switch.

She tossed her fanny pack onto the couch. When she
turned on the Tiffany lamp beside the sofa, a multicolored
glow spotlighted the answering machine. The red message
light winked so fast that it amazed her. Deciding not to fight
the inevitable, Ansel pushed the PLAY button.

Beep... "Ansel, this is Andrew Henderson from the
Montana Museum Association. What's going on down there?
The board has just heard about the murder of Nicholas Capos.
Give me a call as soon as you get in. Thanks."

Beep... "Hello, Ansel. Phil Rodgers at *Science Quest*.
Doctor Andreasson approved your artwork. Once I get it,
we're set to make the proofs. Your check is going off. Are you
interested in doing some more projects? Call me, and we'll
discuss it. Bye-bye."

Beep… "Leslie Maze. Please phone me when you get a chance, Ansel."

Beep… "Hau, Sarcee. When you want the crow gut delivered to the ranch. Lucy needs to know when to start cooking. Jessie. Over and out."

Beep… "Miss Phoenix. Lieutenant Dorbandt. I need to talk to you again. Call me."

Beep… "This is Karen. Nicky's memorial service is scheduled for Thursday morning, eleven o'clock at the Omega Fellowship in Glasgow. Have you looked over the collection? I'd like to get that stuff sold."

Beep… "Sarcee, Pearl and I are worried. The newspaper has us spooked. You call us, hear? Love you, sweetie."

Beep… "This is Cameron. Did you see the article in the *Sky Sentinel* about Nick? He was poisoned with strychnine. We need to do more damage control. Call me immediately."

Beep… "Ansel, I sent my email resignation to you, but can't we talk about this? I'm sorry for what I said to you. I mean it. Please call me when you get in."

Overwhelmed by the messages, Ansel stared at the black device as if it had turned into a crouching beast. Nick had been killed with strychnine? His funeral was on Thursday? Henderson from the museum association sounded upset. Evelyn wanted to rehash everything? And, Dorbandt was trying to track her down for another little interrogation.

"Shit," Ansel cursed, slapping her thigh in frustration.

Could the day get any worse? She'd learned useful information about Nick, but she was emotionally drained and very hungry. All she wanted to do was shut out the world and lick her wounds for the rest of the evening. The one bright spot on the horizon was the money she'd get from Rodgers. Small consolation. As much as she loathed the idea, she needed to get back into the truck and find a copy of the newspaper.

Goosebumps suddenly skittered up Ansel's arms as a primal awareness alerted her to danger. Her back was toward the bedroom hallway, but she had the distinct feeling she wasn't alone.

Ansel froze, listening to sounds inside the trailer. The front door had been locked. *People pick locks*, an inner voice whispered back. The hairs on her neck rose to perilous heights when a noise broke the silence. There was no mistaking the leather-flexing squeak of boots shifting position on the carpet.

Ansel half-turned. An immense man wearing sunglasses, cowboy hat, black leather jacket, and gloves came toward her. A gun glinted in his right hand. Seconds later he grabbed her ponytail and used it as leverage to spin her back around. He quickly forced her toward the breakfast counter.

"Let go," Ansel yelled to the man behind her, pushing, punching, kicking, and bucking despite the painful pull against her scalp.

The cowboy propelled her chest down on the counter top. The Formica edge slammed into Ansel's stomach like a power punch. Tim's bag of oranges flew off the edge and thumped to the carpet. A white ceramic bowl containing delicate fossils percolating in lemon juice exploded into pieces on the kitchen linoleum.

The wind fled from her lungs. With lightning speed, the man released her hair, yanked hard on her right arm, and pulled it behind her back. Her feet lifted completely off the ground. The twisted limb shot bolts of electric fire up Ansel's shoulder, stunning her nearly senseless. A gun barrel, cold and deadly, rested against her right temple.

"Listen, and I won't hurt you," a raspy voice ordered.

Ansel's fragmented thoughts flashed on the night stand in her bedroom. What she wouldn't give for the loaded Colt revolver stashed there. She gasped for breath and fought back the pain. "What do you want?"

"You know what I want. And I want it now."

Ansel groaned. He applied more pressure to the gun. The barrel bored into her flesh while his weight pressed down on her spine. His jacket smelled of sour sweat and old leather.

Her feet kicked air while the counter dug into her stomach. Her twisted arm had gone numb. Ansel swallowed down her fear. She had to think.

"I don't know what you're talking about. I can't breathe."

"Listen, bitch. If you don't want your red ass blown against the walls, you'd better tell me where the money is."

Left cheek squashed against the counter, Ansel saw a plastic bowl next to her head that hadn't been thrown off the counter. A surge of hope calmed her when she looked past the dish toward a white gallon jug next to it.

"There is no money. You robbed the wrong house. Leave, and I'll forget you were here."

The pressure against her temple eased, and she felt the man's body relax. Still her eyes never strayed from the jug.

"You really don't have it?" the man asked with genuine surprise. "You don't have a fucking clue, do you?" A derisive chuckle escaped his lips. "Looks like Capos screwed you more ways than one."

"Nick Capos? What are you talking about?"

Minor relief flooded through her when the cowboy allowed her legs to touch the floor. The hope that he'd let her go evaporated when he pressed harder on her back. More alarming was the way his knee moved slowly between her pant legs and began traveling up her inner calves, slowly separating her thighs.

The brute leaned down and pressed his rough lips to her right ear. "If you can't help me with the money, maybe there's something else you can do, squaw."

Ansel smelled alcohol on his breath. The sweet, fruity pungency of wine. A rapist with epicurean tastes, she thought angrily. Suddenly the fear of death held no power over her. She'd died once. There were things far worse. She had to loosen his hold.

"You killed Nick," she accused, going for shock value.

The cowboy's head pulled away. "Hell, no."

"Let me guess. You're Griffin. No. Maybe you're just the scumbag who poisoned Nick for Griffin."

The cowboy went berserk. "Fuck you," he screamed, releasing Ansel's arm and yanking her upward by the hair. He spun her clockwise, attempting to pull her into his arms. As she made the spin, Ansel's left arm shot out and snagged the jug handle, hefted it, and swung it toward his enraged face.

The cowboy saw what Ansel meant to do and raised the gun. He fired, but the bullet's path intersected that of the moving jug, and an arching, pressurized gush of muriatic acid spit out the puncture hole. Then the jug connected with his head.

The clear, concentrated hydrochloric acid slapped across the cowboy's hat, sunglasses, nose, cheek, and chin. His yelp turned into an anguished scream. He staggered backward, releasing his grip on Ansel and the pistol. The gun thumped onto the carpet. Ansel jumped on the kitchen counter, tucking her legs beneath her to avoid the gurgling acid spraying everywhere.

The cowboy stumbled backward over rolling oranges. He barely escaped more sizzling liquid as it ate away at the carpet near his boots while he slapped at his own melting face. Wherever his gloved hands touched acid, the burning spread, and he screamed anew. Foul streamers hissed like snakes as they ran down the man's jacket and pants, eating through cloth and skin. The felt hat smoked. The leather gloves steamed. His sunglasses cracked. The air reeked of burnt fabric, cooked skin, hot citrus, and putrid fumes. The cowboy had the stamina of a bullock. He glared through one intact lens and located her. "You're dead," he croaked.

Ansel looked at the pistol which had fallen underneath the coffee table. She couldn't reach it, and she'd never get past him. As he stomped across the smoking rug, Ansel swivelled her buttocks and slid across the Formica counter toward the kitchen, putting a barrier between them. Everything crashed to the floor as her knees swept to the left. More bowls shattered. Fossils exploded into dust.

The cowboy lunged at her through the pass-through. He caught her flannel shirt with one hand just as she prepared to leap. Panicked, Ansel twisted around and grabbed his hand. Beneath the glove cuff, her fingers hooked onto a chain encircling his wrist. She twisted it against his skin as hard as she could, and the thug's despoiled face bellowed with pain. He pulled away, and the links in Ansel's fingers snapped.

Ansel fell off the counter, her rump hitting the ground like a bronco rider. Leaping to her feet, she reached for the cutlery in a wood block beside the refrigerator, yanked out a carving knife, and held it defensively. Little protection against a gun, but she would go down fighting.

The cowboy ran into the living room and scrabbled along the floor for the pistol. Then he staggered toward the door. Ansel could see the huge, blood-red blisters erupting on his right forehead and cheek as he gave her one last, hate-filled look. He fumbled with the lock, whipped back the door, and disappeared moaning.

Knife in hand, Ansel dashed to the door and set the deadbolt with shaking hands. She leaned against the wall crying and cussing. God, had Nick really been involved with this monster? As chilling as that thought was, there was no doubt the name Griffin had meant something to him.

Ansel looked down. The knife was clasped in her right hand. A gold chain in her left. The broken links were thick and heavy. A dime-sized charm hung from them. The stylized relief of a single human eye and eyebrow decorated the metal. Ansel had never seen the design, but the bracelet gave her indisputable proof that the cowboy had been there.

Ansel pushed the bracelet into her shirt pocket and hurried into the bedroom. The night stand stood in a corner. She squeezed by a six-foot-high, green rubber, blow-up Godzilla wearing a red cowboy bandana and plastic sunglasses to reach it.

Setting the knife on the bed, she opened the top drawer. The holstered Colt Defender rested next to a box of .45 caliber hollow-point bullets. Ansel removed the loaded, stainless steel weapon. Its perfectly tooled metal curves and customized buffalo horn grip fit her palm like she'd been born with it in her hand.

The odor of gun cleaner brought back memories. The last time she'd fired it had been over a year ago. She'd used it for target practice on empty bottles and vegetable cans. She'd never used the gun on a human being, but she might have to. Although the cowboy was badly injured and probably wouldn't return tonight, it didn't mean he wouldn't come back later.

Stronger locks, Ansel decided. She'd also have an alarm system installed. Until then she would keep her gun handy at all times. Every child on the western prairie learned how to handle a firearm, and Montana women weren't squeamish about picking up a weapon. In this state PMS stood for PASS MY SHOTGUN.

Feeling better, Ansel brought the gun into the living room. She stared at the ruined carpet. The acid jug lay on its side by the breakfast nook. A huge oval of burnt carpeting made the room rank with caustic fumes, mingled with the smell of burnt oranges. If she hadn't planned to mix acid and distilled water for cleaning brachiopods encrusted with chert, the jug would have never been on the counter. She coughed. She needed to open the windows.

Instead Ansel pawed through her fanny pack and drew out Dorbandt's card. She scooped up the remote and punched in the number, followed by Dorbandt's extension.

The phone rang. And rang. Finally there was a click and Dorbandt's gruff voice instructed her to leave her name, number, and the time. For emergencies requiring immediate police aid, he instructed her to stay on the line to be connected with the desk sergeant. She wanted to speak with Dorbandt personally. Annoyed, she turned off the remote.

The unexpected growl of a vehicle engine drew Ansel's attention. Her heart skipped a beat. Had that cowboy bastard come back? Maybe with friends? Ansel turned toward the bay window. Heavy blue curtains shrouded her from view. She moved to a corner edge and peered around the drapery.

Ansel spied a white, double-cab Ford in her driveway, and a huge smile enveloped her face. She rushed to the front door and threw it open. A tall figure with silver hair tied back into a short ponytail and dressed in a white windbreaker, Stetson, and boots stood on the steps.

"Daddy," Ansel yipped, engulfing him in a bear hug.

Chase Phoenix almost dropped the rolled newspaper he was carrying. "Whoa there, mustang." He laughed and gave her a dazzling smile. "You're cinching my girth too tight. Let me get my breath."

Ansel pulled away reluctantly. He smelled deliciously of leather polish and Lava soap, two scents she'd associated since childhood with cattle ranching. "What are you doing here?"

"I figured if Sarcee won't come to the mountain, then the mountain will come to Sarcee." His eyes rolled toward the Colt clasped in Ansel's trembling hand. "What's the Peacemaker for?"

"It's been quite a day."

Chase pulled back at arm's length and squinted at her critically. "I've been worried sick about you." Suddenly Chase lifted his head and sniffed the air. He glanced at the open doorway and his nose crinkled. "Pee Yew. What's that smell? You cooking a sweet and sour Torosaur in there?"

Ansel noticed the *Sky Sentinel* in his hands and frowned. "Daddy, we've got to talk."

Chapter 11

"...The dead are not powerless."

Chief Seattle, Suguamish

Tuesday morning temperatures on the Arrowhead had soared into the upper seventies. A stiff westerly breeze flattened the gumbo grass and rattled the chokecherry bushes. The only tree in sight, a red-stemmed willow planted one hundred twenty years before, rustled and dipped. Scarred headstones surrounded the tree, funneling the wind's breath through a gap-toothed maw of granite. Gusts became moans.

Ansel braced her body against the zephyrs. She had spent the night at the ranch. Before falling into a deep, dreamless sleep, she had made three telephone calls. One to Jessie Whitefish. One to Detective Dorbandt. The last to Andrew Henderson.

The conversation with Jessie had been quick and easy. She'd just left a message with Dorbandt, and he'd returned her call. Even her carefully constructed dialog with Henderson, president of the Montana Museums Association, had gone better than she expected.

She'd explained the known facts about Nick's murder and assured him that the Pangaea Society was just as much a victim of the incident as the MMA would be. Together, they could forge a united front and publically illustrate the merit of their impending long-term relationship with each other through the POP Center. There had only been one hitch.

"We've just got to keep our fingers crossed that none of the Opel heirs use this murder as a reason to contest the memorial gift," Henderson's high-pitched voice announced across the wires from Billings.

"Have you heard something to that effect?" Ansel held her breath.

"Just some whispers. According to a clerk friend of mine at the Lacrosse County Courthouse, Opel's only sister went in and requested a filed copy of the Durable Power of Attorney papers from the will. Seems she was interested in the Power To Make Gifts clause."

"Why?"

"Could be just curiosity. Could be the makings of a family dispute over the way Preston Opel distributed his assets. Too early to tell."

Relatives, Ansel thought despondently, could be a burden worse than your enemies. She cast a glance around the cemetery. She always felt very far removed from her Anglo heritage, even as her father's ancestors now encompassed her on every side. They had immigrated from Germain-en-Laye, France, in 1876. A shiver shot through her as she remembered with vivid clarity how her French blood had almost been spilled the day before.

The graveyard began in 1878 when her great, great grandparents lost their firstborn infant to the scourge of yellow fever. Their grief had led them to choose this upraised ridge with a distant view of the Missouri River for their daughter's final resting place. They buried Brigitte Marie Fenix with a tiny stone cross and wrought iron fencing to keep the wolves and coyotes out.

More fencing had been installed in the early 1900s for other graves. The population explosion hadn't lasted. Most of the Phoenix clan, whose surname had been Americanized, drifted away from Montana during the "dirty thirties" when drought scoured the land.

Ansel sighed and stared at the only grave inside the cemetery belonging to a non-white. She was thirteen years old when piqued Anglo relatives avidly protested her mother's interment. They wanted her body sent back to the reservation, adamant that the Phoenix family tree should be judiciously pruned of dead, Indian branches.

Her father had been furious. As fitting revenge, Chase arranged to have the largest and fanciest memorial marker he could find installed at the front of the cemetery. Mary Two Spots Phoenix was finally laid to rest in a rectangular, above-ground granite vault with a six-foot-high white marble angel on top.

Ansel peered up at the angel. The intricately carved seraphim with her mother's face held her arms open and beckoning for all eternity. Her apparel was chiseled into a ceremonial, fringed buckskin dress, a beaded headband, and laced moccasins. Long tresses fell down her chest. Huge outspread wings rose from behind like a diving eagle. The celestial guardian was both beautiful and imposing. Ansel loved it.

On the tomb's brass memorial plate an inscription read OKIE NIKSOKOWA. This Blackfoot salutation meant "Greetings, Hello my relative!" Ansel had always wondered what the snooty Phoenix clan had thought about that.

She reached out and traced the tall, Raphael-style words with one finger. "*Okie Niksokowa*," she said, wishing she had her Iniskim. After almost two decades without her mother, the hole in her heart was cauterized but gaping.

"You gonna be buried here?" queried a male voice behind her.

Ansel continued to stare at the tomb, fingers attempting to connect with Mary's heavenly spirit through earthly stone. She pulled her hand away and spun around. "You bet I am."

Jessie Whitefish looked totally relaxed. He lounged against the waist-high fence, elbows resting on the ornate crossbar.

His long-fingered hands, burdened with turquoise and silver rings, hung through the spear-tipped finials. His large concha belt buckle flashed like a mirror in the sun.

Jessie chuckled. His shoulder-length hair jumped in the wind gusting beneath his tan cowboy hat. "Gonna piss the pale faces off."

Ansel grinned as she walked toward the gate. "Just keeping up a family tradition." She had known the Siouxian man for years. He owned Frog Skins, Inc., which provided custom shirts and blouses for sale at Indian festivals, rodeos, and souvenir shops. Jessie came up with his own jokes or artistic designs, silk-screened them onto clothes, and sold them to tourists for outrageous prices.

"You shouldn't ambush a girl like that."

Jessie flashed a boyish smile. "Habit. Got to keep you *winyans* guessing."

Ansel noticed Jessie's black tee. There was a color photo of a Cavalry horse tricked out with regulation saddlery, blanket, and bridle. Block lettering asked, "EVER WONDER WHAT WOULD HAPPEN IF INDIANS RAN THE NRA?"

"Turn around, Jessie." He did.

The back of his shirt read, "KA-POW-WOW!"

Ansel laughed. "Talk about pissing people off."

When Jessie faced her, his expression was serious. "Still can't compete with you, Sarcee. Your father told me about you aggravating somebody with a mean streak last night."

"How much did he say?"

"Only that you chased away a guy who broke into your trailer. This son of a bitch didn't hurt you, did he?"

"No, I'm okay. Just a little paranoid."

"I kinda doubted you asked me here to talk about tee shirts. What's going on?"

Ansel lifted the heavy black latch on the cemetery gate, and the barrier creaked on its ancient hinges. The gritty feel of rusted metal chaffed her fingertips like sandpaper. He was right. His wife, Lucy, was a distant Blackfoot relative and could be contacted by phone. She didn't want to expose Jessie or his family to danger, but she needed his help.

"This is just between us. Promise."

He nodded. "Sure."

Ansel opened her fanny pack. "The man who broke in last night wore this." She passed the jewelry to him. "Do you know what that charm is?"

Ansel watched his broad, pock-marked face. He peered intently at the eye charm. Then he bounced the bracelet's weight in his hand as if gauging its importance with the forces of gravity. He grunted and tossed it back.

"High dollar quality, and the charm's custom made. Looks New Age. You know, stars, crystals, hexes. Maybe Egyptian hieroglyphic or that sort of thing."

"You travel all over. Have you seen it anywhere?"

"Nope, and I've seen plenty of weird things. Can't help it with the crowd I sell shirts to. Grabbing a little mystical, Indian spirit is real hip with the Path To Enlightenment crowd. Some of my best wholesale customers are real nut cases, though."

Ansel put the bracelet away. "Shoot. I need to know what this symbol means. I think it will help me identify Nick Capos' killer."

"The murdered guy in the newspaper?"

"Yeah."

"You're looking for a psycho who poisons people?"

"I'm looking, yes."

"You're just as crazy as this killer. You go poking into magic and mischief, you're asking for more trouble. A lot of people who practice arcane arts take it very seriously. They don't want to be messed with."

Ansel's eyelids narrowed. "You think I can't help?"

Jessie shook his head in distress. "No. I think you shouldn't help. This is police business. Let the *wasicuns* handle it."

"It's not just white business. It's my business. Nick was my friend."

Jessie gazed at her. "You don't get hopped up about things unless they're personal. Was Nick more than a friend?"

"Of course not. He was vice president of the Pangaea Society. I have to protect the organization's reputation."

"You want to protect your reputation, make a statement to the papers or the news stations. You want to protect your butt, stay out of it."

Ansel's temper flared. "I can't. There's a lot at stake."

Jessie crossed his arms and sighed. "All right. I don't want to know any more. I hope you have sense enough to give the bracelet to the cops."

"I'm not ready to do that. I need you to do something else for me, Jessie."

"What?"

"Find Freddy Wing. Ask him to get in touch with me."

"Freddy Wing?" Jessie questioned dubiously. "Last I heard, he was in New York. Has his doctor's degree and a fancy Manhattan office where he shrinks rich people's heads."

"Yes, but he's in Montana for a visit. He called Pearl a couple weeks ago. Said he was here for a month doing research on a journal paper. He didn't leave a number. I'd start looking on the rez, but I don't speak the lingo. You grew up there. If Freddy's still here, the pipeline will know about it."

Jessie frowned. "Wing gives me the willies."

Ansel knew what Jessie meant, but it didn't change her mind. She had met Wing through Pearl, who had helped Freddy go to college on a Native American Scholarship. Even before Pearl had met her father, she had been concerned about the cultural direction of twenty-first century Native Peoples. Pearl had been Freddy's mentor since he was ten years old. With the help of an Indian Emergency Relief Fund adoption-sponsor program, she had been his emotional and financial support.

Freddy was very successful. He received his doctoral degree in psychiatry from the University of Montana. Now he de-programmed people involved in cultist organizations or groups. Freddy could also be a gifted shaman. Sometimes the information Indian spirits passed on to him was hair-raising.

"I need Freddy," Ansel insisted. "If anyone knows what this symbol means, he does. And if he doesn't, he'll know where I can find out. Will you help me?"

Jessie sighed, looked toward the cemetery, and then rubbed a hand across his baby-smooth chin. When he turned, his face looked grim. "All right, I'll do it. It may take a few days. I can't go to Fort Peck until Thursday."

"Thanks, Jessie. You want to hear something really spooky?"

"Probably not."

"I lost my Iniskim before I found Nick's body. I still haven't found it."

"What happened to it?"

"I honestly don't know. The stone disappeared after the cord fell off. A bad omen."

"Maybe you just needed to lose it for some reason. A good reason."

She'd never considered the loss of the fossil as a good thing. "Why do you think that?"

Jessie shrugged. "Maybe you're supposed to lose it, so you can grow in some way. Could be your mother wanted it to happen. Could be a message from her. When you get it back, you'll know the answer."

Remembering the crow gut, Ansel pulled a signed check from her pack. "Thank Lucy for me. She's a lifesaver. If you can deliver the crow gut by eleven on Saturday morning, that would be perfect."

Jessie nodded. "I'll keep in touch. See you at the buffet."

"You bet." Ansel waved as Jessie departed. The cell phone in her fanny pack trilled. "Hello?"

"Ansel, he's on his way. Just tore through the main gate."

"Thanks, Seth."

The Arrowhead covered fifteen thousand deeded acres, plus another twelve thousand Bureau of Land Management lease parcels. From nose to tail, the cattle ranch was ten miles long and six miles wide. Asking the ranch foreman, Seth Bartle, to scout the main entrance while on horseback checking range fencing had been a stroke of brilliance. Thank God for cowboys with Nokia phones in their saddlebags.

She took one last look at her mother's grave. *Are you trying to tell me something, Momma?* She couldn't worry about that now. Dorbandt had agreed to come to the ranch.

Time to dance with the devil.

Chapter 12

"Friendship is the severest test of character."

Ohiyesa, Santee Sioux

Dust swirled over Dorbandt's car as he drove through an enormous log beam archway above the east entrance of the Arrowhead Ranch. Winds whipped the pasture land spreading toward infinity on every side and an eight-foot-wide, weathered wood sign knocked viciously at the upper cross post. Creaking corner chains barely tethered it against the elements.

Dorbandt recognized the terrain as true Missouri Breaks country. Once a villainous no-man's-land for rustlers like the infamous Hole-In-The-Wall Gang led by Kid Curry, the open spaces made him edgy.

Born and raised in Billings, he was a citified Montanan proud of growing up in the largest metropolitan area between Spokane and Minneapolis. Nestled within the Yellowstone Valley and ringed by high sandstone rimrocks, the state capital's skyscraper buildings, asphalt arteries, and urban sprawl were his favorite stomping grounds.

At the moment, the only other person around was a grizzled old cowhand riding a buckskin horse. The cowboy gave him a friendly smile and a hearty wave as if he were kin returning home.

At least the ranch hands weren't firing shotgun pellets at him. He drove an unmarked car, but everyone on the ranch had to know he was coming. Given the history between Chase Phoenix and McKenzie, it was a wonder that a lynching posse wasn't thundering down on him. The sooner he got this talk over with the better, though he was anxious to see the rest of the Phoenix clan for himself. Cops didn't rely on hearsay.

Dorbandt gunned the engine. The well-maintained gravel road took him between herds of corpulent black Angus trundling across the grassland. Smaller dirt roads forked off as he drove past an array of ranch structures—feed lot pens, water towers, grain bins and elevators, wood sheds, and pole barns.

"Shit."

Dorbandt slammed on his brakes. Something large and brown flew into his left windshield. The car fishtailed to the right, front wheels locking while the rear tires slid. He watched as a sage grouse thumped against the glass, flapped, and kept on moving, disappearing into the pasture.

A blood smear trickled down the glass. Wedged in the wiper blade, a downy brown feather flapped crazily. He released his breath and thought of the Capos crime scene feather. He wished the DNA results would come back, especially since the forensics results on Capos' car had been disappointing. So far, that feather was all he had in the way of potential evidence.

Dorbandt shifted into PARK, grabbed a napkin, and stepped onto the road. Warm gusts snatched at his suit, billowing his sleeves and pants and twisting his tie and hair. He reached across the hood and plucked the plume off the blade with one hand and scrubbed away the crimson blotch with the other. He released the feather into the wind. It was gone in an instant.

Dorbandt balled up the napkin, pushed it into a pocket of his flapping coat, and walked onto the dirt shoulder. No grouse. He saw only a huge Angus cow. It stood by the barbed-wire fence, mouth grinding side to side. Thick ears twitched while huge brown eyes languidly observed him. A black punch tag in the left ear bore the number 954.

Dorbandt's gaze was drawn toward the sound of an engine. A white double-cab pickup cruised down the road. He hustled to his idling car just as the truck stopped behind it.

An elderly woman with short gray-blonde hair stuck her head out the window. "Hey, you want to buy that cow?" she asked with a laugh. "She's for sale, you know. Her momma's a nice dam from the Black Licorice herd in Red Lodge."

Dorbandt liked her smile. Wide and genuine. No hostility here, he assessed, walking toward the truck. "I'm Lieutenant Reid Dorbandt with the Lacrosse County Sheriff's Department. I've come to see Miss Anselette Phoenix."

"Oh, hello, detective." She pushed her hand out the opening. "I'm Ansel's stepmother, Pearl." Her blue eyes sparkled, made even more compelling by blue-green paisleys on her long-sleeved shirt.

Dorbandt shook her hand, which was warm and surprisingly strong. "Hello, Pearl. Sorry I blocked the road."

"Never mind that. Ansel's waiting for you at the house. Too bad you didn't want to buy Maisey though." Pearl shook her head and withdrew her hand. "She's a rustler's steal for what we're asking."

"I wouldn't think selling her would be a problem. She looks like prime cut."

Pearl blinked, then started laughing. "Lord, you're a hoot, detective. You don't eat our cows. Didn't Ansel tell you? The Arrowhead is a breed ranch. We sell top quality genetic stock to beef ranches all over the country. Maisey's produced up to sixty-nine embryos from three intrauterine egg donor flushes alone. Most of our bulls produce semen at twenty-five dollars a straw. And we'll artificially inseminate anything that stands on four legs around here, too," Pearl announced proudly.

Dorbandt's face burned. It didn't seem right talking about male and female innards with the wife of a man he didn't know.

A mischievous grin dimpled Pearl's rosy cheeks. "You're turning red, Lieutenant. Sorry to embarrass you. Let me pass, and I'll lead the way."

Dorbandt nodded. He maneuvered the car so Pearl's truck could pull by and followed for another quarter mile.

Even before Pearl took another left, he saw the looming, multi-level log home topped by a pale blue, tin roof. The house was built on a nicely landscaped knoll ringed by a wall of Ponderosa pines, alders, Oregon grapes, and serviceberries. Dorbandt whistled as the gravel road turned into a long, brown paver-stone driveway. Pearl stopped the Ford and hopped out.

As Dorbandt exited his car, he noted a red Ford pickup and a blue Saturn parked on the west side of the house. The driveway led around to a detached garage. He took in the rest of the Phoenix homestead: milled spruce log exterior, peaked A-frame ceiling, tempered glass windows. The place had to be four thousand square feet under air.

"Come in and meet my husband." Pearl went up stairs and onto a ten-foot-wide deck that ran the front length of the home. "Then you and Ansel can talk business. Terrible thing about Nick's murder. Unbelievable."

Dorbandt followed up the stairway with thick, hand-carved ornamental posts and railings. Several high-back chairs faced the road. Dusty leather riding chaps were draped over some. Four pairs of dirty cowboy boots in different sizes and colors stood beside the door.

"Pearl, did you know Nicholas Capos?"

"I met him once. I liked him."

Before Dorbandt could ask another question, Pearl opened the door and hustled through. Smiling, she waved the detective forward, then called out, "Chase? Ansel? We have company."

Inside the tangy smell of cayenne spices wafted toward him. Pearl led the way into a great room made entirely of huge spruce timbers. The space was bathed in a warm glow.

Sunshine flowing through tall, clad-wood windows bounced off the honey-colored logs. Intermittent columns of spruce supported a cathedral ceiling.

"They should be down any moment. Sit down. Can I get you a drink?

He walked over white throw rugs that dotted the slatted oak flooring and sat on a brown leather sofa facing the soapstone fireplace. "No, thank you. I had coffee earlier."

"You're sure?"

Dorbandt smiled. "Absolutely sure."

He drank in the walls which were decorated with Indian baskets, pottery, native design blankets, and framed Amerindian art prints. No wonder Captain McKenzie hated Chase, Dorbandt thought. Besides the fact that the cattleman had married an Indian woman, it must really stick in his supervisor's craw that Phoenix lived such a luxurious lifestyle.

McKenzie's father had been an open pit miner in Butte for almost thirty years before the Anaconda Company sold out its copper holdings in the 1980s. When the Berkeley Pit closed, Lee McKenzie had died angry and broke, blaming greedy rich men for his slide into depression and alcoholism. Well, Ed McKenzie's an asshole, Dorbandt mused. Just like his father.

A tall, broad-chested man clad in the usual cowboy attire descended an oak staircase. Except for the long white hair pulled back in a ponytail, he bore a startling resemblance to the actor Gary Cooper, who had been born in Helena.

Dorbandt held his breath, wondering how Chase Phoenix would react to having a Lacrosse County detective in his house.

"There you are," Pearl chimed. "This is Lieutenant Reid Dorbandt. He followed me up. I think he was staking out one of our cows. Detective, this is my husband, Chase."

A broad smile was etched across Chase's long, thin face, creating deep, leathery creases along his cheeks and nose. He moved quickly, crossed the distance between them, and stretched a large open palm in Dorbandt's direction. Dorbandt went with the flow.

"Good day to you, sir." Chase clasped Dorbandt's hand, pumping it with gusto. "Welcome to the Arrowhead."

"Pleasure to meet you, Mister Phoenix. I've come to talk to Anselette. She called me," he added.

"So she tells me." Chase stared the officer in the eye with undisguised appraisal. His grip on Dorbandt's hand never slackened. "Have a seat for a minute. Ansel knows you're here, and I won't hold you up very long." Chase released his grip and folded himself into a brown suede wingback chair.

"If you two bulls are going to kick up dirt, I'll just leave you to it," Pearl said with a knowing smile. "A pleasure meeting you. Don't be a stranger. Come over to the Beastly Buffet this weekend. We'd love to have you."

"Thank you for the invitation."

Pearl gave Chase one last glance and left the room.

Dorbandt felt his insides twist. He knew Chase's informal chat and his daughter's noticeable absence had been pre-arranged. This was it. Chase was going to let fly and tell him what he thought of the department. Things might get ugly, but that wouldn't stop him from doing police business.

Dorbandt looked expectantly at the rancher. Chase leaned back in his chair and met his gaze. The seconds crawled by as both men silently waited for Pearl's footsteps to become inaudible. Chase leaned forward and cleared his throat. Dorbandt's hands tightened into fists.

"Somebody tried to kill Ansel last night," the rancher declared, his voice steely. "I'd like you to see to it that nothing more happens to her in the future."

Dorbandt's anxiety melted. Despite his surprise, he switched gears and went into cop mode. "Was she harmed?"

"No, thank God. I happened to stop by her place right after it happened. She spent the night here."

"Tell me what you know."

"Just the basics. A big, nasty cowboy, carrying a gun, ambushed her inside the trailer and roughed her up. He was looking for money. Money Capos had. He thought Ansel knew about it. She didn't, and things got ugly. The bastard insinuated he was going to rape her. She poured acid on him, and he ran out smoking skin."

Dorbandt reached into his coat pocket for his pad and pen. "I don't want to miss anything relevant."

"I don't want you to miss anything either," Chase echoed. "I wouldn't be truthful if I didn't say that I'm not fond of the sheriff's department, Detective Dorbandt, but I blame that on certain people, not the whole shop. I'm approaching you with this request because Ansel's first impression of you is favorable. I trust my daughter's intuition. I don't want you to bush-tail if she gets herself into trouble. This Capos hoopla has nothing to do with her."

Dorbandt wasn't so sure. If this thug thought Ansel knew about money, he had his reasons.

"I'll do whatever I can to protect your daughter. That's my job. Breaking into her trailer with a gun is an assault with a deadly weapon. The information Ansel can provide could be a turning point in the Capos case. Once she files a report, I can examine the trailer for fingerprints or trace evidence. With a description of this creep on file, I can get an APB out on him."

Chase sighed and leaned into the chair. "Ansel won't file a report."

"She has to. I need it to proceed. Is she afraid or does she just dislike the department, too?"

"You'll have to ask her. I can tell you that Ansel's afraid of very few things. She didn't know anything about my problems until a few days ago."

"If she files a report, I can protect her much better."

"It's her decision." Chase sighed again, swiped a hand across his tanned brow, and bent forward. "She's like her mother. Stubborn."

"Stubborn doesn't catch the bad guys. Stubborn could be viewed as obstruction of justice."

"I understand, Lieutenant, and I agree with you. Ansel's being muley. You can't bully her. You've got to convince her to see things your way."

None of this made any sense to Dorbandt unless Ansel Phoenix knew more about Capos' murder than she admitted. His antenna vibrated like a lightning rod into his gut. She was a well of information he needed to siphon. If he handled her right, he might get something solid. And maybe he could get McKenzie off his back. That newspaper article had side-swiped him.

"I'd better talk to your daughter, Mister Phoenix." He stood and straightened his suit jacket before slipping the pad and pen into his pocket.

"Then we have a deal?"

"Deal?"

"You'll keep a special eye on my girl." Chase's gaze was unwavering.

"You bet I will, Mister Phoenix."

"I'll take you at your word. Thank you." Chase stood, relief smoothing his furrowed brow. "Ansel's in the study. Follow me."

Chase paced across the great room and took a sharp right-hand turn into the east wing of the house. They walked down a small hallway and passed a dining room. Another right past a kitchen and they reached a heavy cedar door.

"In here." Chase stood aside.

Dorbandt moved into the room, to be enveloped in the delicious smells of cayenne, mustard, and garlic. The study contained built-in, floor-to-ceiling bookshelves, an antique redwood desk, and plenty of cushioned chairs. It looked empty.

Ansel walked through an archway to his left which he hadn't noticed. "There you are," she proclaimed, a large silver platter of orange-red crustaceans resting on a garnished bed of Romaine lettuce in her hands. "I hope you're hungry. You're having homemade Crouching Crawdad Boil, baked potato, spinach strawberry salad with raspberry vinegar dressing, and sourdough bread. These raspberries came right from Kalispell. Dessert is pastry with chocolate mousse."

He walked a step further and saw a wooden table with four brown leather armchairs. The table faced a long row of partially opened casement windows. Formal table settings for two included a satin tablecloth, woven place mats, linen napkins, gold flatware, and china dishes.

Dorbandt also noticed Ansel's pretty smile and sparkling brown eyes as she gazed back at him. She was packaged in tight black jeans, a white short-sleeved shirt with a low zippered neckline, and black, spike-heeled boots. She looked damn good for a problem child.

Chase caught Dorbandt's gaze by leaning closer to his shoulder. "Whatever you do, buckaroo," he whispered, "don't mention the pond."

Before Dorbandt could ask what he meant, Chase retreated and firmly closed the door.

Chapter 13

"We are all children of one God. The sun, the darkness, the winds, are all listening to what we have to say."

Geronimo, Chiricahua Apache

"These are great crawdads." Dorbandt snapped off the tail, forked out the tender meat, and swallowed.

The conversation had been formal but relaxed. Neither had jumped into a discussion about the real reason for Dorbandt's visit.

Ansel watched his movements with fascination. He opened and dissected the three-inch-long crustaceans with large, dexterous hands. Every muscle in his arms bulged from beneath a white short-sleeved cotton shirt. It had been a long time since she'd enjoyed such ordinary delights. Too bad Dorbandt was a cop.

She gazed at the magnificent panorama visible through two corner windows. An east wall overlooked the Ponderosa pines and well-tended grounds. The south wall framed a pastoral view of a horse pasture, filled with beautiful pinto horses frolicking and grazing among wind-blown grasses. A large pond sparkled beneath the sun. Ansel quickly averted her eyes, vertigo spinning the room for a moment. She focused on Dorbandt.

"It's a beautiful day. Warm but windy. The horses love weather like this."

Dorbandt looked at her. "Are those overo or tobiano pintos?"

"Both. Overos have large black and white patches all over their body. Tobianos have white patches over any color except black. Pintos are Indian horses. My mother gave me that brown and white gelding when I was ten years old."

"What's his name?"

"War Bonnet. He's twenty-eight."

"He has more seniority than my boss."

Ansel stopped chewing. "I hope your boss won't mind you eating at the ranch."

Dorbandt sighed with contentment. "Don't worry. Do you ride War Bonnet?"

Ansel shook her head. "I'm not at the ranch much, and he's got laminitis. Bad hooves. He rarely gets to graze like he is today. Most of the time he's paddocked. I'll never get rid of him, though."

"Sounds like you and your mother were close. How did she pass away?"

Ansel reached to touch her Iniskim, then dropped her hand away. "Diabetes."

"She liked horses?"

"She lived and breathed them. In her twenties she performed as a professional barrel racer. She also worked the rodeo crowds wearing a ceremonial Blackfoot buckskin dress decorated with elk teeth. She charged four bucks a Polaroid. Tourists got a souvenir photo of themselves standing next to a 'real' Indian maiden. It was a lucrative gimmick for her. That's how she met my father."

"Really?"

"Yes. My father had his picture taken and never left her side. It was fate."

Dorbandt appeared to be enjoying himself. He was making small talk and working his way through a creek-full of crawfish. Good. Ansel flashed him a smile.

"Would you like more salad?"

"Yes. Thank you."

Ansel rose, grabbed the large wooden salad bowl, and walked around the table. She stood close to Dorbandt, leaned over, and dished out more of the raspberry and spinach mixture. She made sure that Dorbandt could smell her musky Shalimar perfume as well as get a good view of the mocha-colored curves within her blouse.

"Is that good for you?"

Dorbandt's breath hitched in his throat. He blinked, and heat pulsed into his cheeks. "Great. Just right. I mean, this is the best meal I've had in months."

"And you haven't even had dessert." Softening Dorbandt up was easier than she had thought. "Just yell if you want more."

Ansel walked slowly around the table, swishing her hips before taking her seat and continuing her meal. She decided the time was right to start the inevitable conversation about her attack. Dorbandt remained silent and shoveled food into his mouth.

She forked a limp crawdad across her plate. "I suppose my father told you what happened last night."

Dorbandt stopped eating. "You were lucky. Changed your mind about filing a complaint?"

"No."

"Why not?"

"I have my reasons."

"That's unfortunate."

A long silence prevailed. Ansel stared. That's all? Wasn't he going to demand the facts or try prying the info out of her? Maybe she'd softened him up too much.

"Makes me wonder though," Dorbandt added.

"Wonder what?"

Dorbandt wiped his mouth. "Why you called me. If you want to put your life in danger by allowing a maniac to go free, that's your business. I can't force you to make a report. So Miss Phoenix, why am I here?"

"I thought you'd want to know what happened. My family certainly feels better knowing the police have been told."

Dorbandt speared raspberries with golden fork tines. "This guy was looking for money he claimed Capos had?"

"Yes."

"So maybe you got a look at Capos' killer, and you don't want to help me catch him?" Dorbandt shook his head. "Not very logical for a smart scientist-type like you."

"You'll probably never understand me."

"I'm not your psychiatrist. I'm a homicide detective. You want to cut the cards and deal or not?"

Ansel bit back a sharp retort. This was no time to let her temper run away with her. She had called him.

"All right. I'll deal, but everything I tell you is unofficial."

Dorbandt nodded. "May I take unofficial notes?"

"Go ahead."

Dorbandt dropped his fork and wiped his hands. He grabbed his pad and pen from his coat jacket draped over the chair. "Shoot."

Ansel sighed. "Before I describe what happened, I want to tell you that Nick and I slept with each other. Just once. After the last society meeting I told you about earlier. He stayed and we started drinking. One thing led to another."

She scrutinized Dorbandt's reaction. The guy was a pro. He scribbled notes, a bland expression stamped across his face.

When he looked up, his gaze was inscrutable. "So Capos stayed over on June second, and you lied during our first interview."

"I didn't think it had anything to do with the murder. Afterward we were just friends."

Dorbandt scribbled again. The scratchy noise of the ball-point tip sounded like a personal indictment. "When did Capos leave?"

"I'm not sure. I woke up at noon on Sunday. He was gone. I had made a mistake."

"Did Karen Capos know about this mistake?"

"No."

"You're sure?"

Ansel was sure about Karen, but she remembered Evelyn Benchley and suppressed a shudder. Could Evelyn have found out and gone crazy, poisoning Nick for revenge? She couldn't tell Dorbandt about Evelyn's affair because she'd promised she wouldn't. And what about the man in her trailer who seemed to know about that one night?

"Karen didn't know, but that cowboy made a snide comment about Nick and me. I thought he'd just assumed we had sex."

"Maybe Nick told him," Dorbandt speculated. "And he figures Capos and you were working together. The last time anyone admits to seeing Capos was Sunday morning. Landlord spoke to him around ten o'clock when he was leaving the Sky View Apartments. Tell me about your attack."

Ansel told about coming home, listening to phone messages, and being jumped. She took her time. Dorbandt interrupted to ask questions or to clarify some detail. He took copious notes. Then she described the cowboy as best she could. She said nothing about the bracelet. If he knew about it, he'd want to see it. Then he'd want to take it.

"Now that we're finished with that, detective, would you like dessert?" Ansel, relieved, hoped to move the conversation on to something else.

Dorbandt closed his notebook. "Sure. There's just one more thing."

Ansel rose and went over to a walnut server where she picked up two plates, each laden with a large chocolate mousse. "What?"

"You're a professional artist. Draw the face of this cowboy and fax it to me."

Ansel considered the request. "I draw dinosaurs, not people. Besides, I didn't see much. He wore a big hat and sunglasses."

"Give it a try. I'll run it through the sketch artist databases. I also need to look over your trailer. Can I do that today?"

Ansel stopped beside him. "Today?"

"The sooner the better. I can dust for prints and collect evidence. I especially want to retrieve that bullet." He looked expectantly at the dessert plate in her hand.

Ansel set the china plate down hard. "This is supposed to be an unofficial report, remember?"

Dorbandt moved the dessert closer. "I'll need evidence to work with even if I don't report collecting it. You want me to catch the perp, don't you?"

"Of course. I just don't want it to be obvious that I helped."

"Hey, I'm doing you a favor. I could get in big trouble for sneaking evidence through the labs without proper authorization. I'm doing what your father asked—keep you out of trouble."

Ansel turned and went back to her seat, dropping her plate with a dull thud on the table. Suddenly she wasn't hungry, and she loved mousse.

Dorbandt ate a huge forkful of cream-filled pastry, chewing with ecstasy. "He's right, you know. Somebody has to watch your back. We could go to your place from here. I've got my evidence kit in the trunk."

"I have something planned after lunch."

"Then, tell me when," Dorbandt grinned.

He's too agreeable, Ansel thought angrily. What had her father been thinking? She loved him dearly, but she wasn't a child that needed a guard dog, especially a rough-edged, muscle-bound, hungry one. She already had a gun. God help the next person who sneaked into her trailer and tried to man-handle her. Still she had to walk a thin line between her father and the sheriff's department. She had to appear cooperative.

"Tonight at seven."

A muffled ringing erupted from his jacket. "Hold that thought." He fished out a black cell phone. "Dorbandt." His expression turned sour. "Hold on a minute." He glanced at Ansel. "Excuse me."

When she nodded, Dorbandt stood and walked toward the archway. As Ansel inconspicuously tried to eavesdrop, she managed to hear the word, "Capos," just before Dorbandt disappeared into the study. The house was like a soundproof fortress. She considered leaving the table under the guise of clearing the dishes, but never got the chance.

Dorbandt shot into the room. "I've got to leave." He reached for his jacket, pushed the phone into a pocket, and slid his arms into the tailored sleeves with practiced speed.

Ansel stood up. "Bad news?"

"Very."

"Nothing personal, I hope."

Dorbandt half-turned in the archway. "No, this is business. I'm sorry to rush out. Lunch was very good. Thank you."

"What about tonight?" Ansel trailed behind the detective as he opened the cedar door.

"I'll try to make it by seven. If I'm running late, I'll call. I need to collect evidence and get it processed as soon as possible."

"Because of the call?"

"Yes." Dorbandt hurried down the hallway.

Ansel rushed behind him. "Can you tell me what happened?"

Dorbandt slowed a bit. "I'm sorry. No."

Ansel stopped in the hallway. The truth behind Dorbandt's upsetting call hit her like a brick wall. "There's been another murder, hasn't there?"

Dorbandt halted abruptly. His piercing blue eyes met hers. "Dispatch just got a call. Evelyn Benchley was found dead at the Roosevelt Museum. When you go back to your trailer take somebody with you. Don't touch anything. Good-bye, Miss Phoenix."

Ansel was left speechless. She watched through a window as the detective raced to his car, shock and disbelief paralyzing her. She heard Pearl draw up beside her.

"Lord. He left like a jackrabbit in a brush fire."

Chase stood by Ansel's other side, hands on his hips. "Sarcee," he said, an ominous tone lacing his voice, "what in blazes did you do to that man?"

Chapter 14

*"If you have the honesty to pray for real,
from your heart, you will be heard."*

Good Lifeways Woman, Lakota Sioux

After Dorbandt rushed away, Ansel explained to Chase and Pearl what had happened. They empathized and consoled her, but she saw a deepening fear in their eyes. Under the circumstances, coming home had not been a kindness to them. Ansel urged them to go about their regular activities: Pearl had to make final arrangements with a local band to perform at the party, and Chase had to supervise the vaccinations of heifers.

Then Ansel had forced herself to sit down and write a pleasant and supportive recommendation letter for Tim Shanks. With the events of the night before, the letter had completely slipped her mind until that morning. She couldn't let Tim down. The letter waited on the foyer table to be mailed. She spent the rest of the afternoon holed up in her childhood bedroom. Alone with her morose thoughts.

Evelyn Benchley was dead. Not only drained by her emotions of grief and shock, Ansel was also riddled with guilt. In her mind's eye, she replayed the angry parting scene at the Roosevelt Museum the previous afternoon.

She had every right to have been angry. Evelyn had disparaged the Pangaea Society and had shown her vulgar intolerance of Indian Peoples. Still Ansel berated herself for allowing the secretary to get to her. Firing Evelyn as society secretary was a knee-jerk response to confrontation and, perhaps, a gross misuse of her presidential power.

All she wanted was to step down next June with a successful term record which included securing the POP Center money that would propel the Pangaea Society into a new era of statewide recognition. Nick and Evelyn had put everything at risk.

I should have returned Evelyn's call, Ansel chastised herself. *If I'd warned her about the cowboy, could I have saved her life?* She prayed that wasn't the case. As these tortuous reflections whirled through her mind, the doorbell rang.

Ansel forced herself to rise. The Timex clock on the pine night stand read four o'clock. She didn't want to answer the door, but anything would be better than suffering endless mind loops over Evelyn and Nick.

The doorbell chimed two more times before Ansel climbed down the stairs. She peered through the peephole on the heavy spruce door and didn't see anyone. When the doorbell rang again, she jumped backward. Was someone hiding from view? She turned to dash upstairs and retrieve her gun when a voice called through the door.

"Hey, Sarcee. Open up. I'm getting blown off the porch."

A smile eclipsed her fearful grimace as she unlocked the door. Freddy Wing looked up at her. All sixty pounds of him.

The psychiatrist and part-time tribal spiritualist had achondroplasia, a defect in the formation of cartilage of the long bones which produced a form of dwarfism. Despite his four-foot stature, he was a dominant presence wherever he went.

Ansel leaned down and hugged him, feeling the mounds of beefy muscle inflating his shoulders, chest, forearms, and calves. To offset progressive bone and ligature problems, Freddy weight-trained daily. He smelled of sage and fry-bread.

"I've missed you," she said.

The wind tousled Freddy's waist-long, ebony locks, as he flashed her a knee-weakening smile, revealing perfect little alabaster teeth. "I was told to come. So here I am," he declared, throwing up his child-like arms.

Ansel's heart fluttered. He had the same effect on all the ladies. She eyed the gray truck with driver parked out front. "Why don't you have your friend come in, too."

"Lenny's fine. He likes to wait," Freddy said, gazing at her with black sloe-eyes. His coffee and cream complexion was flawless, his masculine facial contours rivaling any cover-boy's good looks.

"Grab a seat."

Ansel closed the door, as Freddy moved inside with a short-legged quickness. He headed for the living room, hopped onto the sofa, and scooted backward on the leather cushion. Slightly bowed legs dangled above the floor. She sat beside him.

"The place looks great, Sarcee. How's Pearl and Chase?"

"They're great, too. They're out doing chores. Pearl will be upset that she missed you."

"I won't be in Montana long, but I'll catch them before I leave."

"Are you coming to the Beastly Buffet?"

Freddy folded tiny hands on his lap. "Gonna try. I'm supposed to be in Corwin Springs on Saturday morning doing interviews for an article."

Ansel nodded. "I hope you'll come. Pearl is pulling out all the stops. What are you researching?"

"The Church Universal and Triumphant. I'll be doing intervention and exit-counseling with ex-CUTs when I get back to New York. If it goes well, I can get something into print about the cult dynamics from a psycho-clinical perspective."

Ansel knew plenty about the New Age cult started in 1958 by Mark Prophet as a New Age retreat. Later renamed by his wife, Elizabeth, as The Church Universal and Triumphant, the church touted a combination Christian-Reincarnation philosophy.

The thirty-two-thousand-acre religious retreat had always been a burr under the saddle for state residents. The cult dallied in controversial activities that included selling expensive bomb shelters after making dire apocalyptic predictions, allowing dozens of leaking petroleum fuel tanks to contaminate the environment, stockpiling weapons, committing tax evasion, and even identity fraud.

"I don't envy you working with confused and needy people, Freddy."

Freddy gave her the once over. "Speaking of needy people, you look wrung out. I read the newspapers. How are you? "

Slightly flustered at his scrutiny, Ansel nervously brushed hair from her face. She felt too emotionally raw to deal with her problems. She wanted a good, stiff drink.

"Fine. Would you like something to eat or drink?"

"No thanks. How are your panic attacks? Had any flashbacks lately?"

At least he'd branched toward a topic she could handle, Ansel thought. "I had an episode a few days ago while I was drawing, but I got over it quickly."

"What triggered it?"

"Water leaking from a paper cup."

"Interesting. How are you sleeping?"

Ansel smiled. "Like a rock. No bad dreams."

"That's good. You want to tell me anything else?"

Ansel fidgeted. "I guess you're wondering why I sent Jessie Whitefish to find you."

"Didn't see Jessie."

"Pearl talked to you?"

"Wrong again, Sarcee."

Ansel fixed him with a wry grin. "Then how did you know I wanted to see you?"

Freddy's eyes sparkled. "A meadowlark told me."

"Uh huh. And what did the meadowlark say exactly?"

His brow furrowed. "It was a short message, but I had a hell of a time figuring it out."

Ansel couldn't resist taunting him. "Why? Did the bird have a cheep accent?"

"Hah, hah. No, the bird spoke French. I had to find somebody who could translate. Do you know how hard it is finding a local who speaks that? I finally called a language professor at Bowie College. Imagine my surprise when I realized the meadowlark was talking about you."

Ansel was dumbfounded, but decided to move forward. "How did you come to that conclusion?"

"I realized the meadowlark spoke French because of all that French-Indian angst you cart around all the time."

"You're joking."

"I wouldn't kid about this," Freddy protested.

Ansel fell against the cushions. She'd heard the Indian gossip that Freddy could talk to animals, but she'd never believed it.

"So what was the message?"

"It said, '*Burnt honey keeps the bees warm.*'"

"What does that mean?"

"I don't know," he said with a shrug. "It's your job to figure it out."

Ansel scowled. "That's not very helpful, Freddy."

"It's all I've got. So tell me why you were looking for me."

"I've decided I don't want to talk about it."

Freddy regarded her for several seconds. Then he shook his head. "Sounds like post-traumatic avoidance behavior with a dominating superego. Self-punishment through irrational free association is characteristic of a neurotic anxiety state."

"Good job. Go back and tell the meadowlark I'm cured."

He ignored her sarcasm. "You wanted to show me something. What is it?"

Ansel nearly fell off the sofa. "You know about the bracelet?"

Freddy grinned. "No. That was just good old psychological guesswork. I don't get the big bucks in New York City for nothing."

If anyone deserved to be successful, it was Freddy Wing, Ansel reckoned. When she had been suffering through the monumental decision of whether to choose a Tasco 450X Reflector telescope or a Bushnell 1200X Deluxe Zoom Projector microscope for her eighth birthday, Freddy was a kid living in a reservation shack with fifteen other family members surviving on sowbelly.

"You're sure a little bird didn't help you?" she kidded.

Freddy reached out and took her right hand in his miniature one. "Come on, Sarcee. Didn't your mother ever tell you that you can't fight the spirits? Get the bracelet."

How could she resist his brown eyes, soothing voice and sensitive touch? What a charmer he was.

"I guess if that's what the spirits want, I'd better oblige."

Ansel left the living room and took the stairs two at a time. In her bedroom, she retrieved the gold bracelet. By the time she'd returned, Freddy had spread out a handkerchief-sized black cloth on the burled wood coffee table.

As she stood watching him, he pulled a narrow, braided rope and some matches from his size ten boy's jeans. He lighted a match and held it to the brown plait. Blue smoke curled upward. Sweet grass. The pungent, incense-like smell filled the room, purifying the area, according to Indian tradition.

"Set the bracelet in the middle of the cloth."

Surprised at his serious tone, Ansel stretched the heavy link bracelet out with the eye charm visible. When the great room was hazy with vapors, Freddy snuffed out the burning braid with a quick twist of his thumb and forefinger. He pushed the sweet grass into his shirt pocket, jumped down from the couch, and stood staring at the jewelry in deep concentration for several moments. He rotated the cloth occasionally, not touching the bracelet with his hands.

"Hai," Freddy exclaimed with disgust. He carefully pulled the cloth corners over the bracelet. Jumping back onto the sofa, he slid as far away from the coffee table as he could.

Ansel's eyes widened "What's wrong?"

"Tell me where you got this."

Ansel told Freddy of her attack and how the cowboy implicated himself in Nick's murder by admitting he was searching for money. Freddy never interrupted, unlike Dorbandt, but nodded encouragement as she relived the worst parts. When she'd finished, Freddy steepled his hands and thought quietly for a long time.

"Freddy, what is this thing?"

"This is what my people call *wihunge*. Witch medicine. A conjurer's charm."

"Not Indian," Ansel concluded.

"No. This is white power, not red. Magic power is either good or bad. Somebody bad made this. I believe it's very relevant to your friend's death."

Ansel sat down. "Do you know what the symbol is?"

Freddy looked at her gravely. "It's called an *utchat*. The Eye of Horus. Usually a charm to protect against evil."

"Why would a cowboy have it?"

"Hard to say. The *utchat* is Egyptian in origin and can represent either the left or right eye of the falcon-headed god Horus. This sky deity is associated with the sun or the moon. The charm represents the All-Seeing eye of the mind. That's all I know."

What in the world did Nick have to do with a gun-toting jerk into Egyptian mythology? Obviously Nick had either owed money or taken it from somebody. Evelyn might have known about Nick's activities. Now she couldn't tell her anything.

Freddy slid off the sofa. He pulled out a bent business card and a pencil stub from another pants pocket. A quick scrawl, and he passed it to Ansel with an enigmatic smile.

"He'll tell you about the charm." Freddy headed for the door in a fast, bobbing gait.

Ansel sprang off the couch. "Wait. That's it?" Freddy stopped short, and she almost bowled him over.

He gave her a gorgeous, machismo look. "All you need is that card."

She looked at the name and phone number. "Mortimer Peyton. He's not one of your loony patients, is he?"

Freddy opened the door, turned around, and said sweetly, "Pick up the phone and call Peyton. Do it, or I'll come back and shove your dominating superego up your neurotic id."

In the blink of an All-Seeing eye, Freddy Wing was gone.

Chapter 15

"Do not grieve. Misfortunes will happen to
the wisest and best of men. Death will come
always out of season."

Chief Big Elk, Omaha

The first thing Dorbandt heard as he entered the autopsy
suite was the ratchet sound of the diener opening a white
body bag. Used for making pipes, the polyvinyl chloride
material had been fashioned into a tough, leak-proof storage
compartment for the thirty-eight-degree Fahrenheit cadaver
of Evelyn Benchley.

Dorbandt halted beside the stainless steel autopsy table
where two other smocked and masked detectives stood with
notepads and pens handy. "Traffic was bad."

"I'm Dr. Thomas Avery," said the oldest man across from
him. "My attendant, Dan Newpoint. To your right are detectives Wherle and Carter. Wherle's the tall one. Gentlemen,
this is Detective Dorbandt from Lacrosse County. Grab a
smock, mask, and gloves from that cart, Detective."

"Dorbandt?" queried the older, balding detective. "You
working the poison case?"

"Yeah."

"Don't think these cases are related, do you?"

Dorbandt shrugged. "Could be."

Wherle's eyes grew wide above the paper mask. "Our vic was poisoned with strychnine?"

"That's what I'm here to find out."

Detective Carter, short and dark-haired, gave Dorbandt a challenging stare. "Seen your name in the papers. Getting a lot of free publicity, aren't you?"

Dorbandt let the needling remark slide. He was on their turf. "Too much."

"Don't mind Carter," Wherle said. "It's his first official autopsy. Only been in Homicide three days."

"That's none of his business," Carter said.

Dorbandt grinned beneath his mask. "A rookie? You'll be fine, Carter."

The coroner cleared his throat. "Let's get this horse out of the barn, shall we?"

The diener threw back the flap, revealing the sheet-wrapped corpse. Final vinyl, Dorbandt mused. There were endless nicknames for body bags. Squish dish. Soap envelope. Gag bag. Droop scoop. All designed to vanquish death with a chuckle and transform darkness into light.

And no place in the world was more dehumanizing than this cold, green room located in the hospital basement and furnished with stainless steel coolers, tile walls, floor drains, grocery scales, dissection hardware, and human body parts pickled in formalin-filled jars. And the smell was a cloying presence, a hellish, amalgamated scent of disinfectant, rot, and blood.

"Dan, turn off the air conditioner. It's going to get hot, but I can't have trace evidence blowing off the corpse." Avery eyeballed Carter. "If you puke, do it outside."

The diener walked to a rusty window air conditioner and switched it off. The room became much quieter, disturbed only by the sound of huge, stainless steel morgue coolers cycling on and off and whirling ventilation fans.

Avery bellied up to the table. A corpulent, elderly man with cool gray eyes resembling dirty ice chips, he was dressed in an extra-large, green scrub suit, a disposable plastic apron, sterile latex gloves, paper booties, plastic goggles, and a surgical face mask. Clipped to the collar of his scrub shirt was a small microphone.

Avery looked at Wherle. "Tell me what you've got so far."

Wherle consulted his notepad. "The vic is Evelyn Bench-ley. Found dead at six this morning in the employees room of the Roosevelt Natural History Museum. Director found her when he came to work. She was lying on her back. ME found defensive wounds on her hands and a needle puncture between her shoulder blades. Might be drug-induced. Estimated time of death is between six to ten last night."

Avery glanced at Dorbandt. "What makes you think this is related to your case?"

"Benchley and Capos knew one another."

"Any leads I should know about before I examine her?"

"Capos got a dose of concentrated strychnine solution injected in the nape of the neck. There's some missing money involved. I'm thinking this was a vendetta killing. Trace evidence was minimal, but I'm tracking down the poison's source."

The coroner nodded. "Suspects?"

"Lots. Nobody's leading the pack."

Avery motioned to the diener. They removed Benchley, sliding the body bag from under her deadweight. "Well," continued the coroner, "you're probably looking for a layman who can get strychnine and knows how to use it. Check hospitals, dispensaries, labs, and pharmacies. Don't forget feed stores, warehouses, storage areas, vet supply houses, farms, and ranches."

Dorbandt wrote a note. Arrowhead Ranch? Phoenix had known both victims.

The swishing noise of the diener slowly unwrapping the starched sheet caught Dorbandt's attention. Evelyn Benchley had been a tall, older woman wearing a matching long black and white skirt and short-sleeved top. Tan hose encased her legs. Shoulder-length strands of blonde hair had slipped from their restraints and flopped against her face.

Her hands and feet were covered with brown paper bags, carefully tied to the wrists and ankles. Approximately eighteen hours after death, her body had become locked straight at the elbows and knees, a board of frozen muscles. Her head and arms looked reddish-green. Benchley's face was doll-like: cold, lifeless. Open, glassy blue eyes stared upward: dilated, fixed.

Avery checked the I.D. tag on Benchley's right ankle. He moved up to her chest and used a stethoscope to check for a heartbeat. Then he compared a driver's license supplied with the transfer paperwork to the corpse's stony face.

"It's a match. Wherle, while I get her measurements, describe the crime scene."

"She was a fossil cleaner who often worked late at the museum. Museum entrance was locked. Rear exit wasn't. Don't know if the perp hid in the museum at closing time, or came in the unlocked rear entrance, or maybe the vic knew the person and opened the door. Evidence of a struggle. Room was tossed. Not a robbery. Director said nothing is missing. Vic had her purse and wallet. Money, credit cards, and jewelry all there. Defensive wounds on the vic's hands included broken fingernails and blood. A search of the premises didn't turn up any drugs, syringes, or needles. Not much trace evidence. So far no prints, finger or shoe. The perp is either very good or very lucky."

"Sexual assault?" Avery queried.

"Nothing we could see. Clothing was intact, and there were no bruises, blood, or body fluids consistent with rape."

"How about the body transport? That go okay?"

"Yeah. She was pronounced dead by the ME, bagged, and transported straight here by the EMTs."

"Any over-the-counter drugs in the victim's possession?"

"Just buffered aspirin in her purse."

Avery nodded. "Check the victim's home for prescription drugs, illegal drugs, and drug paraphernalia. Look in the cupboards for household poisons or pesticides. Try everything, including food goods where things can be hidden. And get me the medical history ASAP. I want to know if there's drug abuse."

"Will do," Wherle agreed, writing in his notepad.

Avery grabbed a full-plastic face shield and adjusted it over his surgical mask. He set his microphone volume. Dorbandt noticed how pale Carter looked beneath his mask. The rookie stood stiffly, nervously wiping his face with a gloved hand.

"Let's get started. This is case number 01-2515, Evelyn Benchley. The body is that of a well-developed and well-nourished fifty-two-year-old Caucasian female with blonde hair and blue eyes. The body is seventy-one inches long and weighs one hundred forty pounds. The skin is slightly greenish-red and cold to the touch. Rigor is resolving. The jaw and neck are slack. The limbs remain rigid. The corneas are cloudy."

Avery dictated as he removed the hand bags, placing them into separate evidence bags and labeling them RIGHT or LEFT. "She fought all right," said the coroner, pointing to dirty and bloody nails. "Maybe we'll get DNA."

He used rape kit collection envelopes and took fingernail parings as well as fingerprints. Everything was recorded on tape, including the physical appearance of the bruised hands themselves. The coroner removed the bags on Benchley's feet, revealing low-heeled, black leather pumps.

Avery grabbed a small, flashlight-like device from an equipment cart and clicked off the huge overhead autopsy lamps. "Turn off the regular overheads, will you, Dorbandt? Behind you on the wall."

When Dorbandt hit the lights, Avery searched Benchley's clothes with the Woods Light, looking for semen stains that would fluoresce beneath the ultraviolet rays. With the help of the diener, Avery moved the beam over the front side of Benchley's clothing. Occasionally odd pinprick patterns of purple-white light appeared. "Just some lint," Avery announced. "No signs of sexual activity."

"Just like Carter," Wherle said.

Carter didn't move, his eyes riveted to the corpse. "Very funny."

Avery put aside the Woods Light and clicked on the surgery lamps. "Turn on the lights," he directed Dorbandt. He dictated more findings, cataloguing everything Benchley wore by color, size, label, style, and location. He removed non-clothing possessions and bagged them separately for delivery to forensics.

"One Elgin watch, white metal. Two pierced earrings. Black stones in silver metal settings. Two rings. One diamond in a yellow metal setting and one blue stone in a yellow metal setting. One necklace with charm. Yellow metal."

Avery stopped the tape. "This gold necklace with charm is weird. Have a look." He held up the eighteen-inch-long chain with a dime-sized charm. "Eye design. Anybody recognize it?"

Sweat coursed down Dorbandt's forehead. And the smell inside the suite had reached a new revolting intensity. He stole a glance at Wherle and Carter. Wherle was sweating profusely, too. Carter looked greener than the cadaver.

Wherle shuffled closer. "Nope."

Carter just shook his head, so Dorbandt moved in as Wherle backed away. "Looks familiar, but I can't place it." He quickly sketched the charm in his notebook, then watched as Avery continued gathering evidence for DNA testing. Avery plucked single hair samples from the scalp and bagged them. He collected blood stain samples from Benchley's fingers via water-moistened swabs.

"Dan, let's flip her," Avery directed before dictating again. "There are numerous ante-mortem contusions on the undersides of the arms, legs, and head, suggesting the victim suffered extreme ante-mortem trauma. The bruises progress vertically up the limbs and are symmetrical on both sides of the body. There are no cuts or abrasions above the bruising, and I see no patterns or marks imprinted on the skin from a weapon. This suggests the wounds were self-inflicted during a state of intense paroxysmal, involuntary muscular contractions common to convulsions or seizures."

Dorbandt's stomach twisted. "Capos had those. Bruises on the undersides from thrashing around after he was poisoned."

The coroner pursed his lips. "Could be coincidence."

Carter's voice exploded inside the room. "Shit, we've got a serial nutcase."

Avery shook his head and glared at the young detective. "Don't put words into my mouth. I haven't determined strychnine poisoning as the mode of death. The body will reveal everything to us in its own good time. Let's have a look at this puncture mark."

Avery's gaze swept over Benchley's shoulder blades and lingered there. "What's this?" He leaned closer to the blouse. "There's a small hole punched through the cotton. Dan, hand me a swab."

"Find something?" Wherle moved closer, careful not to touch Benchley's stiffened arm.

"There's a tiny, oily-looking stain around the puncture hole. It's visible even on black fabric." Avery swabbed a sample. "I'll cut out a swatch and send it to the lab."

"What do you think it is?" Dorbandt held his breath.

The coroner's face was pensive. He stood quietly, staring at the puncture. "I'm not positive, but I think it's silicone or Vaseline. Did your ME mention that in his report?"

"No. Capos' needle puncture went directly into the skin. How did you know what it was?"

"I've seen it before. I had a case where a wildlife officer accidentally shot himself in the leg while loading a tranquilizer gun. The dart was filled with enough Ketamine to immobilize a nine-hundred-fifty-pound bull. He died in five minutes from seizures and respiratory failure. His trousers had the same stain. Sometimes hunters use lubricants to facilitate needle penetration."

"The bastard's using a dart gun?" Wherle asked.

Avery nodded. "Possibly."

"That's great for us. The sale of cartridge-fired dart rifles is regulated by federal law. Interstate shipment is restricted to government agencies or holders with a state or federal firearms license." Wherle's eyes gleamed over his mask.

Carter nodded. "We can check with local gun dealers and see who's been buying cartridge rifles and darts."

"It could be a compressed air pistol," Dorbandt added. "Easier to handle and with an accuracy up to thirty yards. That's better for close hits within small areas. No matter whether the perp used a rifle or a pistol, you need an explosive charge to fire darts. We should track down sales of CO_2 gas cartridges and powder blanks, too."

Avery snipped away a three-inch swatch of Benchley's blouse and transferred it into an evidence bag with forceps. "If it's a dart gun, tissue and fabric analysis will reveal the presence of CO_2 or gunpowder."

For two more hours, Dorbandt watched as the body was stripped, X-rayed, inspected, photographed, and washed. Finally, a nude, pale husk of the living Evelyn Benchley lay face up on the autopsy table, her head centered on a black rubber block.

Dorbandt glanced at his watch. He had to be at the Phoenix trailer by seven and it was already six. The final exam on Benchley hadn't even started yet.

Finally Avery said, "Turn the air on, Dan."

The diener followed Avery's command, then returned to the autopsy platform and opened a water spigot. A trickling fountain of clear liquid ran down the perforated tier and dripped through holes onto a flat stainless steel catch basin below.

Dorbandt shot a glance at Carter. "How're you holding up?"

The young cop's eyes were as big as casino tokens. "Shut up, Dorbandt," he grumbled.

Dorbandt chuckled. "Listen, I'm history. Thanks for letting me stand in, Dr. Avery."

"Leaving so soon?" asked the coroner. His gaze raked over a dissection tray containing a generous supply of gleaming steel instruments which included a bread knife, pruning clippers, and a vibrating bone saw.

"I have another appointment."

"Too bad. I guess it's just us chickens." Avery picked up a shiny scalpel and grinned eagerly at Wherle and Carter. "Let's dig in."

Dorbandt reached the exit and pulled off his mask. Once through the swinging double doors, he stripped off his latex gloves and smock as well. The last thing he heard as the doors flapped closed was the thud of Detective Kevin Carter hitting the floor.

Chapter 16

"All birds, even those of the same species, are not alike, and it is the same with human beings."

Shooter, Teton Sioux

Ansel yanked the steering wheel to the right, guiding the truck safely onto the two-lane road five miles east of Big Toe. She'd taken the corner too fast. A cell phone at her ear didn't help.

"Daddy, I'm running late. Has Dorbandt arrived?"

"No. I'm the only steer at the trough," Chase drawled. "I'm airing out the trailer. Place smells like a Fourth of July sparkler. Where are you?"

"I'm on Barnum Brown Road. I've got to talk to Bieselmore for a few minutes."

Chase sighed. "I'll be here, Sarcee."

"Thanks, Daddy. See you soon." She tossed the phone on the passenger seat, her eyes focused on the asphalt roadway slowly disappearing behind a curtain of darkness as a magnificent orange sun set, dragging an artist's palette of pastel colors with it.

Barnum Brown Road, named for the early twentieth-century bone digger who unearthed dinosaur fossils near Fort Peck, was a bumpy turnoff snaking through rolling pasture beside the Redwater River. Part of the lower Missouri River watershed, the narrow, serpentine tributary ran southwest and petered into hundreds of streams and seasonal creeks.

Ansel remembered when the surrounding three thousand acres had been a working Hereford ranch. Two hundred cow-calf pairs had wandered these live-water birthing grounds from March to October. The previous owner, Chester Dover, had been a friend of her father's since high school. When Chester died of a heart attack in the late nineties, she and her parents had attended his funeral.

Soon after the federal government moved in, claiming that Chester had leased Conservation Reserve Program acres from the Bureau of Land Management and failed to make annual lease payments for several years. Since Chester's relatives hadn't wanted to pay the fees, the warranty deed had been signed over to the BLM as payment for the unpaid balance and back taxes.

Luckily the Big Toe town council had recognized a commercial opportunity when it banged on the courthouse door. As part of a city rejuvenation project, they had made a proposal to the BLM to lease a portion of the forfeited property, including the fifties-era Dover house.

The business-savvy councilmen had no interest in the ranch land. What they wanted was access to the quarter mile of riverbank around Chester's house. Two years before his demise, a violent flash flood had exposed fossilized dinosaur tracks.

Slowly their municipal dream of a commercially viable tourist attraction had been transformed into a sign-on-the-dotted-line reality. The deal permitted the city to manage the dinosaur park and tourist revenues, and gain limited public access to the entombed national fossil treasures. In exchange, the council was responsible for securing the area against trespassers or vandals and paying a portion of the commercial income, plus lease monies, to the BLM. It was a bureaucratic match made in heaven, Ansel reflected.

The front gate was open and the parking lot empty except for Bieselmore's spit-and-polished black Explorer. Ansel parked close to the entrance where a lighted sign proclaimed she'd arrived at the Big Toe Natural History Museum.

A twenty-one-foot-long fiberglass sculpture of a rare Montana Torosaurus stood adjacent to the concrete walkway. The triceratops-like beast had a head as long as a compact car, an enormous neck frill, two three-foot-long brow horns, a small nose-horn, and a narrow, parrot-like beak. Ansel rubbed the dinosaur's nose-horn for good luck as she walked by.

Surprised to find the door unlocked after hours, she entered. A laser sensor gave a tonal beep. The blast of cool air felt invigorating. Even more enjoyable was the elemental smell of dirt, rock, and bone.

Ansel adored the new building. Thanks to funds anted up by the council and volunteer labor supplied by local citizens, the old two-story, wood-frame farm house had been gutted and modernized. The second floor had been removed, the interior walls knocked down, and the original foundation and roof trusses expanded outward on all sides.

She closed the door and scanned the main entry room. The museum walls were a pleasant, pale beige color and lined with huge display cases and prehistoric murals. The middle of the room had been tastefully crammed with small dinosaur skeletons and spectacular indigenous rock and mineral samples. Any remaining space was filled with books, dinosaurian models, museum souvenirs, and educational toys for children. Behind this room was a larger display hall with fossil replicas and dioramas.

Motion from above caught Ansel's attention. A huge, winged Quetzalcoatlus model hovered over her as if gliding on Cretaceous air currents. Thirty-nine feet across from wingtip to wingtip, the long-necked, toothless flying Pterosaur swayed on its cable supports during the summer months when the ceiling fans twirled at top speed.

"Ansel." Cameron Bieselmore stood in an open doorway to her right, his bald head gleaming beneath the fluorescents. "I've tried to reach you for two days. You never returned my calls."

"Hello to you, too, Cam. I can't stay long." She quickly circumnavigated a short counter advertising five-dollar-a-head tours of the tracks located on the fossilized mud flats out back.

"Let's talk in my office." He scooted through the door.

Ansel followed, dreading Bieselmore's tiny, ten by ten inner sanctum. The room overflowed with shabby-chic, maritime decor reminiscent of a wharf-side seafood restaurant. For a man who lived and breathed to study the recycling of land masses and their associated life forms, she could only rationalize Bieselmore's split personality as a result of being born and raised in Boston.

Nothing had changed. The walls swelled with prints: floundering galleons, intrepid whalers, and swift clippers. Nautical lamps made from old sea lanterns and miniature Fresnel lighthouse lenses filled the room. Ancient-looking glass barometers, storm scopes, and tide clocks covered any extra space. Against one wall, a fifty-gallon saltwater aquarium belched bubbles above a coral seascape complete with neon-colored fish, creeping mollusks, sea anemones, and aquatic plants.

Ansel got down to business. "I need to borrow Leslie's membership file."

Bieselmore stared. "May I ask why?"

"I'm going to write an article about his career and his new book for my Pangaean column. Is there a problem?"

"Don't tell me you liked his book?"

"I think it's very clever." Ansel forced a happy face. What a pretentious bore Cameron could be.

The director tapped a right index finger against his lip. "I can tell you what you want to know about Leslie. I've known the crotchety old goat for ten years."

"I'd rather read the facts for myself, Cam. Can you get the file, please?"

"Of course. You're the president."

Cameron walked to a battered four-drawer file cabinet in a rear corner, dug into his pants pocket, and pulled out a tiny brass key. He inserted it into the button-lock on the top drawer. When the key hole popped out, he opened the third drawer down, flipping through a jam-packed row of manila folders. He removed a slightly soiled, inch-thick file. He also slammed the drawer and quickly locked it.

"This is it. Bring it back as soon as you can. We don't want membership files floating around. Not professional."

You mean that you want private information at your disposal, Ansel ruminated. How much dirt could Bieselmore extrapolate from public information that fell into his beefy paws? What did he know about Nick, Evelyn, and Leslie? And what had he gleaned from her file?

Ansel stepped forward and plucked the folder from his hand. "I'll return it in a couple days."

"Now can we get on to important issues?"

"I can't stay, Cam."

"This can't wait. Have a seat."

He directed her to an empty chair as if she were a recalcitrant child, then sat in his executive chair behind a faux-wood desk. Cameron stared officiously past the mounted, two-foot-long specimen of a herring gull. The bird's slightly crossed, yellow glass eyes watched her with disdain. Ansel gritted her teeth as she dropped into a plastic, sea-green chair.

"What are you going to do, Ansel? Nick was killed with strychnine, for God's sake. You must publicly disassociate the society and us from Nick immediately."

Despite her annoyance at Cameron's attempt to place all the repercussions from murder and mayhem upon her shoulders, Ansel kept her feelings hidden. She imagined him dressed in a frigate Admiral's uniform, holding his nose with one hand and jumping ship with a piggy squeal and a splash.

Cameron's glower etched deeper. "You're in charge. Do something or we're going to lose the money to build the paleohistorical center. When the museum association finds out that Nick was poisoned, they're going to blow us out of the water."

Ansel's mood darkened. What she was about to say was truly painful for her. "I have more horrible news. Evelyn Benchley is dead." She watched his reaction carefully. She was beginning to suspect everybody.

The man's disapproving frown changed into mortified disbelief. "What?"

"The police discovered her body a few hours ago."

"Are you sure?"

"Yes. Detective Dorbandt was talking to me when the call came from the sheriff's office."

"My God. This is shocking. How did she die?"

"She was murdered."

"Was she killed with strychnine?"

"I don't know the specifics, Cam." She noted that, despite his obvious shock, not one tear spilled from his squinty eyes.

Cameron bolted upright, his gaze fierce with revelation. "You know what this means, don't you? Somebody's killing off Pangaea officers."

"Nonsense."

Though the idea of a murder plot targeting the society had never occurred to her, Ansel believed that Nick and Evelyn's deaths had more to do with dirty linens or dirty monies rather than dirty bones. Trust Biesel the Weasel to turn the tragic deaths of two people into a devious conspiracy.

"Ansel, it's so obvious. Someone's killing us off." He shivered.

"Why would anyone do that?"

"I don't know, but there's only three of us left. You, me, and Leslie. Who have you pissed off while you've been president?"

"I don't go around pissing people off."

"Somebody's gone berserk," Cameron insisted.

Ansel scowled. If he shared this epiphany with anyone, the society would be torn apart by false rumor and suspicion. And God forbid the press got wind of his crazy idea.

"Cameron, stop it. Don't mention this theory to anyone. You voted me the society's mouthpiece during this catastrophe, and I'll handle it."

"You'd better speak to Henderson of the association board, Ansel. Especially if Evelyn's murder is going to become public any time now."

"I already have. Andrew assured me that the board fully intends to support us. They want this deal to go through just as much as we do. According to him, the only problem may be Preston's sister. She's been looking into the terms of Preston's will filed at the county courthouse. I'm worried that the money wouldn't be transferred from Opel's lawyer if a relative steps forward to contest the memorial gift."

Cameron snorted through his nose. "Well, Evelyn's murder certainly isn't going to fill this woman with more confidence about the Pangaea Society's respectability. And we still must face the press."

"Tomorrow I'm sending out email statements or snail mail letters to members as well as associate societies. I've already made statements to the newspapers. The TV stations are next." She fixed Cameron with a severe stare. "Besides, you should stay away from any discussion connecting you to strychnine."

Cameron blinked beady eyes. "Why?"

"The extinction diorama you worked on with Nick contained Tertiary, alkaloid plant models in the display. He wanted them. You didn't. Those botanical models were based on strychnine-like, poisonous flora. Somebody might think you used the idea to kill him."

"Why would I want to kill him?"

"You fired him, then had to find a paleobotany expert to replace him. It cost a bundle to re-contract. The museum incurred financial hardship when it was closed so the diorama could be rebuilt."

Cameron leaned back and laughed. "You sound like Leslie. He tried to prick me with that murder scenario on Sunday. It's rubbish."

"Is it? The town council called you on the mat about it. Bad blood between a municipal employee and a professional consultant. It caused ripples in society circles, too. It gouged your pride when your reputation was sullied by Nick."

The director sat forward, his mirth dissipated and fists clenched on the desk blotter. "All that happened over a year ago. It's old news, Ansel. You think I sat around plotting retribution and deciding to lash out at Nick just when everything in my life is going nicely? That doesn't make sense."

"I don't think you did, but what will the police think?"

"Are you trying to intimidate me?"

"Absolutely not, Cam. I'm making a point. Don't spread conjecture about these murders. It will backfire on you, and that would hurt the society even more."

Cameron gave her a pained look, then relaxed. "Point taken, but you'd better tell Leslie about Evelyn before he hears it somewhere else. Otherwise, he'll have a coronary occlusion."

Ansel rose. "Leslie's a big boy, and I'm not scaring him with the notion that somebody's out to kill him because he's our newsletter editor."

"Wait. Did you talk to Karen Capos about Nick's fossil collection?"

She stopped to face him. "There is no collection. It's gone."

"Gone? What do you mean?"

"Karen gave me permission to appraise it, but when I went to Nick's apartment to start cataloguing there wasn't a fossil to be found."

"What happened to them?"

"I don't know. Did you know Nick was interested in Baltic amber?"

"I don't know what you're talking about."

Ansel believed him. Cameron looked truly appalled that Nick's collection of fossil flora had slipped through his fingers into unknown hands. Even the heartless director knew how woeful it was that a lifetime of collecting rare paleobotanical specimens had ended, leaving nothing to show for it. Nick had cherished his collection more than his marriage or his wife.

"I've got to run." Ansel took a last glance at the dead sea gull and walked out, Cameron on her heels.

"Call me. We must monitor this situation," he commanded.

"Uh huh."

Ansel swung open the entrance portal and a brilliant light cascaded inward. She was blinded. The sound of whirring machinery accompanied the white-hot glare. She raised Leslie's file in front of her eyes and peered around its edges.

A woman stood in front of her. A man with a high-intensity lamp and a minicam perched on his left shoulder dogged her side. Grinning triumphantly, the media huntress shoved a bulbous, foam-covered microphone directly into Ansel's face.

"Nancy Kilpatrick. Channel Three News. Are you aware, Miss Phoenix, that your Pangaea secretary, Evelyn Benchley, was found murdered this morning at the Roosevelt Museum?"

At the same moment, Ansel felt a firm shove against her back. Propelled forward, she almost toppled down the steps. The white steel door behind her slammed shut. A deadbolt echoed in her ears like a gunshot.

God damn, Bieselmore. He was throwing her to the wolves.

Chapter 17

*"I have seen that in any great
undertaking it is not enough for a
man to depend simply upon himself."*

Lone Man, Teton Sioux

Ansel's hands shook from fury even as she gripped the steering wheel and guided the Ranger onto her driveway. How could Bieselmore thrust her into the clutches of Kilpatrick and her video toady? Cameron was despicable. And how had the media found out about Evelyn's murder so quickly?

She couldn't remember exactly what she'd said during the interview. The rapid-fire round of questions and answers had accelerated with dizzying speed. She had tried speaking calmly and succinctly to Kilpatrick while striding toward her truck. Had she come across on film as a harried, professional spokesperson or a simpering idiot?

The headlights washed over the trailer. Ansel sighed with relief. She was home. Even if she wouldn't stay there, it was comforting to see the boxy dwelling. In contrast to the night before, the double-wide blazed with brightness.

Light poured through the open windows and front door. Her father's truck was backed up near the front steps. A white sedan sat next to it, trunk open. Dorbandt. Ansel grabbed

Maze's folder with one hand and hurriedly stuffed it beneath her seat. She didn't need the hawk-eyed detective prying into her affairs tonight.

Ansel parked the truck and jumped from the cab. The spiked heels of the button-laced half-boots she'd worn since the luncheon sank into the grass like pylons as she went to the steps. She could hear Dorbandt and her father talking. Their words jarred her to a halt.

"Why did you tell me not to mention the pond outside your study?" Dorbandt asked, his voice resounding from the left-hand side of the living room where he couldn't see her.

"Oh. I didn't want you upsetting Ansel," Chase said. "She almost drowned in the pond when she was a little girl. She's never really gotten over it. Me either, if truth be known."

"An accident?"

"Not hardly. It was Thanksgiving day, and a boy pushed her through an ice hole. She was under for forty minutes before I got her out."

Ansel stood frozen where she was, hand on the wood railing, right foot raised and about to land on the bottom step. Their voices seemed unnaturally loud in her ears, amplified so she couldn't miss hearing them. A foul, slimy taste rolled across her tongue, and the air around her felt heavy, soapy. Cold. Her breathing stopped.

The instinct to flee the property was almost overpowering. She squelched the panic response and forced her leg to move backward. Breathe, she ordered herself. It's just idle talk. It means nothing. Still she wished that she hadn't heard them.

Dorbandt whistled. "Forty minutes. That's a long time."

"The cold water saved her life. She sank to the bottom and balled up like a hibernating ground squirrel. I pulled her up by snagging her coat with a fishing rod the kids were playing with. Had to find and re-string the damn hook because the old one was gone."

"You showed amazing control under the circumstances, Mister Phoenix."

"Don't know how I did it. Lordy, dinner guests were crying and screaming that she was gone. I wouldn't give up on my little girl, though. I couldn't. Not with her momma watching me. Mary believed in me, and I had to, too. Ansel came up blue. Just about then the paramedics arrived and took over. They got her breathing, then carted her off to the hospital. She stayed there three weeks fighting off a bacterial infection from the water in her lungs."

Ansel couldn't stand any more. She turned and hurried away from the doorway, their voices fading to nothingness behind her. When she reached the truck, she stopped for several seconds to regain her equilibrium. She didn't have time to do much else.

Suddenly her father's back appeared as he dragged a huge chunk of living-room carpet and padding through the trailer doorway and down the front steps. Once it hit the ground, he tossed the rolled-up mess into the flatbed. The smell of burnt nylon pile and foam assaulted her nose. Her blue mood turned black. What a hell of a day this had been.

"Hello, Miss Phoenix," Dorbandt called from the open doorway. His white shirt sleeves were rolled up to his elbows and his forehead beaded with sweat. He looked disgruntled. Ditto, Ansel thought.

Chase turned, surprised to see her. "Hey, darlin'."

He slapped his glove-covered hands against his jeans. A cloud of dust, rubber fragments, and robin blue rug fibers rose around him like prairie smog. "I'm almost done. Figured you'd want the ruined carpet out."

Her smile was weak. "Daddy, you're a prince."

Dorbandt snapped off his rubber gloves and came down the steps toward her. "I've completed my investigation. I have good news and bad news."

"Me, too, Detective Dorbandt. Do you mind if I change into more comfortable clothes and shoes? My feet are killing me."

That seemed to leave Dorbandt speechless, and Ansel wobbled past him. He walked over to his car and fussed around inside the open trunk. It gave her a moment to speak with her father.

She rolled her eyes in Dorbandt's direction. "How's he been?"

Chase scratched an ear. "Not real chatty but when he does talk, he's a straight shooter."

"I'll be out in a minute. Keep him entertained, okay?"

Chase bobbed his head, and Ansel went inside. Even with the windows opened and ceiling fans running, the trailer was hot and stuffy without air conditioning. The living-room rug was stripped away from kitchen to bedroom hallway. The acid jug and its noxious contents were gone. So were Tim's oranges, of which she'd never tasted one juicy drop.

Without carpet, the interior smelled better, but her living-room decor was a disaster. In order to cut the carpeting out, her father had pushed her furniture against the walls in jumbled groups. A single lighted ceiling fan globe bombarded the room with an unnaturally brilliant white light, washing out colors and highlighting the barren plywood floor.

"Perfect," Ansel snorted with disgust. Her spike heels click-clacked across exposed sheathing and nail studs as she trekked to the bedroom.

Closing the door, she sank onto the bed. The boots were the first things to come off. Blood rushed to her stockinged toes, numb feet tingling painfully. Wearily, she pulled off her beaded Indian belt and form-fitting black jeans, then dropped them to the floor. Her knee-high nylons and flimsy shirt were added to the mound.

She stood in her bra and panties and rummaged through a bureau drawer for an old Moose Drool Ale tee. She also grabbed some paint-splotched carpenter jeans off a ladder back chair. So much for blinding Dorbandt with her exotic, Amerind beauty. Tonight he'd have to grill her in her work fatigues.

Ansel headed for the kitchen, not paying attention to the disheveled living room but unable to ignore the grit and sawdust on the floor beneath her bare feet. She noticed that everything knocked to the linoleum during her fight with the cowboy had been cleaned up, too. Her father. She opened the fridge and searched for something to drink, then grabbed a Coke can.

"You ready to talk now?"

Ansel jumped as if she'd been slapped. Dorbandt stood in the kitchen holding a silver briefcase. "Please, don't sneak up on me like that."

"I didn't mean to."

"Do you want a drink?"

"No, thanks. I have some questions."

She pulled out a second Coke anyway. "Let's go to my workshop. It's air conditioned."

Ansel slipped on some old, suede Minnetonkas by the kitchen pass-through, and they went outside. Her father had finished loading the rug remnants and was tying down the bulky, stinking trash with rope. A headache building momentum in the back of her skull every minute, Ansel popped the pull-tab and took a long swig of caffeine. Maybe the chemical rush would help her cope with Dorbandt's questions.

"I'm going to head home." Chase peeled off his gloves and tossed them into the truck bed. "Tomorrow I'll move the furniture back. You're sleeping at the ranch, right?"

"Yeah, I'll be there soon." She passed him the extra Coke. "Drive carefully."

"Thanks for the drink. Rug scalping is thirsty work. Good night, Lieutenant."

"Good night, Mister Phoenix."

Chase gave Dorbandt a lingering look and got into his truck. Ansel saw the silent glances. A man thing, she figured. She watched the pickup until the rear tail lights winked out behind the driveway's curve.

"This way," she said.

Ansel led Dorbandt around the east side of the double-wide. They walked along a worn dirt path. Crickets chirped, bluegrass rustled, and stars twinkled. The front of the hangar had a single personnel door as well as a fifty-foot-wide, bi-fold door. Two huge, light-sensitive, halogen pole lamps had tripped on at sunset so the area was well lit.

"Quite a workshop," Dorbandt said, pacing behind her. "You have a plane?"

"No. The former owner had a Bonanza." Ansel stopped at the personnel door and punched the alarm keypad. "I need the space. Besides my art room, I have my fossil collection out here."

Ansel pulled a plastic Tilly key chain from her coverall pocket and unlocked the door. A flick of a light switch, and the front half of the divided hangar flooded with fluorescent lighting. Skylights in the peaked roof directed moonlight into the forty-by-eighty-foot space.

Ansel watched as Dorbandt stood transfixed. She knew the room was quite impressive with its collapsible tables filled to brimming with fossil bones and reconstructed fossil replicas, long glass display cases, shelving filled with small dinosaur sculptures, and artwork depicting reptiles from the ancient past.

Dorbandt's eyes focused on her largest sculpture. The life-size, wooden beast stood over twice his height and six times his length. It was made from cut plywood pieces shaped into a gigantic, head-to-tail silhouette of an upright dinosaur. Two trunk-like wire legs and short wire forearms comprised the limbs. The head was more complete, a yard-long skull resting on a tubular frame attached to the plywood neck. The menacing skull had a jaw filled with top and bottom rows of three-inch-long, razor-sharp teeth.

"That's my work in progress. It's an Allosaurus."

"Is that a real skull?"

"No. It's a casting made from one. I'll have to get castings of the entire skeleton from a museum and position them on the plywood support."

"Sounds like a lot of work."

"It is. Then I have to add a clay musculature to the skeleton using body shape and ligature attachment clues on the bone castings. That fleshes the model out, but the skin makes the dinosaur come alive. Hide work requires applying tiny, wart-like bumps one by one to simulate carnosaur skin."

Dorbandt shook his head. "And I think police work is tedious."

Ansel led him further into the hangar. "Building the clay model is the easy part. The hard part is creating this beautiful creature and destroying it."

"Why?"

"The clay I'll use to build the dinosaur is oil-based so it never hardens. When the original model is finished, I'll create a mold of it in separate large pieces. To do that I have to paint the Allosaurus with several coats of latex, add cheese-cloth to strengthen the back of the rubber mold, then build up successive layers of fiberglass over everything to hold the latex mold in place until it hardens. When the latex mold pieces are cut away, the underlying clay dinosaur is destroyed."

"But you'll be able to make all the copies you want with castings from the latex mold. It's not a total loss."

"True. And I'll be able to sell the mold castings of a complete dinosaur to museums and tourist attractions. It's still strange spending months recreating a once living, sixty-five-million-year-old creature, knowing you'll destroy it. In a sense, I gave birth to it and nurtured it. Hacking it apart will be like killing my own child."

"If that were the case, then it would be my business."

Ansel looked at the detective. If she didn't know better, she'd think he'd actually made a joke. The corners of Dorbandt's mouth had turned up. Could it be that the pragmatic cop had lightened up a bit?

As Ansel walked into her office, a chill coursed up her spine. Evelyn had been here. She'd sat on this very sofa and expressed grief over Nick's hideous death only two short days before her own.

Ansel sat on the left arm of the horseshoe-shaped furniture. "Have a seat."

Dorbandt surveyed the stylish office, mini-kitchen, and artist's studio with a single panoramic glance as he sat next to her. Heat from his body rushed over Ansel and she hitched in a breath. A tingle of pleasure ran through her, then irritation. She had to be severely addled when a hard-nosed cop about to interrogate her sent dormant hormones flooding across her body.

Dorbandt opened his briefcase and pawed through it with deep concentration. "I examined the trailer. No signs of forced entry. My guess is the lock was picked since I found a couple small scratches on the knob plating. Found plenty of latent fingerprints, but they're small. Probably yours. Makes sense if the perp wore gloves."

He pulled out a manila folder and a pen. "No other obvious trace evidence at the scene, but I took vacuum samples. Lab might find something."

Ansel rubbed her aching neck. "Is this the bad news or the good news?"

"Neither. Good news is I found a single .45 caliber pistol slug."

"Great."

Dorbandt exhaled. "Bad news is I found the slug inside the acid jug."

"I don't like the sound of that."

"Yeah. Acid may have etched away the bore marks. Means ballistics can't match the slug to the gun."

"So even if you find the cowboy's pistol, you can't prove he fired that bullet at me."

"With the slug casing, ballistics could link the jacket back to the gun barrel, but it wasn't in the trailer. Perp must have grabbed it before he ran."

"So where does that leave me?"

Dorbandt fixed her with a stern stare. "It leaves both of us waiting for the lab results. Won't come quick. Got to push them through on the sly. Want to change your mind and file a report?"

"No. Maybe my sketch will help."

Dorbandt opened the folder. "When was the last time you saw Evelyn Benchley?"

"I saw her yesterday at the museum."

He looked up. His cool blue eyes were intense. "About what time?"

"I arrived around five and left by five-thirty."

"Why did you see her?"

Ansel swallowed. "I went to talk to Evelyn about Nick. I found out, by accident, that Nick and she had an affair."

Dorbandt's eyes narrowed. "Tell me about it."

Ansel explained the series of events that had led her to get the key to Nick's apartment, how she'd seen that Nick's fossil collection was gone, and how surprised she'd been by Evelyn's unexpected entrance. She also informed him how she had identified the missing paperweight Evelyn took from Nick's glass collection and what she had learned from Evelyn.

Dorbandt listened, but his expression darkened every minute. "Why didn't you mention this at lunch?"

"Evelyn begged me not to. She was afraid it would ruin her reputation. It wouldn't have made any difference if I'd said anything at lunch. Evelyn was dead."

"I'd prefer to decide what's important to my investigation, Miss Phoenix."

Ansel crossed her arms defensively. She didn't like his tone. "Something odd was going on with Nick before he was killed," Ansel declared. "He used Evelyn to get access to museum computers. He worked with software to evaluate and reconstruct digital images of fossils. Evelyn never knew what he was working on. Nick was secretive about it."

Dorbandt scribbled some notes in his file. "When did this happen?"

She had his full attention again. "During their affair from June to December last year. When Nick didn't need the computers, he dumped Evelyn. She was devastated."

"His having a pet project and his getting killed might be coincidence."

"I might agree if it weren't for Nick's missing fossils. I'm talking about a life-long collection he loved. Nobody seems to know what happened to it."

"Maybe he sold it."

"Some of his specimens were very rare. Nick would have thought long and hard before selling them. The only items in his apartment of interest are new Baltic amber pieces with plant and insect inclusions. Nick never expressed any interest in fossil resins to me."

Dorbandt shrugged. "I saw the amber. There wasn't much of it. Capos was desperate for money and sold everything else. End of story."

Ansel thought about Leslie Maze. Had Nick borrowed money for daily expenses? It made sense, but... "It's not that simple. Nick was a fanatical collector. Yes, he might have sold the collection, but he also changed the direction of his hobby interests for some reason. Did you take Nick's fossil files and field notebooks?"

"Why?"

"Because a clue to what he was doing may be in them."

"I've got them, but I haven't gone through them."

"I can help you," Ansel volunteered. "Everything in them would be familiar to me. I'd spot inconsistencies."

Dorbandt placed the pen and folder in his briefcase. When he turned around, his face was pensive. "I'm more worried about other inconsistencies in this case. How did you feel when you learned about the affair between Capos and Benchley?"

"Why would you ask me that?"

"You slept with Nick. I'm wondering what your reaction was."

"I was disgusted. I felt used. And they had also risked causing problems for the Pangaea Society with their behavior."

"So you went to the museum and confronted Evelyn. The next morning she's discovered dead there. You spent time with Capos before he died. As far as I know, you're one of the last people to see either victim right before they were murdered."

"I'm a suspect?" Ansel blurted, incredulous.

"Everyone's a suspect until I make an arrest."

"A man tried to kill me yesterday. I'm the one in danger."

"So maybe you're setting up the victims or just leading the killer to them. Either way, people die after they've been with you."

"I'm innocent."

"Prove it. Don't withhold information. It's counterproductive. And stay out of the sleuthing business. That's probably why you're in danger."

Ansel fumed. He was totally disregarding her observations about Nick's inexplicable new interest in Baltic amber and the disappearance of his fossils. She wanted to shake Dorbandt off his blue-steel pedestal. Why wouldn't he listen to her?

"Get that sketch done as soon as possible. I'll get back to you about the lab reports." Dorbandt rose from the couch in one swift movement.

"You know where to find me, Detective."

"Aren't you coming? You shouldn't be here alone."

"I'll be leaving in a few moments."

"I'd advise that you do. Good night."

"Goodbye," Ansel said.

Dorbandt left. Ansel heard the airplane hangar door open and close. Sheer stubbornness prevented her from giving him the opportunity to herd her off her own property as if she were a helpless female in need of male supervision. Ten minutes later, she had locked up the workshop and grabbed some extra clothes. She drove toward the Arrowhead, feeling hurt and angry. Damn Dorbandt. All she wanted was a good night's sleep.

Ansel was tired, but not so tired that she failed to notice the unmarked patrol car pulling out to follow her truck. It escorted her more than ninety miles until she safely reached the Arrowhead Ranch.

Chapter 18

"The rains are cold and bone chilling...
Without the rain, we would not live."

Evening Rain Calling Crow, Cherokee

The Montana Monitoring Cooperative was housed in a small concrete block building. Dorbandt pulled the sedan into one of eight parking slots outside the windowless gray structure. His watch read nine o'clock. The morning drive from Mission City to Glasgow had gone faster than expected.

He went through the dusty glass door decorated with gold decals and stopped before a yellow counter. Stacks of agricultural pamphlets and fliers held down by small slate rocks fluttered underneath a ceiling vent. The front room was tiny and functional, containing two church pew benches set against whitewashed walls covered with insect and plant identification charts.

"Welcome to the Cooperative. Nice morning outside."

Dorbandt estimated the woman behind the counter to be somewhere in her thirties. Her brown hair was cut short and freckles dusted her cheeks. A broad smile hung beneath a glitter of gold wire-rim glasses and silver earrings.

Adhering to western etiquette where conversations with strangers began with the weather, Dorbandt said, "Heard there's a storm coming."

"We could use the rain. I'm Dottie. What can I help you with?"

"Lieutenant Dorbandt. I have an appointment with Dr. Stoopsen."

Dottie leaned toward him, fingers playing with a bone button on her blue western blouse. "Bet you're here about Nick. Any idea who killed him?"

Dorbandt avoided the question. "Did you work with Capos?"

"Gracious, yes. I don't know why anyone would hurt him. He really knew his plants, and he was smarter than smart. Had that sexy dark and dangerous look going for him, too."

"Was he?"

Dottie's face scrunched up. "Was he what?"

"Dangerous?"

"Heavens, no," she said, pushing the glasses up her nose. "Nick was a nice fella and very polite. Never had a bad day or snapped at anyone. Doctor Stoopsen lost a real asset when he quit."

"Is Doctor Stoopsen in?"

Dottie's thoughtful look dissolved. "Sure is. I'll tell him you're here."

The woman moved through a door behind the counter. Dorbandt looked over the printed handouts and shook his head. EPA soil regulations, BLM irrigation district rules, Federal Court cattle management laws, Conservation & Reinstatement Act land acquisition forms, Department of Agriculture pesticide use rules, and National Forest Service system guidelines.

Such was the world of a rancher living in the twenty-first century American West. He wondered how Chase Phoenix managed to keep his business running while fighting a losing battle against the federal government.

Dottie appeared and waved him through a swinging half-door. "He says come on in."

Dorbandt walked into a narrow hallway. Dottie pointed to an office. A black plastic nameplate read DR. BARCLAY STOOPSEN.

He walked into another sparsely furnished room. Its walls were covered with color charts and posters brimming with educational information on dangerous plants, endangered grasses, and agricultural dos and don'ts.

Barclay Stoopsen remained seated behind a gray desk holding only a white remote phone and a huge monthly calendar blotter. A single green folder lay across the month of June.

"Good morning," he said, glancing at a gold watch on his right wrist with a perfunctory quickness.

"Lieutenant Dorbandt. Lacrosse County Sheriff's Department." He took a seat in a battered, brown office chair.

Dorbandt surveyed Stoopsen carefully. He was a small man with neatly barbered salt and pepper beard, hair, and moustache. The white lab coat over his down-home, red plaid shirt was starched to a painful-looking crispness. Dorbandt took his time pulling out his pen and notebook. Then he gazed at Stoopsen again with a steady, unblinking stare. Dead air pressurized the room as he waited for the man to speak.

Stoopsen cleared his throat. "A terrible thing about Nick. Let's get started."

Dorbandt shot an obvious look at the folder. "That Capos' personnel file?"

"Yes, but I've told you all I know on the phone."

"Actually, I'd like to know what your position is and how long you've been here."

Stoopsen couldn't hide his surprise. He hesitated, then said, "I'm a USDA agronomist and the chief researcher. I've been here eight years."

"What type of work is conducted at this facility?"

"This is an Agricultural Research Service field station for monitoring local rangelands, forestry parks, and other areas used for livestock ranching. We study plant ecologies to assure federal lands are not destroyed by overgrazing."

"What do these studies entail?"

Stoopsen's jaw clenched. "What has this got to do with Nick?"

"It's routine." He shot Stoopsen a solicitous smile.

Stoopsen's fingers tapped a nervous staccato on the blotter. "Vegetation studies are conducted on lands where suspected over-grazing by cattle and sheep needs investigation. Lab testing is performed on samples, and a report is written with recommendations for improvement. My job is to assign research duties, oversee their progress, and review and approve the final recommendations."

"How many people work under you?"

"Three. Dottie Clausen, the receptionist. Jack Kittredge, a researcher. And Dan Morgan, an assistant researcher."

"Are Morgan and Kittredge here?"

"No. They won't be in the lab until this afternoon. They're attending a day-long forestry seminar in town."

"The lab's in this building?"

Stoopsen nodded. "Behind these offices."

Dorbandt made a note. "What did Capos do?"

"Nick was employed as an assistant researcher. He collected plant samples in study areas, then conducted specific experiments or tested them using standard laboratory techniques. He was also responsible for general laboratory maintenance. He made common lab solutions and stocked supplies."

"What happened with Capos' test results?"

"He sent the information to Jack Kittredge. Jack compiled a report based on the lab data and other factors. I approved the final draft."

"How long did Capos work here?"

"Five years."

"What kind of employee was he?"

"Overall, he was quiet, reliable, and very good at lab procedure and interpretation. I don't think his talents were being used to their fullest. Nick had an IQ of one hundred sixty, but he never showed any interest in career advancement. Claimed he liked the outdoors and fieldwork more than the office grind a job promotion would have entailed."

Dorbandt gazed carefully at Stoopsen. "How did you get along with him?"

"I didn't see Nick much. I'm not in the office a lot, but I liked him. Everyone did."

"You had problems with Capos, though. Explain that."

Stoopsen inhaled deeply. "I didn't have any difficulties with Nick until the last few months of his employment."

"When was that?"

"About twenty months ago. October I believe."

"What happened in October?"

"Nick started coming to work late. Then he failed to make study deadlines. In particular, his lab reports for range investigations weren't completed on time."

"Anything else?" Dorbandt asked, scribbling.

"Nothing I could put my finger on. He just seemed disinterested in the job."

"Did you talk to him about his performance?"

"Several times. He was apologetic and promised to pick up the slack, but he didn't. After a while I gave Nick a warning that he'd have to improve or he'd lose his job. A week later Nick gave two weeks' notice without animosity. He worked his remaining days, picked up his last paycheck, and I never saw or heard from him again."

"Did Capos have problems with his co-workers?"

"None that I know about."

"How about his case studies? Any problems with the people whose property he investigated?"

Stoopsen shook his perfectly trimmed head. "No. Sometimes ranchers and farmers get upset when the Cooperative is contracted to do environmental studies on their land, but nothing ever happens except they cuss us out. Our studies are quick and unobtrusive. We don't hassle landowners."

"Did Capos ever confide in you about personal problems?"

Stoopsen grimaced and looked at his watch. "I never saw him depressed or heard him complain about anything."

"You mentioned that Capos was responsible for maintaining chemical solutions and supplies. Is strychnine used in any of your lab procedures?"

Stoopsen glowered. "Now I know where you're going with this, and I don't like it."

"Answer the question."

"No. We don't even have strychnine in the lab." His voice grew louder.

"Anywhere else?"

"Absolutely not. The Cooperative is not responsible for Nick's murder." His face turned a light shade of red.

Dorbandt looked at the folder on the desk. Stoopsen hadn't cracked the cover.

"I want to see Capos' file."

"Sorry, I can't do that." The researcher picked the folder up with fastidious speed.

Dorbandt made a show of glancing around the room. Everything was very neat: books aligned in rows, surfaces free of dust, and papers bound or filed in organized niches. A real bureaucratic neatnik.

Too bad the real world didn't work this way. In the real world, chaos ruled. It was his job to wade neck deep through the shit and garbage and find a bright shiny spot people could stand in and be proud of. He didn't like Stoopsen on principal.

Dorbandt closed his notebook, capped his pen, and pushed both items into his jacket before fixing Stoopsen with a gaze icier than a Canadian Northeaster.

"Why can't you show me the file?"

"Because Glasgow isn't in your county jurisdiction. Not to mention our employment records belong to the Cooperative Board. The file simply isn't mine to give you."

"Your Cooperative Board won't appreciate your obstruction of justice, and I doubt that your high-dollar University of Montana and BLM contractors would like your entanglement with a murder investigation. In fact, I think you should have Dottie photocopy Capos' file while I get a friendly tour of your lab."

Stoopsen's face turned to stone. "I think you should leave this office right now."

"Don't call my bluff. Fold your hand, or you're going to see my aces the hard way."

"Which means what, Lieutenant?"

Dorbandt stood and leaned forward on Stoopsen's picture-perfect desk, making sure his shoulder holster was visible. He towered above the agronomist, his lean, athletic body adding to his intimidation factor.

"Two people have died from strychnine," Dorbandt began, his voice frighteningly calm. "They convulsed in agony. Their backs arched, heels to head, so long that they beat their arms and legs into bruised pulps. They finally died by suffocating in their own lung fluids. Do you seriously think that I will leave this office willingly without that file? If I do, I'll come back and search this lab with so many sheriff's deputies, and TV reporters to catch it all on film, that you'll wish you'd gift wrapped the file, put a big, red bow on top, and given it to me the first time I asked. Are you following my lead, Doctor Stoopsen?"

Stoopsen's face went progressively whiter as Dorbandt spoke. He sat frozen, staring at the detective in horror. Finally he looked toward the door. "Dottie, come here."

Dottie rushed in, grinning gaily. "Sure thing, Doctor Stoopsen. What do you need?"

"Photocopy this while I show him the lab."

"All of it?" Dottie asked as she accepted the bulky file from his shaking hand.

"Just do it."

"Be done in a jiffy." She glanced at Dorbandt as she turned for the door. "It's starting to rain. Gonna be great for the ranchers."

Dorbandt gave her a genuine smile. "Downright perfect, Dottie."

Chapter 19

*"It is from Wakan-Tanka that the holy man has the wisdom
and the power to heal and to make holy charms."*

Flat-Iron, Oglala Sioux

At three o'clock on Wednesday afternoon, Ansel arrived in a
middle-class suburb where all the houses looked cut from
the same head on a giant Cab-Mate mineral-faceting machine.
Mortimer Peyton had made a stab at individuality, painting
his home beige with brown trim. She parked on a concrete
drive behind a customized yellow Isuzu Trooper.

Her morning had been spent on presidential correspondence.
While she wrote letters to society members and other
organization leaders about the murders, her father moved her
living-room furniture back into place. Pearl donated a large rope-
braid rug to throw on the bare living-room floor. After these
tasks were completed, she'd called Mortimer Peyton. He had
agreed to meet her that afternoon.

Peyton lived in Poplar, a small northeastern agency town
for the Fort Peck Indian Reservation. Poplar traced its begin-
nings to an Indian trading post and a freighting center for the
Great Northern railroad. The town's claim to fame was the
tribally owned A & S Industries, which manufactured camouflage netting and medical chests for the U.S. government.

Ansel went up to the door and rang a buzzer. On the phone, Peyton had been cordial and anxious to meet her. Suddenly a rail-thin, elderly man stood in the doorway. He smiled and a fluffy white moustache twitched. It reminded her of an albino Woolly-Bear caterpillar that might have crawled under his nose in search of shade.

"Welcome, Miss Phoenix."

"Hello, Mr. Peyton. I appreciate you seeing me on short notice."

When he moved back to allow her entry, Ansel stepped into a small living room. She didn't know whether to stare at Peyton's cottony hair and long, ladle-shaped sideburns or at the eclectic decor, which had a noticeable bent toward a historic, western motif. She settled for stopping beside a brown Naugahyde couch, over which hung a pair of Texas longhorns wider from tip to tip than she was tall, and watching Peyton's eyes sparkle like polished topaz nuggets.

Peyton closed the door. "Any friend of Freddy's is a friend of mine. How about something to drink?"

"No, thank you, Mr. Peyton. I'd really like to get this over. Freddy didn't tell me much. Just to show you the bracelet."

"Before I take you to my office, I want to tell you a little about myself."

"That's not necessary. I trust Freddy's recommendation."

"You're as nervous as a snake in a hog pen, and I don't want you upset by what you'll see or imagine me to be. I'm just a regular guy working forty hours a week as a construction foreman, collecting his pay, drinking Wolf Pack beer, and watching TV. You've got to listen without thinking I'm a crazy ol' crackpot. The fact is, I don't solicit my services, and I don't try to convert anyone."

Peyton eyed her silently. His likeness might have been that of an aged sheriff or a weathered wagoner of the 1800s. A leathery, paternal face and dignified mannerisms captivated her and radiated a character brimming with self-reliance, truth, and wisdom. What in the world was she going to see?

she wondered. Chasing down information about Egyptian *utchat* charms and New Age spiritualism was so alien to her compared to the grounded academia of earth sciences.

"I'm ready, Mr. Peyton."

Peyton's gray snakeskin boots scuffed the wood flooring as Ansel followed him past a wagon wheel ceiling fixture, white cedar pole end tables and coffee table, cowhide throw rugs, and bucking bronco lamps. They entered a kitchen rich in gingham accents. When Peyton opened a basement door next to the magnet-encrusted refrigerator, Ansel smelled cinnamon incense.

They descended a white birch staircase into a much cooler realm. At the bottom, Ansel stifled a gasp. This wasn't the average cellar outfitted with tool benches, rec-room pool tables, or storage boxes. In fact, the basement was unlike any she'd ever seen.

Two-foot-square white marble tiles covered the floor. The walls were solid panels of white birch. Every basement window had been draped with white velvet. There was no furniture, only an enclosed expanse filled with a veritable jungle of live potted flowers and plants. From somewhere behind the wall of greenery, the relaxing cadence of tumbling water echoed across the room.

"Being a pagan used to mean you practiced a type of Christian folk magic," Peyton said as they left the stairs. "We knew about herbs, healing, and how to find wells, stones, rivers, and the like. It's only been the last two centuries that our beliefs have become distorted to imply pagans are demented or dangerous people who cavort with supernatural beings and practice destructive magic."

Ansel walked through the indoor garden of burgeoning plant life including violets, geraniums, chrysanthemums, carnations, ponytail palms, philodendrons, and drooping ferns. She inhaled air thick with the smell of mulch, flowers, and growing greenery. Strategically positioned grow lamps in the ceiling not only kept the plants healthy, but gave the basement a soothing, sheltered atmosphere. It was beautiful.

Peyton walked beside Ansel, talking nonstop in his deep, hypnotic voice. "Magic isn't really a proper term to describe what I do. This is my religion. I listen to the earth just like Indians listen to the spirits of nature. I try to achieve a joyous union with all of nature and to use natural energies as a tool to sanctify ritual areas so I can improve myself and the world. You may pray in a building, Miss Phoenix, but my temple is a meadow or a desert."

They stopped at the north end of the cellar. Ansel felt as if she'd stumbled into a secret forest grotto. This area had been reconstructed into a large, floor-to-ceiling waterfall with a fish pond. Just below high ceiling timbers, water cascaded down through a maze of slate outcroppings into a large, crystal-clear, oblong pond filled with tropical fish.

Ansel's gaze was drawn to a nine-foot-wide circle fashioned in front of the waterfall and outlined with crystals. Inside the circle was an oak altar where a variety of items were carefully positioned. She surveyed the small black cauldron, knife, bell, wooden staff, bowls of assorted liquids and powders, candles, and sticks of incense. In a bowl of dirt, a small upright pentacle had been drawn with colored sand.

Peyton moved to the southern rim of the sphere. "This is the Circle of Stones," he intoned. "Its circumference is made of forty pre-selected quartz crystals. This is where all of my rituals take place. The other implements inside the circle are very important in helping to invoke the power of a particular God or Goddess whose essence reflects my needs."

Ansel stared at him. She could see why Peyton and Freddy had hit it off. Freddy would have found Peyton's religious philosophies quite compatible with his own beliefs, which embraced Mother Earth, Wakan Tanka, and the spirits of nature.

"I'm impressed, Mr. Peyton, but I'm confused. I assumed you were a scholar on occultism."

Peyton, magnetic green eyes gazed back. "Freddy sure didn't spill the beans, did he? No, I'm not one of those lambskin theologists from the university. I practice Wicca. I run a coven. I'm a witch."

Ansel silently cursed Freddy for not warning her. This trip was going to be a complete waste of time. Trying not to show her annoyance, she replied, "Technically speaking, wouldn't you be a warlock?"

The foreman threw back his head and bellowed out a jolly laugh. When Peyton stopped, he regarded her with his twinkling eyes. "You sure do speak your mind. I like that. Most people with a peck of opinion are four quarts low on honesty. Come into my office, and I'll show you what a blue-collar warlock can do for you."

A moment later, Ansel stood in the tiny office situated behind the grotto. The walls were raw cedar panels covered with long cedar bookshelves. All of Peyton's books concerned either nature studies or New Age topics. There was a small sofa and a desk with a computer as well.

"Let me see the bracelet."

Ansel gave it to him still wrapped in Freddy's black handkerchief. He opened the cloth and took out the jewelry with one wrinkled hand, stooping beneath a halogen desk lamp to inspect it. Ansel told herself to listen to Peyton with an open mind. She really liked this spry man who had invited her into his home, sight unseen, and shown his secret lifestyle to her with unconditional candor. Few people treated her so openly in the outside world.

"This is interesting. Want to tell me where you got it?"

Ansel had considered what to say to this question on the drive to Poplar. Should she hold details back from Peyton as she had with Dorbandt? She decided she had to level with somebody and gave Peyton a brief synopsis of the circumstances behind Nick's death and her attack. Peyton's concentration never wavered from the charm.

"It's an *utchat*, isn't it, Mr. Peyton?"

"You know about *utchats*?"

"Just what Freddy said. It's a protection charm associated with the Egyptian god Horus."

Peyton nodded. "The *utchat*, also called the *wedjit*, is known primarily as an ancient, Egyptian symbol resembling a heavily made-up eye with a symbolic beard and ostrich plume beneath, but it means a lot of things to a lot of different people. It usually represents the eye of Ra or the Eye of Horus, the Egyptian hawk-headed sun god who was the son of Isis and Osiris. Egyptians believed that pharaohs were the living incarnation of Horus."

"Have you seen an *utchat* charm like that before?"

Peyton pursed his lips. "Never saw one on a bracelet, but I've seen a few. An *utchat* is either the right or left eye of Horus. This is the right. It represents the sun. The left eye is the moon. An *utchat* is usually worn around the neck as a charm for drawing protection or good health. It's also associated with metaphysical endeavors and the study of mathematics."

Peyton handed her the bracelet. "So what is something like this doing on a Montana cowboy?" she asked.

"I gather from his name that your friend Capos was of Greek descent?"

"Yes, he was."

"That's your answer. To the Greeks, the *utchat* represents the eye of Apollo. In Greek mythology, Apollo is the god of the sun. The cult of Apollo began from Egyptian roots and gained great power over the centuries. Apollo is the beautiful, golden-haired solar man and the patron of prophecy, art, and music. One of Apollo's divinatory aids, along with the lyre, the bow, and the dolphin, is the stylized, All-Knowing eye. Sometimes it's called the Eye of Apollo. There's a group right here in Montana that worships the deity Apollo," Peyton said as he sat down in a creaky rolling desk chair.

Ansel stood behind him. The idea that such a bizarre group lived in Montana didn't surprise her. What else could she expect in a state known for its militant survival groups, racist militias, religious extremists, and all other manner of unconventional organizations that gravitated here for some uncanny reason.

"Do you think the cowboy belongs to this group?"

The computer was booted, and Peyton quickly logged onto the Internet with a few clicks of the mouse. "Probably. That charm is a classic example of Greek magic generated through those who follow the Heroic Path and initiate their powers through mythic forces. Besides the *utchat*, the gold metal links represent the yellow-gold color associated with Apollo."

Once he was on the Internet, Peyton's fingers tapped across the keyboard with amazing speed. He pulled up a Web page devoted to the Greek god Apollo and scanned it quickly. Ansel looked over his shoulder. A statue of Apollo, both the left and right *utchat* designs, and information on the god's position in the Greek pantheon of deities filled the screen.

Ansel's heart quickened. "Do you know where this cult is?"

"Yes," he said with a smile. "There's some fraternal bonding between different esoteric societies. Since we're all under fire from traditional world religions, we tend to keep tabs on each other. I know exactly where your disciples of Apollo are and who leads them."

Ansel couldn't believe her luck. "Tell me."

"The group is called the Avis Arcana. They're based just outside of Lustre, near the Fort Peck reservation. Dr. Athanasios Stouraitis runs the group from a private retreat. He's a very wealthy Greek who immigrated from the old country. He's educated, popular in academic circles, and fully devoted to his religion. He is also a practitioner of augury."

Ansel's brows knitted. "What's augury?"

"Augury is the divination of future events through the interpretation of the flight, sound, and feeding of birds. Usually this is done by taking twelve seeds or pieces of grain and feeding them to a chicken. Each piece of food is individually inscribed with a meaningful Greek symbol. As the bird eats, the diviner keeps all the grains that fall from the augury bird's mouth and reads them as prophetic messages from the gods. This type of divination is called alectryomancy."

Peyton made a moue of disgust. "Stouraitis believes he's communicating directly with Apollo, who reveals the future to him. He divines the meanings and shares his messages or predictions with his disciples."

"It doesn't sound like you approve of him, Mr. Peyton."

"I don't. Greek magic is a powerful mythic force, but Stouraitis reduces it to a game of serendipity. If our lives depend on crop-stuffed poultry, we're in a sorry mess, Miss Phoenix."

Ansel smiled. The idea of witches looking down their noses at oracles was amusing. However, Stouraitis could be a murderer. People killed for their religion every day.

"Do you know anyone associated with Stouraitis named Griffin?"

Peyton thought for several seconds. "Nope. Why?"

"Nick talked to somebody named Griffin before he died. They seemed to have a falling out."

"Are you sure it's a person?"

"I assumed so. Why?"

"Well, there is a mythological Greek beast spelled G-R-Y-P-H-O-N, which is sacred to Apollo and associated with the sun. A Gryphon had the body of a lion and the head, wings, and talons of an eagle. Several of the beasts were said to pull the chariot of Apollo across the sky. The Gryphon is also an avenging bird that lays a solar egg."

Ansel considered Peyton's information. Had Lydia overheard enough of Nick's phone conversation to know for sure if he'd been speaking about a person or about a creature?

"I need to know more about Stouraitis. Where can I get that information?"

Peyton turned back to the keyboard and tapped in a volley of letters. "Just a second."

The Apollo Web site vanished. Up sprung a home page labeled *Avis Arcana*. "Stouraitis isn't the shy type. He's gone global. I'll print this out." He typed in a command and the laser printer next to the computer spit out copies.

Ansel smiled. "That's great, Mr. Peyton. I can't thank you enough for your help."

"Seeing your pretty smile is all I need. Just be careful. Stouraitis deals with some unsavory people. I'll call upon the Mother Goddess in a ceremony this evening and draw a rune of protection for you. Perhaps that will help your quest, but you've already got something going in your favor if you face Stouraitis' power."

"What's that?"

"Your last name. A Greek diviner is going to think twice before messing with a Phoenix," Peyton said, giving her a conspiratorial, emerald-eyed wink.

Chapter 20

"The love of possessions is a snare,
and the burdens of a complex society
a source of needless peril and temptation."

Ohiyesa, Santee Sioux

Ansel parked the truck at a convenience store a mile from Peyton's house. She purchased a Coke and a candy bar, then snacked on the junk food as she read over the pages about Dr. Athanasios Stouraitis and his Avis Arcana. The printout contained an overview of the historical origins of augury, its mythological credos, qualifications for membership, and a detailed biography of Stouraitis. She started to read.

Born in 1950, Stouraitis had resided in Athens forty-seven years before coming to the United States. He acquired a zoology degree and a biology Ph.D. from the University of Crete. He had been employed for twenty years by the Greek Department of Environment as an expert on Aegean birds, serving numerous times as an officer for prestigious international organizations such as the Greek Ornithology Society and the Hellenic Ornithology Society.

Ansel perused a long list of published works, which included more than two hundred ornithological journal papers, magazine articles, and associated materials. Stouraitis had been a guest speaker at a staggering variety of European symposia on birds. Retired for five years, he still officiated over several American environmental conservatory committees and boards. Stouraitis was also a member of the Bowie College Board of Trustees. He'd had a productive life for a man who worshiped Apollo and believed he was a western oracle.

There was no doubt that his entire countenance radiated the authority and power of a formidable adversary. Stony eyes stared at her from the printed sheet. Medium-length graying hair curled over undersized ears and a broad, smooth forehead. A narrow chin hung beneath full lips pinched and unsmiling. Peyton had told her that Stouraitis dealt with unsavory characters. Had Nick and Evelyn crossed him?

Ansel folded the printouts and stuck them into the glove compartment. She considered driving north to Lustre for a quick reconnaissance of Stouraitis' estate and decided against it. Better to stick to her plan of driving to Mission City. After reviewing Leslie's membership file earlier, she had questions to ask him.

She arrived at Leslie's residence in fifteen minutes. His blue Oldsmobile Regency sat parked on the driveway. A battered white Econoline van, looking vaguely familiar, shadowed Leslie's car nose-to-trunk. She halted the truck by the curb.

Leslie owned a fairly new, L-shaped, light tan, concrete block house with a white fascia. A decorative gray board fence with a gate ran to the left of the garage and around half the house. The sod lawn was green but sparse. A scrawny pair of prickly junipers formed twin sentinels along the driveway. Ansel went through the gate and up the angled walkway leading to a white door set between two multi-pane windows. She had raised her hand to push the doorbell when the door opened and a man pushed through the screen door.

"I'll see you later," he said over his shoulder, then stopped short, realizing Ansel blocked his path.

Ansel lurched backward, avoiding the swinging aluminum door before it struck her. Her eyes widened. "Shane? What a surprise."

Shane Roco, her seminar student, glared at her. She hadn't heard from or seen him since they'd left Pitt's ranch the day Nick's body was discovered. Shane was clad in the same immaculately pressed shorts and shirt ensemble he'd worn on Saturday.

"Ansel, is that you?" Leslie's spectacled face appeared beside Shane's. "Good to see you."

Shane stepped through the doorway. "Hi, Miss Phoenix."

"You know Doctor Maze?"

Shane's mouth became a smirking half-smile. "He's my grandfather. Are we having a seminar this weekend?"

His grandson? "Yes, Sunday afternoon. We'll meet at my workshop. I'll email the details. Are you coming to the buffet?"

"I'll think about it. I've got to run. See you later." He slid past Ansel and hurried toward his van.

Leslie held the door open. "Come inside, Ansel."

She pulled her gaze from the antisocial student and stepped into the house. They stood in a medium-sized living room, very neat and new-looking with a modest sofa, recliner, television, and stereo unit in contemporary styles. The walls were relatively bare, the dowdy lighting fixtures profuse. If not for the interesting three-dimensional bird sculptures placed around the entranceway and living room, the house would have been very austere, almost monkish.

The birds of all sizes were intricately detailed with real bird feathers. A bald eagle was absolutely stunning. More life-like than Bieselmore's pathetic seagull.

"My wife did those," Leslie said, noticing her interest. "It was her hobby. As an artist yourself, you would appreciate the time it takes to make one of these. Each bird is made from wire, papier-mâché, acrylic paints, and real feathers. Takes several hundred sessions to make them right. She won several exhibitions, you know."

"They're beautiful. Where did she get the feathers?"

"From craft catalogs and local pet stores. They throw out feathers by the bagful when they clean the cages. Sit down. Coffee?"

Ansel picked a flowery, brown and white sofa. "No thanks. I didn't know Shane was your grandson. Why didn't you mention he was taking a Pangaea seminar?"

"Shane is my daughter's son. I didn't know he was in the seminar until Monday when Ellen told me. I called you Monday night. Left a message to call me, too."

She vaguely remembered his recording among those she'd listened to before being attacked. She'd never called him back. "You're right. Sorry."

Leslie lowered his bony frame into the recliner. "Don't worry about it. You're here about this awful mess with Nick and Evelyn, I suppose. A Detective Fiskar came to see me this afternoon. When will this madness stop?"

Ansel turned off her thoughts about the police and Dorbandt, a sore spot at the moment, and concentrated on Leslie. "I'm handling the society's involvement with as much decorum as I can. I think the society will weather the storm all right."

"I hope so. I'd hate to see us lose the POP Center funds when we're so close to finishing the deal. I saw you on the news. Your presentation under pressure was commendable. You're right. Time will sort this tragedy out. I don't know how I'll get through the funerals." Leslie heaved a huge sigh. "Thanks for coming by."

Feeling pleased somebody had seen her television interview and found it acceptable, Ansel smiled. She respected Leslie's opinion. "Actually, I wanted to ask you something."

"What?"

"Karen Capos asked me to appraise Nick's fossil collection. When I went to Nick's apartment to begin cataloguing, I found some Baltic amber pieces with plant and insect inclusions. Since I don't know a lot about amber and you do, I wondered if I could ask you some questions?"

Leslie stared, as unmoving as a statue for several seconds. "What makes you think I know about it?"

"You're a geologist," Ansel said, grinning so she wouldn't seem threatening.

"Yes, I am. However, fossil resins and their subgroups aren't my field. Those types of organic materials are relegated to techno geology studies pertaining to oil and coal. My field is physical geology."

Ansel was flustered. Leslie had never been shy about his accomplishments or talents. Normally, he expounded on any subject relating to geology. Backpedaling over his professional expertise defied everything she knew about him.

"That's strange," she replied bluntly.

"What is?"

"Evelyn told me she'd seen a copy of your Yale University paper on resinous caustobioliths inside Nick's apartment. She said it appeared in the *Metamorphic Geology Journal.* I wanted to read it."

Leslie's face shot through expressions of shock, annoyance, and fear in a matter of seconds. His wrinkled face turned ashen. His intense gray eyes enlarged into nickels beneath his thick prescription lenses. His hands clenched upon his lap, skeletal fingers turning pale.

"Are you all right, Leslie?"

"Just tired. Evelyn made a mistake. I didn't write the paper."

"Really? She was quite astute when it came to knowing about scholarly publications and their authors."

"Well, she was confused. I'd hardly forget a journal paper if I wrote it. I may be archaic, but I'm not senile." He managed a brief, forced smile.

"You taught at Yale."

"Yes. I worked in the geology department for ten years before I retired to Montana. Now I just want to live out my life writing and enjoying the fruits of my labor. No hassles."

"You must have been really annoyed when Nick asked for money."

Leslie's mouth flew open. He leaned forward defensively, the survival instincts of a startled animal preparing for battle. "What?"

"Cameron told me you lent Nick money."

"Biesel the Weasel," Leslie scoffed. "I should have known. That prig. He sticks his snout into everyone's business."

"You didn't give Nick money?"

"Yes, I lent Nick some money. One time. Is there a law against that?" Leslie fixed her with a challenging glare.

"Of course not. I'm just curious why he came to you."

Leslie snorted. "I guess Nick thought I had money to spare. He came to see me after I received my first royalty check for *Walk Your Dinosaur*. Said he'd made some bad investments and needed something to tide him over until the next paycheck. I was flush so I loaned him five hundred dollars. It was no big deal. I don't appreciate Bieselmore gossiping about it."

Ansel shook her head. "Nick lied. He didn't have a paycheck coming. He'd quit his job and left his wife. His old fossil collection is gone. He probably sold it to pay for expenses. I want to know why you're lying to me now, Leslie. If you were so flush, why couldn't you pay your dues to the Pangaea Society?"

"You're blowing this out of proportion. The fact is, I'm displeased that you've been perusing my personal files. I thought we had an amicable relationship, Ansel."

Ansel nodded. "You don't have to explain anything but, believe it or not, I'm trying to help you. The police would have asked you the same questions if they'd known you loaned Nick money. Eventually Cameron will tell them, and they'll be back. I could have told Dorbandt about this loan several times, too, but I didn't."

Leslie fiddled with his entwined hands, then studied his lap for several seconds before looking up again. "I haven't done anything wrong."

Ansel saw through Leslie's deception. Guilt etched its way across his haggard face as a spider web of new worry lines. He was stonewalling about something. Something that hinged either on the journal article he denied writing or on Nick's loan. She had to turn up his fear factor a few notches.

"Having anything to do with Nick during the last year could be dangerous. I was attacked in my trailer two nights ago by a man looking for money Nick owed."

"You were attacked?" Leslie swiped a bead of perspiration from his face. "My God. Were you hurt?"

"No. I was lucky." Ansel leaned toward the geologist. "Please tell me what you know, Leslie."

"There's nothing to tell."

"The paper on caustobioliths is yours."

"No," he insisted.

"I can call the Yale library and find a copy. I'll get one faxed to me and read it."

Leslie leaped from the recliner. "There is no paper."

"I can also call the Dean of the Department of Sciences and inquire about it. If that doesn't work, I'll contact the editor of the *Metamorphic Geology Journal*."

"Leave this alone," Leslie yelled, his face turning fuchsia.

"Tell me why I should," Ansel shot back.

"You're out of line, Ansel."

"I'll call Detective Dorbandt."

"Don't," Leslie wailed in fear. "What do you want from me?"

"I want you to level with me."

"Why can't you forget about it? That paper has haunted me for years. I made a mistake. One stupid, stupid mistake."

Leslie stumbled and practically fell backward into the recliner, his hands over his face. He moaned several times and then regained control. He pulled off his glasses and wiped his eyes. When he looked up, his face was flushed, his gaze watery and weak. Ansel feared he would have a stroke. He looked totally drained and defeated.

"Nick was blackmailing you," she said.

In his private hell, Leslie could barely nod. "Yes. The filthy bum was bleeding me dry."

Chapter 21

*"Birds make their nests in circles, for
theirs is the same religion as ours."*

Black Elk, Oglala Sioux

Leslie's confession didn't surprise Ansel. The Nick she'd been
learning about was capable of anything. An unbidden sense
of alarm crept into her mind as she sat on the couch across
from the distraught man.

Leslie was truly distressed over Nick and Evelyn's deaths,
but were his feelings those of remorse and guilt rather than
sadness and loss? Had they blackmailed Leslie? Had Leslie
decided to free himself from their stranglehold forever?

"Did you kill Nick and Evelyn?"

Leslie's head snapped up. "My God, no. How could you
think that?"

"I don't know what to think. How did Nick blackmail you?"

"I was a senior researcher in the Yale School of Geological
Sciences and held an extracurricular job for the *Journal of
Earth Sciences*. As a referee reviewer I scrutinized the work of
researchers who submitted their papers for publication. Two
independent reviewers have to approve a research paper for
merit and scientific accuracy before it's printed.

"One day I received a paper from *Earth Sciences* entitled, 'Pyrolysis Processes in Caustobioliths: Destructive Chemical Breakdown by Heat,' authored by two Harvard researchers. The senior scientist, Carolyn Ryes, had received her first review approval and was one step away from publication."

Leslie peered nervously over his glasses at Ansel. "I haven't spoken about this for a long time. I'm so ashamed."

Ansel gave the tortured man an encouraging smile. "Please, go on."

"At that same time, I was coauthoring a paper on processing caustobioliths via heat with Jack Kittredge, a senior author. Kittredge held a fellowship at Yale and taught as a member of the faculty. Ryes' research resembled the exact research we'd done for two years, but hers demonstrated a more efficient experimental technique and superior writing."

Ansel was familiar with the "publish or perish" mentality of professorial politics, where research grants and tenure slots depended on the gospel of the printed, scientific Word. The bickering and backstabbing between academic departments and colleges maimed careers. She'd experienced firsthand the corruption and deceit of fellow students chasing a career and big money.

Ansel nodded. "I can see why you'd be upset."

"I panicked. The research was my final manuscript submission before retirement. My last few years of work would have been for nothing. The odds that Ryes' paper would come to me for review were astronomical. I believed Fate had brought it to me, and I decided to do something about it."

"What?"

"I rejected Ryes' paper, sending it back to *Earth Sciences* with a recommendation for revision. Before I returned the paper, I sent it to Kittredge. A week later, he sent me an updated copy of his research data, which was transformed into a thoughtful, well-written, and well-documented analysis of our project. We submitted our paper to the *North American Journal of Metamorphic Geology*. It was printed two months later."

Ansel hitched in a ragged breath as the shock of his words registered. Leslie had tutored Kittredge in the fine art of scientific fraud. Tidying up experimental data or pulling whole scientific experiments out of thin air by copping Carolyn Ryes' work challenged every popular conceit about science being the search for truth through objectivity.

"Did Ryes find out?"

Leslie nodded. "Ryes didn't see our paper in *Metamorphic Geology* until several months later. By then her revised manuscript was going to the *Journal of Earth Sciences* for review again. She went ballistic."

Maze squirmed in his seat. "Aside from being a top-notch scientist, Ryes was as tenacious as a bulldog. She insisted that Kittredge and I had plagiarized her manuscript. She also charged we conspired to thwart her from getting her work published first. The ensuing upheaval over her claims continued for a year."

The woman's persevering nature impressed Ansel. Normally such a serious accusation by Ryes would have meant nothing stacked against Leslie's protests of innocence. Only a few staunch college administrators would have questioned Leslie's esteemed judgment or prowess as senior researcher, even if the Maze-Kittredge study wasn't worth the paper it was written on. The academic elite rarely endured the rigorous peer scrutiny that others did and suffered the consequences for their actions even less.

"How did it end, Leslie?"

"The college dean ordered an impartial review audit of Kittredge's experimental data. Kittredge buckled and admitted he saw Ryes' manuscript. On top of that, Kittredge's experimental data didn't add up as authentic. The backlash resulted in our paper being retracted from the *Metamorphic Geology Journal*. The university succeeded in raking over this embarrassing pitfall in their collegiate landscape. None of this ever became public."

"What happened to Ryes?"

"Her manuscript was published in *Earth Sciences*, and she left Harvard, taking an oil corporation job. Kittredge resigned his fellowship. He acquired a position with the federal government. The Dean of Sciences insisted I take a slightly early retirement."

Ansel steered the conversation back on track. "How did Nick get the paper?"

"I'm not sure, but he knew about the scandal. He came to see me in January and demanded a thousand dollars. Not a loan. A gift. I refused. He pulled out the paper. From then on, Nick wanted installments every two weeks up until four weeks ago. When Nick didn't show up to collect, I was relieved. I thought he'd gotten what he wanted from me and would stay away."

"Those payoffs must have hit your wallet pretty hard."

"It was draining my savings account, but what else could I do? I couldn't have the incident revealed to the newspapers."

"Surely, a scandal that old wouldn't impact your life here that badly," Ansel probed.

Leslie looked at her with hooded eyes. "There's something I didn't tell you."

"What?"

"During the investigation, Ryes made certain allegations about my relationship with Kittredge. I simply can't have those preposterous slanders repeated again. Not after I've become nationally acclaimed for my young adult books."

His tone told Ansel the truth. "Were they allegations of homosexuality?"

Leslie bobbed his head. "I didn't know Kittredge was gay. I had a wife and family, and the repercussions in my private life were horrible. I won't go through that experience again."

"You hated Nick, didn't you?"

Leslie gazed toward the living-room windows. His face slackened as if his mind had flown far away from the tiny room. "Yes, but I didn't kill him."

Ansel stood. "Do you have a copy of the paper?"

Slowly rising from the recliner, Leslie left the living room on shaky legs. Ansel watched as he disappeared into an adjacent hallway. Tired of sitting, she spent the next few moments walking around the room, gravitating toward the TV/stereo wall unit to survey a large color portrait of Leslie and a small elderly, gray-haired woman.

Leslie wore a brown wool suit. The woman wore a long-sleeved, brightly flowered dress with a pleated front. A gold-tone pin fastened over her heart read "Anna." The bird sculptress. His deceased wife and Shane's grandmother. Ansel wondered how Shane would react if he knew Nick had been blackmailing his grandfather.

Footfalls caused Ansel to turn. Leslie approached carrying a sheaf of folded papers. "Take the damned thing out of here. When you're done, destroy it."

Ansel took the papers from his trembling, liver-spotted hand. "Thank you. Everything will be all right."

"I wish I could be so optimistic." Leslie adjusted the glasses on his hawk nose. "Nick had a sick side to his personality we never knew about, Ansel. He had a devil inside him."

"We all do, Leslie."

✦ ✦ ✦

"You want something else?" asked the burly man behind the cheap oak counter at the Red Rose Bar.

For the first time in an hour, Ansel looked up from the wood bar shellacked to a reflective sheen. The shiny surface acted like a fun house mirror, distorting her scowling features into a goblin leer. She pushed two empty glasses toward the huge, muscle-bound Indian and nodded.

"Sure. Make it the same. No ice. I hate ice."

"Yeah, yeah," said Omaha Henry. "I know how you like 'em, Sarcee. You been coming here for years, ain't you?"

Ansel peered at Henry thoughtfully. She'd known the Sioux bartender since he'd lost his job as a professional wrestler fighting under the Mandan pseudonym of Chief Omaha. A spinal injury ended his celebrity status, and he'd taken up tending bar. Henry's calloused hands eclipsed the beer mug and the shot glass, but he handled them with the grace of an Austrian crystal cutter as he carted them away.

Ansel gazed around the seedy interior and pondered the lethargic crowd in attendance. The jukebox pumped out Waylon Jennings' "Ruby, Don't Take Your Love to Town," though nobody listened, and the demands for Henry's services were few and far between. A couple of Indians drank beers at a front table, but most of the action was happening in the back. A crowd of five Indians gathered around a large table, watching as a raucous gambling game ran its inevitable course, and the jobless men went broke.

She didn't come to the Red Rose often, only when she felt her Blackfoot bloodlines chafing against her whiteness. Touted in the reservation newspapers as a "Native American Tavern," the disintegrating wood structure was just off the Fort Peck Reservation so a liquor license could be procured. The joint was nothing but a hooch shack.

Omaha Henry returned and set another boilermaker in front of her. He wiped down the scarred bar with a blue rag that foamed with dish soap and smelled like lemons. "My advice is to slow down. It's late, and I don't want to call your father and have him pick you up because you can't drive."

Ansel didn't reply right away. When she was seventeen her father had caught her hanging around the bar and accused her of slumming with underage Indian boys for cheap thrills. She paled at the memory. She and her father hadn't spoken for days after the incident. She'd finally gone to Chase and explained that he'd misjudged her. The Red Rose represented one of the few places where she felt truly comfortable. It was far easier to be half-Indian near the reservation than to be half-Anglo near the Arrowhead Ranch.

"I'm not drunk," Ansel protested, flicking a strand of hair away from her face. "I'm deliciously numb."

"What's the occasion?"

"I'm going to a funeral tomorrow." Ansel picked up the whiskey shot, poured it into the beer, and chugged down half the drink in one swallow. She set the mug carefully on the counter.

"Sorry to hear that. Anyone I know?"

"Nobody you'd want to know."

Henry studied her for several seconds. "What do you have there?" He pointed to a piece of paper in her hands.

Ansel squinted at the small note clutched in one hand. A pencil scrawl read HMN-1880. She'd been trying to figure out what type of fossil specimen Nick had scanned into the machines. Maybe she was too close to the problem to see the answer.

Ansel pushed the slip toward Henry. "It's a puzzle. Any idea what this stands for?"

Henry stared at the line with chocolate eyes. "Phone number?"

Ansel sipped her drink. "Nope. I called every area code for 466-1880 in Montana. No such number. Try again."

"Okay. The first three letters are initials. The last four numbers are a year. Somebody did something in 1880."

"Without periods between each letter, I don't think they're initials, and the year eighteen-eighty doesn't ring any bells."

Henry shook his head. "How about a Zip code but with a zero at either end like 01880 or 18800?"

"Tried it. Massachusetts had a 01880 hit at Wakefield Station in Greenwood. There is no 18800 Zip code. Massachusetts doesn't seem related to HMN."

"Then the HMN letters are an abbreviation for something. Eighteen-hundred and eighty of them."

Ansel laughed, the first time in hours. "Yeah, that's the big question, isn't it? What's the something? I thought about abbreviations, so I looked up HMN in a book. I found Her Majesty's Navy. That's definitely not it."

Henry snapped his fingers. "I got it. The number's to a post office mailbox. Maybe HMN is a business."

"No go. Can't find any businesses online called HMN, and God forbid it's a postal box. I'll never be able to track it down."

"No wonder you've been drinking," said Henry. "That would drive me nuts. Why don't you take a break. Go over and see that chicken with a brain." He pointed toward the rear table. "Lenny claims that Kangi is over forty and played in Hitchcock's *The Birds*. He's got a great scam going on."

Something about the "chicken with a brain" statement tweaked Ansel's memory. A red buoy of inspiration floated past her synapses, then sunk out of sight. Damn, she'd almost had it. Disgusted, she swivelled her stool around and watched the betting Indians with sudden interest. Could this be the same Lenny who had driven Freddy to the Arrowhead?

"Maybe I'll do that. Thanks for your input on the note." She dug deep into her fanny pack and passed a Grant to Henry. "Keep the rest."

"*Pilamaye*, Sarcee."

Ansel slid off the stool. The chicken with a brain turned out to be a foot-and-a-half-long crow. Kangi stood on the center of a large pine board table. Ansel could see only the raven's head, thick black beak, and piercing, ebony eyes over the shoulders of the Indians hunched around it. She stood behind the swarm of bettors and watched as the quick, aggressive raven went through its routine for jerky rewards tossed by a short, fat Indian wearing an MSU Bobcats sweatshirt. Lenny.

"You know how to play?"

She turned. One of the Indians who had been sitting at a front table smiled at her. A cigarette smoldered between his dirty fingers. Middle-aged with short-cropped black hair going gray, he resembled a lot of Arrowhead ranch hands. Except the breath coming from behind his crooked teeth reeked of cheap whiskey.

"No, I've never seen this game."

"For a buck, you set two sticks down on the table in front of the bird. One stick is an inch shorter than the other. The bird picks up a stick and tries to drop it lengthwise into a slot in that box. You bet that the bird won't pick the right stick. If the Kangi picks the long stick that won't go in, you double your money. If the he picks the short stick, you lose your dollar."

At that very moment, Kangi picked up the short dowel and dropped it into the box slot. The crowd roared in disappointment as a gambler lost. The raven let loose with a chilling *caw-caw* that reverberated like a diabolical chuckle.

Ansel knew that ravens, though highly intelligent, couldn't judge an object's length. When the birds built their nests, they often brought back sticks too long to fit sideways into the entrance hole. Instead of pushing in the stick end first, the birds dropped long branches onto the ground and searched for another. Only luck helped them complete a nest.

"Ernie Vogue," said the man loudly in Ansel's ear.

"Excuse me?"

"My name. Ernie Vogue. What's yours?"

A switch flipped in Ansel's head. Amazing. She stared at Ernie, knowing without a doubt what fossil Nick had scanned into the Roosevelt Museum computers.

"The chicken with a brain," Ansel remembered with delight.

Ernie's uplifted mouth fell. "That's not very nice," Ernie slurred. "I'm just trying to be friendly."

"I've got to go," Ansel replied. She turned on her boot heels and headed for the exit with a jaunty, slightly wobbling gait.

Behind her, Kangi trilled a shrill *caw-caw* of victory.

Chapter 22

"One man's shrine is another man's cemetery."

Lame Deer, Sioux

Eyes burning even with sunglasses on, Ansel squinted against the bright sunlight streaming across the Resurrection Garden of the Omega Fellowship. She tried not to throw up. Payback for her binge at the Red Rose had ambushed her at the ranch the night before. She'd been too ill to tell Pearl and her father that she'd figured out Nick's secret project. Instead she'd silently suffered Chase's scornful gazes and Pearl's pragmatic, medicinal ministrations in between rushes to the bathroom. She had barely managed to get a couple hours of sleep.

By some perverse quirk of fate, she'd arrived early for Nick's memorial service. Ansel remembered hearing the Fellowship's ads on local radio stations. The organization promoted "low-cost, non-funeral, nondenominational ceremonies for transitional loved ones." From what she could see, that equaled cheap, generic cremation. Karen could probably count the ceremony's final price on her fingers.

Ansel sat in an end-row, folding wooden chair situated beneath a large green, canvas canopy with scalloped edges. Seven other rows spanned before her. Recorded mood music with ethereal overtones burst from two loudspeakers attached to canopy poles. An oak veneer dais with a microphone stood centered before the cluster of chairs.

Two huge floral sprays on Roman pedestals were positioned on each side of the dais. They repelled her. The gaudy blood-red vases displayed artificial lilies and ferns. Only a stippling of dust on the fabric leaves provided the illusion of living plants threatened by the onset of an insidious fungal disease. A few genuine flower sprays graced the aisles, including one large bouquet of red roses and ferns contributed by the Pangaea Society.

Dressed in her mourning outfit, a black ankle-length broomstick skirt with concha-style side buttons, a black whipstitch blouse, and flat-heeled, black shoes, Ansel sat rod-straight and prayed for an errant breeze to drift across the treeless field. Every time she inhaled, dust particles the size of coal soot seared her parched throat.

She coughed and tugged at a hand-crafted, silver Pico earring. Sweat dripped from her hairline. She'd gone all out for the service, twisting her hair into a chignon and applying heavy makeup to hide her pasty, hangover complexion. Now trapped body sweat prickled her skin like an icy sponge bath.

Ansel stared at the large, metallic-gold urn placed on a smaller scrolled column before the dais. Beyond the reach of mortal concerns, Nick had been reduced to several pounds of burnt calcium chips and funneled into a vessel resembling a brass spittoon with a lid.

"Hello, Ansel."

Karen Capos had definitely shopped for bereavement attire. She wore a black satin, double-breasted jacket with padded shoulders and a matching above-the-knees skirt that zipped up the front. The satin bustier under the jacket was white. Karen also wore black hose and black satin, strappy sandals with covenant heels. A black purse with a satin flowerette latch hung from her cushioned shoulder.

"Hello, Karen."

"Did you see Nicky's collection?"

Ansel looked as inconspicuously as possible for Alex King. She didn't see him. Had a sense of propriety kept him from attending? Or was it something else?

"I went to the apartment, but the bulk of the collection is gone. Some small amber pieces, not of much value, are the only things left."

"What do you mean the collection wasn't there?"

"That's all I know." She opened her purse and pulled out Nick's apartment key. "You should take this back."

Karen grabbed the key. "That doesn't make any sense. Those fossils have to be somewhere. I wonder if that's what that man who called was talking about," she said, crinkling her perfectly plucked, blonde eyebrows.

"What man?"

"Oh, he called this week and left me a message. I have no idea how he got my number, but he babbled something about needing to speak with Nicky about fossils. I didn't pay too much attention."

"Do you remember the caller's name?"

"Nope. He did mention a store called Rockheads in Butte. I remember that. Why don't you check it out? Alex and I are planning a cruise to the Caymans. I'm swamped with details."

Ansel had heard of Rockheads. It was a large gem and mineral shop. Keeping in contact with Karen didn't appeal to her, but a man calling about Nick's fossils sounded intriguing. Could he have any connection to Athanasios Stouraitis or Nick's computer project?

"All right."

"Good. I've got to get my seat. Keep me informed."

Ansel forced a smile as the merry widow sauntered away. More people arrived in batches. As she waited, numerous society members passed her or stopped for a few seconds to exchange comments about Nick's untimely passing. A few tried to gossip about the murders, but she discouraged them with monosyllabic answers and polite nods.

When more shadows hovered beside her, she looked up to see Lydia Hodges and Tim Shanks. She couldn't hide her surprise. What was Lydia doing here? She still remembered how Lydia had rushed from the trailer, proclaiming she wanted nothing more to do with Nick.

"Hi, Miss Phoenix," said Tim. "We were hoping to see you."

Lydia looked sheepish and said nothing. She moved nervously from foot to foot within the folds of a navy blue dress and fingered a white pearl necklace. Ansel hardly recognized Tim without his straw hat and camera. His dark blue suit made him look much younger than he was.

"Nice to see you, too. You came together?"

"No. We met here," Tim said.

Lydia nodded. "Tim talked me into coming. He thought it was the right thing to do. After all, we found him."

An uncomfortable lull invaded the space around them. Ansel wanted to ask Tim about the pictures he'd taken at the crime scene. She wished Lydia wasn't present. The girl was acting very edgy. Maybe she just didn't really want to be here.

Tim took Lydia's elbow. "We'd better take a seat. If you need anything, Miss Phoenix, just call me."

"Thanks, Tim. See you both at the next seminar."

They nodded and walked toward the front of the canopy, taking seats directly in front of Leslie Maze, who had apparently arrived during the last few minutes and hadn't bothered to approach her. She hadn't yet reviewed his research paper. Was he still smarting from his confession yesterday? She would keep her distance.

Slowly her row filled with mourners she didn't know. It appeared there would be a fair turnout for the service and that pleased her, despite her conflicted feelings about Nick. She watched the gathering crowd, hoping her stomach would settle by the time the service began.

"Good morning, Miss Phoenix."

Ansel flinched when the voice spoke directly into her right ear. She looked up. Detective Dorbandt, wearing his usual suit and smelling of spicy cologne, leaned toward her. He was immaculately groomed today, thick hair combed and parted, tanned face shaved, blue eyes sparkling. Ansel felt a spark ignite in her chest and drowned it with a wave of annoyance.

"You scared me again. I wish you'd stop that, Lieutenant."

Dorbandt straightened. "I'm sorry."

Ansel noted that he didn't look repentant. "What are you doing here?"

"Looking for you. We need to talk."

"Now?"

"After the services." He thumbed toward the parking lot. "I'll be waiting."

Before she could protest, Dorbandt walked away. Her stomach flip-flopped with apprehension. What did he want? She watched him move beyond the canopy, heading toward the parking lot adjacent to the Omega crematorium. There was no way she could sneak past him and reach her truck.

Ansel turned and glanced at the man who had taken the seat next to her while she talked to the cop. Damn. Cameron Bieselmore's hulking mass had spread into her personal space, and he positively reeked of Old Spice aftershave. Clad in a midnight-black suit with vest and shiny black loafers, he must be in heaven, she considered angrily. At last his dreadful fashion tastes doubled as suitable apparel. If she didn't vomit on them first.

"Good day, Ansel. Though I guess such a salutation is inappropriate given the occasion."

"You have some nerve sitting next to me, Cameron," Ansel said, a vitriolic edge deepening her voice, "after shoving me out the door. I faced those press piranhas alone."

Cameron frowned. "I didn't shove you. I gave you a firm, supportive tap of comradeship."

"You deserted me and slammed the door," Ansel uttered between clenched teeth so other people wouldn't hear.

"Nonsense. The museum was closed. I had to secure the premises. If anyone should be indignant, it's I. A neanderthal named Detective Fiskar visited me. He grilled me about my relationship with Nick, and he knew all about the dispute over the extinction diorama and the strychnine connection. You told the police about it."

"Not about the strychnine. Somebody else did. I warned you this would happen."

"Yes, I suppose," Cameron acquiesced. "This is excruciating for all of us." He scrutinized her. "You look terrible. You're not going embarrass me by fainting, are you?"

Before Ansel could make a justifiably nasty retort, the area quieted as a short, mousy man with a goatee silently positioned himself behind the dais. A taller black man, who served as an usher, approached the cassette player and cut off a harp-infused, symphonic melody with a loud, amplified crackle.

Ansel hardly listened as the squeaky-voiced man delivered a dreary, uninspired eulogy about a murdered man he never knew. For the next thirty minutes, she forced herself to sit calmly and observe the people around her. Was the killer here, flaunting his or her invulnerability?

Throughout the service Leslie Maze didn't move an inch. He stared ahead like an automaton. Cameron hunkered down in his wood-slat chair looking extremely put out and staring at the urn with undisguised loathing. The eulogy abruptly ended when the speaker, acting as a spiritual shepherd, gave a wave of his hand and dismissed the mourners.

Karen Capos bolted down the aisle toward the parking lot. Would she return later and pick up Nick's remains for the trip to the Caymans? Ansel wondered sarcastically. Other mourners walked by the urn, paying their last respects.

Lydia and Tim stood, and a swirling stampede of exiting mourners enveloped them. As Ansel rose, Cameron bumped her while lumbering upward from his own seat, knees popping. Ansel almost lost her balance on the grassy terrain. When she looked again, the students were nowhere to be seen. Was she ever going to get to ask Tim about those pictures?

"Such an inspirational eulogy," Cameron said. "Can you imagine Nick 'at slumber within the Eternal Flame'? I bet Nick's a tempest in a cinerary pot after hearing that drivel."

Disgusted, Ansel bit her tongue and simply walked away.

Chapter 23

"I am of another nation, when I speak you do not understand me. When you speak, I do not understand you."

Spokan Garry, Middle Spokane

Ansel followed Dorbandt to a nearby restaurant called the Rincon Grill. They shared a booth in a small bustling diner serving breakfast twenty-four hours a day. Food didn't interest her, but sitting someplace cool felt wonderful.

She pulled off her sunglasses and stared at Dorbandt. "What is this about?"

"I haven't received your suspect sketch."

"It's in my truck, for all the good it will do."

"I'll get it before you leave."

"Anything else?"

Dorbandt swivelled toward his steel briefcase sitting on the seat beside him. He popped the latches, pulled out a paper and placed it on the table. "Ever see this man?"

The photocopied color print was a blow-up from a driver's license. Flash glare had overexposed it. Ansel half-hoped it was her cowboy attacker, but it wasn't. The man wore a plain white tee shirt and looked in his mid thirties with short, dirty-blond hair and a dark complexion. Crows' feet latched onto the corners of his brown eyes. Black stubble peppered his cheeks and jaw. He had a tough, weatherbeaten look that reminded Ansel of someone used to hard, outdoor labor.

"No. Who is he?"

"Theodore Melba. Ring any bells?"

Ansel pushed the photo back. "No. Is he Greek?"

Dorbandt gave her a double take as he picked up the paper. "He was."

"Was?"

"He's dead. Committed suicide a year ago. Hanged himself in a barn."

"That's terrible, but why are you showing it to me?"

Dorbandt pinned her with a hard look before speaking. "This doesn't go any further than you."

"Fair enough."

"I looked into Capos' employment history. I ran the names of every person mentioned in his personal file through the computers. Melba's name popped out."

A harried, brown-haired waitress wearing a "Cindy" name tag appeared at their booth. "Sorry I didn't get here sooner. What can I get y'all?"

"Water for me, please," Ansel replied.

Dorbandt eyeballed her. "That's it?"

"Yes." She hoped her face didn't look as inhuman as she felt.

Without using a menu, he said, "I'll take the Durango Special."

Cindy scribbled on a tiny pink pad. "How do you want your steak and eggs?"

"Medium rare and sunny-side up."

"Be right back." She smiled and hurried away on squeaky, rubber-soled shoes.

Dorbandt gazed at Ansel. "Hard night?"

She had expected him to jump back into his Melba story. "Funerals aren't pleasant."

"That's some hangover. You should eat something."

Not appreciating his fishing expedition inside her head, she changed the subject. "Was Melba's death suspicious?"

"No. Everything looked plumb in the police report. Melba ran a small cattle ranch along the Big Hole River. A passel of federally protected sage grouse lived there, too. The Cooperative came in and said Melba was overgrazing the grassland ecosystem, driving the grouse out. The BLM revoked Melba's federal land-use permits so the birds got their habitat. Melba went bankrupt and committed suicide during a fit of depression. He lost the ranch his family had owned for more than a hundred and fifty years."

"What has that got to do with Nick? The government made the decision to close Melba down."

Dorbandt nodded. "Sure. A faceless tree-hugger lowered the ax, but Capos sharpened the blade. He was the drone doing the government's dirty work, and he helped chop down a fellow Greek. Maybe that stuck in somebody's craw."

"Maybe somebody could blame Nick, but his actions weren't personal."

"At least Melba's a lead." He put the paper in his briefcase and snapped it shut.

Cindy returned, carrying a tray with a glass of water, a stainless steel carafe of coffee, and a plastic basket brimming with fresh blueberry muffins. After she'd left, Dorbandt poured his coffee, adding two sugars and creams to the steaming caffeine brew before stirring slowly.

Ansel watched Dorbandt. His motions were always fluid, as well coordinated and efficient as his police demeanor. For the first time, she noticed he wasn't wearing a wedding ring, only a gold college ring with a red-faceted stone. If Dorbandt had a girlfriend, what did she look like, and how in the world could she put up with his overbearing cop attitude?

"I may have some other leads for you," she volunteered.

Dorbandt glanced up, his face unreadable. "Such as?"

"I know what fossil Nick scanned into the museum computers."

Dorbandt sipped his coffee and reached for a muffin. "What?"

"*Urvogel*," announced Ansel. "In German it means 'first bird.' It's an *Archeopteryx*."

"How do you know?"

"Evelyn saw the phrase HMN-1880 in Nick's research notebook. I remembered that's the catalog number for an *Archaeopteryx* fossil found in Solnhofen, Germany, in 1861. HMN stands for the Humboldt Museum für Naturkunde in Berlin, where the specimen is housed. The fossil's famous because it's a remarkably well preserved and complete specimen with a head. The first one discovered didn't have a skull."

Dorbandt finished his muffin in three bites. "That's important? It's just a bird."

"No. *Archaeopteryx* is a small, feathered reptile that lived during the Upper Jurassic one hundred and fifty million years ago. It's believed to be the evolutionary link between dinosaurs and modern birds. Have you ever seen a picture of *Archaeopteryx*?"

Dorbandt nodded. "Ugly-looking thing. Reminds me of a prairie chicken with fangs and claws. If they weren't already extinct, I'd shoot them on sight."

Ansel almost smiled. "Right. *Archaeopteryx* was a pigeon-sized dinosaur with bird-like feathers, wings, perching feet, hip bones, and a wishbone. The long bony tail, scaled snout, sharp teeth, and three claw-like fingers positioned midway down the wings are reptilian features."

Dorbandt's breakfast arrived. The waitress set down a cattleman's spread consisting of two eggs, hash browns, and a sizzling T-bone steak.

Cindy grinned. "Anything else?"

An air-sick bag, thought Ansel desperately. The smells of cooked bird ova, fried spuds, cow muscle, and grease assaulted her digestive tract with a vengeance.

Dorbandt gave her a gracious smile. "Nothing, thanks." He speared his steak with a fork, then spied Ansel. "Don't heave on me."

"Very funny. Where were we?"

"Old bird. Big choppers." Using a wicked-looking steak knife, he lopped off a large chunk of blood-tinged meat and pushed it into his mouth, chewing heartily.

Beneath the table, Ansel clutched her stomach. Was he taunting her or just ravenous? "The point is, Nick was a paleobotanist. It makes sense that any new research he did on *Archaeopteryx* might be connected to his new interests in amber inclusions."

"In what way?"

"I'm not sure," Ansel admitted. "I do know that Nick had research material concerning pyrolysis in amber. Pyrolysis is the destructive action of heat. Amber is a poor conductor of heat, and it oxidizes when exposed to extreme temperatures. This changes its natural physical and chemical properties."

"Sounds pretty thin to me. You may never know what Capos was researching."

"Well, I know that experts have claimed that finding *Archaeopteryx* in lithographic limestone was the paleo-historical equivalent of finding the Rosetta Stone. If Nick found some new trace fossil evidence relating to *Archaeopteryx* and amber, specifically DNA materials, it could be the equivalent of finding the Ten Commandments."

"Just speculation. I can't use it."

"Wait. I have something to show you." Ansel removed the bracelet from her black purse and placed it on the table.

Dorbandt's pupils transformed into cold pinpricks of black. "Where did you get that?"

"The jerk who attacked me left it behind."

Dorbandt set his fork down. "Impossible. I examined your trailer, remember?" He pulled out his leather notebook and flipped it open.

"Sorry, but you missed it," Ansel lied.

He slid his notepad across the table. "Benchley wore a necklace with the same design."

Surprise widened her eyes as she looked at his *utchat* drawing. "You're sure it belonged to her?"

"Yeah, I'm sure. I watched her autopsy from body bag to Y-cut. She was killed by a dart filled with enough strychnine to stiff a cow, so quit yanking my chain. When did you really find the bracelet?"

The shocking image of Evelyn on an autopsy table with the detective observing every medical debasement hit home hard with Ansel. And Evelyn had been murdered with strychnine, too. Bile rose in her throat. "Right after I was attacked."

"You mucked up potential fingerprint evidence, and then didn't tell me? That's not only stupid, but suspicious behavior." He shoved both the notebook and the bracelet back into his coat pocket. "What's the matter with you, Ansel? When are you going to trust me?"

"Why should I? Nobody trusts me because I'm..." She clamped her mouth shut.

Dorbandt nodded his head as the revelation hit him. "So the big bad, white world is oppressing the little misunderstood Indian girl. That's your excuse? Did I ever give you any reason to think I'm prejudicial because you're half Indian?"

Ansel stiffened. "You have no right to sit there and label me as some paranoid female."

"Then don't label me as a male bigot. Tell me everything you know about this case right now, or I'll haul your pretty hide down to the Sheriff's Department and let Captain McKenzie browbeat you for a day or two. Maybe that will teach you the difference between my investigative techniques and extrajudicial racism."

"That's not fair."

"Life ain't fair and death don't care." He crossed his arms and gazed at her, eyebrows cocked.

Ansel glared back. Neither of them spoke for a full minute. Finally she snorted in exasperation. "All right. I'll level with you."

Dorbandt picked up his fork. "Get to it."

"I visited a warlock and learned the charm is called an *utchat*. It represents the Eye of Apollo. Ancient Greek religions believed the *utchat* brought good luck. There's a rich Greek, Dr. Athanasios Stouraitis, living in Lustre. He's an oracle who runs a New Age group called the Avis Arcana. They're reviving the old Greek religion of augury, foretelling prophesies by using birds. This bracelet may connect Stouraitis, the cowboy, Evelyn, and probably Nick together. And Stouraitis would probably be very interested in a half-bird reptile like *Archaeopteryx*."

Ansel stopped and took a big breath. She also gulped down a few swallows of water. Dorbandt had shoveled eggs into his mouth until she finished. He still looked angry.

"A warlock and a Greek oracle. You've been busy."

"I'm not done. Lydia Hodges told me that she overheard Nick talking on a Bowie College pay phone before he was murdered. Nick mentioned a 'Griffin.' I thought Griffin was a person, but now I don't think so. When the first headless *Archaeopteryx* was found, it was given the temporary name of Griphosaurus, which is a taxonomic description that literally means 'the problematical griffin lizard.' Nick might have used the term 'griffin' to refer to *Archaeopteryx*."

"A griffin, too? Anything else?"

Ansel ignored Dorbandt's sarcasm. "Yes. That paper on pyrolysis and caustobioliths I mentioned was written by Leslie Maze. Nick used the paper to blackmail him over an old scandal at Yale. Nick found out that Leslie and a man named Jack Kittredge had stolen research material from a Harvard researcher, Carolyn Ryes. They used it to pad their own research data and got it published first."

"Jack Kittredge?" Dorbandt considered. "He's a researcher at the Cooperative."

"Really? So that's how Nick found out about the scandal. Oh, I also found out that Shane Roco is Leslie Maze's grandson."

Dorbandt pushed his near empty plate away from him. "Finished?"

"Yes. Are you going to check out Stouraitis?"

"I'll be going out of town for a bit first." Dorbandt waved to catch Cindy's notice.

"Are you checking out Melba?"

"I can't talk about that."

"Will you come to the Beastly Buffet?"

"Don't think so."

Damn. She'd really messed up with him. He was shutting her out. Time to move on. Ansel gathered her sunglasses and purse. She waited while he paid the bill. Then they walked out to the hot parking lot in silence. Dorbandt escorted her promptly to her vehicle.

As Ansel handed him the eleven by fourteen pencil sketch of the cowboy's face, her eyes met Dorbandt's. "May I ask you one question, Lieutenant?"

His piercing stare was all business. "What?"

"Do you really think I have a pretty hide?"

Dorbandt blushed and Ansel savored his discomfiture. The perverse pleasure was almost as satisfying as blowing off Moose Drool bottle necks with her Colt .45.

Chapter 24

*"Treat the earth well: it was not
given to you by your parents. It
was loaned to you by your children."*

Indian Proverb

Ansel arrived in Butte by three. Born from a bonanza silver camp, the industrialized city sprawls across the "Richest Hill on Earth," which yielded treasure-trove quantities of copper, silver, and by-product gold and metals from one thousand acres of mines.

As she passed steel architectures, lighted tennis courts, flower gardens, picnic grounds, swimming pools, and a landscaped baseball diamond, she wondered what Old West desperados would think of the changes. The Plummer gang, who ran amok through early mining towns until vigilantes hanged them, probably wouldn't believe their eyes.

And what would Chief Joseph think had he lived to see the World Museum of Mining, the Cooper King Mansion, Berkley Pit, and the ninety-foot-high statue of Our Lady of the Rockies set atop the continental Divide?

Ansel parked the truck beside the huge aluminum-sided warehouse called Rockheads, Incorporated. A gigantic, phallic-looking logo shaped as a rose quartz crystal with googly eyes and a sappy grin was emblazoned across the panels. She chuckled. Seeing that tacky cartoon figure made the long trip worthwhile in spite of her hangover.

A surprised gasp escaped Ansel's throat when she walked through the door. Rockheads bulged from seam to seam with towering metal shelves, glass cases, and a maze of narrow rows packed with wooden bins offering a myriad of high-quality gems, minerals, rare metals, lapidary supplies, and jewelry.

Ansel felt like a kid in a candy store. She pulled off her sunglasses. On one immense shelving unit she spied rows and rows of upright rock slabs displayed on metal stands. The fossils exposed on their surfaces resembled finely drawn etchings rather than prehistoric flora and fauna trapped between silt and dirt during the processes of decay. She experienced the same sense of wonder she'd felt when her mother gave her the blue copper-carbonate sea urchin.

Once these mineralized copies of creatures and plants had existed as organic matter. They grew and reproduced. Lived and died. The miraculous process of fragile life preserved as timeless imagery never failed to humble her. Touching a fossil meant touching the past. If such wondrous artifacts could be reduced to collectibles, she reasoned, they were art by God.

Ansel reached a long, glass case where an obese man wearing navy twill coveralls finished ringing up a girl's purchase of a six-inch slab of malachite. She waited patiently, staring into the display below her with pure lust. A breathtaking selection of luminescent minerals resting on black velvet cloth vied for her attention. Beneath small ultraviolet lamps, rock chunks of all sizes fluoresced with fiery blue, red, orange, green, and yellow hues.

The man gave a hearty farewell to the teenager, then grinned at Ansel with bright, white teeth. "I'm Gunther Osgoode," he said with a good-old-boy twang. "What can I do for you?"

"My name's Ansel Phoenix. I'm acting on behalf of Mrs. Nicholas Capos. I've come to discuss a fossil collection belonging to her deceased husband. You called her the other day."

Osgoode scratched a stubbled, doughy cheek and eyed her suspiciously. "Deceased?"

Judging from Osgoode's distrustful appraisal, Ansel wondered whether it was her formal black apparel or her mixed-blood heritage that had the shopkeeper buffaloed. Maybe both.

"Yes. I'm a close friend of the family."

"How'd he die?"

"An unexpected tragedy."

"Man, that's terrible. I'm sorry to hear that."

Ansel gave him a deprecating smile. "Thank you. If you want to verify I'm representing Mrs. Capos, I have her number in my purse."

Osgoode shook his head, the wattles beneath his chin shaking. "Naw, that's not necessary. I sold his fossil collection."

"He placed the collection up for sale here?"

"Oh, yeah. Put the whole kit-n-caboodle in the store over a year ago. Fantastic stuff. His fossils and tools were top quality. Never saw such great petrified woods and fossil seed pods. Books and magazines went, too." Osgoode squinted at her. "You saying Nick's wife didn't know about it?"

"No. She didn't. Do you know why Nick sold it?"

Osgoode shrugged and skin jiggled beneath his ballooning coveralls. "For money." He grinned. "I pulled in over thirty grand for him with quick sales, minus my commission, of course."

"Are there any items left?"

"Just a used orange pick hammer back in aisle seven."

Sadness coursed through Ansel as she listened to Osgoode speaking about Nick's beloved artifacts, tools, and reading materials as articles of barter. He stared at her with beady gray eyes cushioned within folds of baby-pink flesh.

"Can you get the check, please?" Ansel asked, hoping to move things along.

"Sure."

Osgoode waddled from the counter on trunk-like legs and disappeared through a curtained opening. Ansel searched for aisle seven. She found it toward the rear of the store. On her left, large rock cutting and spool polishing machines occupied floor space. The other side of the aisle held a pegboard wall which contained new and used tools organized in neat, well-labeled rows.

Various brands of picks, chisel hammers, and gad pry bars hung on metal clips. Ansel didn't look long before locating Nick's Estwing rock hammer. The fluorescent orange paint made it impossible to miss.

Ansel pulled the hammer down. She read the white tag hanging from the twenty-two-ounce head, immediately recognizing Nick's writing. The leather grip was sweat-stained and the neon paint sprayed on the neck and head looked atrocious. He had listed a ten-dollar sale price.

She knew Nick had painted the tool so he wouldn't leave it on an outcrop where dull colors of rock and dirt could camouflage it. She ran a finger across the cold, smooth surface of the strike edge. Ansel remembered kidding Nick about the orange monstrosity during a fossil-hunting trip. He had proclaimed that as long as he had the hammer in his hands, he'd never get shot by hunters. Something much worse had happened to him.

A loud, metallic sound startled Ansel from her reverie. What in the world was that? She looked left, then right. A person at the end of the aisle jetted across the opening. She caught only a split-second glimpse: bright red and green shirt, dark pants. Male or female she didn't know, but the movement was furtive. Was someone watching her?

Ansel paced to the aisle opening, clutching Nick's hammer in her right hand. Determined to locate the person skittering past, she turned right. She passed several deserted aisles. A few customers in rows much farther away caught her attention, but none wore the shirt she'd seen.

Ansel went toward the front. Maybe the mysterious patron had moved in that direction. She rounded a corner and almost ran head first into Osgoode's elephantine chest.

"Been looking for you. Here's the check." A blue paper flapped in his sausage fingers.

"Thank you, Mr. Osgoode. I'm sure Mrs. Capos appreciates all you've done." Ansel took the check, looking over Osgoode's shoulder. "Have you seen anyone with a red shirt?"

Osgoode's face turned quizzical. "Hmm. Haven't paid any attention, ma'am. Tell the widow I'll be glad to sell any other fossils or minerals she doesn't want. Even amber."

Ansel's head snapped toward Osgoode. "Amber?"

"That's right. I figure if her husband asked where to buy it, he probably did."

"When did Mr. Capos ask?"

Osgoode shuffled toward the checkout counter, coveralls swishing as he gained momentum. "Last summer."

Ansel tagged behind step for step. "He bought amber from you?"

"Naw, I didn't have anything but small pieces. He wanted something big." Osgoode walked behind the register and hefted himself onto a rickety stool. "I sent him to the board."

"What board?"

"Bulletin board. Outside." Ansel bolted away. "Ma'am, you gonna buy that hammer?"

She stopped short. She'd forgotten about it. Ansel set the tool on the counter. "Yes," she said, hurriedly digging in her handbag for a twenty-dollar bill.

"Can't get a better pick. Too bad it looks like a Halloween toy. This for you?"

"Uh huh." Ansel passed him the money.

Osgoode made change and dropped the tool into a bag. "You're a rockhound?"

"Uh huh." She grabbed the sack. "I'll see you. Thanks."

"Thank you, ma'am. Come again, you hear?"

The sunlight outside was brutal. Ansel winced, scrabbled through her purse, and pushed on her sunglasses as if her life depended on it. A twenty-four by thirty-six cork bulletin board hung next to the entrance beneath a home-built wooden overhang. Multicolored push-pins speared through thick stacks of accumulated personal advertisements.

As Ansel set the purse and hammer on the concrete walkway, she hoped any amber ads posted had remained on the board. A year was a long time, but even a current sales notice could lead her to someone who knew another person selling amber. Word of mouth worked wonders in mineral and fossil collecting circles.

"Help me, Nick," Ansel muttered, as she pawed through curling notepaper messages, faded photos, yellowing three-by-five cards, and stained business cards for several minutes. When her fingers lifted a flier offering Web site construction services, she found a piece of aged notebook paper offering amber for sale. She hooted with joy.

A man named Pete Becker had sold Baltic amber. There was a Helena address. No phone. She found no other ads. Could this be one Nick had responded to?

Ansel looked nervously over her shoulder toward the Rockheads entrance. Nobody wearing a red shirt had exited. She picked up her purse and hammer, then headed quickly to her truck. Along the way she inspected the few cars in the parking lot to see if she recognized any of them. Nothing. Well, she could reach Helena in less than an hour if she cruised north on Interstate Highway 15.

And she'd make sure nobody followed her.

Chapter 25

*"Live your life that the fear of death
can never enter your heart."*

Tecumseh, Shawnee

Pete Becker lived in a two-story, gray stone house sitting on a rolling, two-acre lot. Surrounded by immense oak trees, the home's dark rock profile melded perfectly into the late afternoon shadows cast by foliage.

Ansel drove around the block twice. As far as she could tell, nobody had tailed her. Her suspicions about being watched in the lapidary aisle bothered her, but the loaded gun in her purse made her feel safer. She reached for the tactile comfort of her Iniskim and a wave of sadness crashed over her.

She liked the state capital area, and it brought back fond memories of a trip she and her mother had made when she was eight years old. Mary took her sight-seeing and told her the history of Helen Piotopowaka Clarke, the daughter of a Blackfoot princess born in 1848.

Her mother told her how Helen had started her career as a classical actress of great acclaim in Europe, then returned to Helena to become a schoolteacher. She eventually became the first woman elected to county office as the superintendent of schools. Later Helen had worked in Indian affairs as an interpreter and mediator for several Blackfoot tribes. During that visit, Mary had made it very clear that if Helen Clarke rose above negative circumstances in her life, Ansel could, too.

"Never give up your dreams, Sarcee," her mother said. "There is freedom in dreams that gives you power. A man dreams of fitting the landscape. A woman dreams of being the landscape. Your dreams make you a force of nature to be reckoned with."

Fortified by those words, Ansel parked on the river stone drive behind a black and white Bronco. As she exited, she heard a dog barking inside the residence. The animal's powerful voice contained a deep intonation of alarm.

She went up a serpentine, natural stone walk surrounded by blooming beds of forget-me-nots and pushed the doorbell. Westminster chimes reverberated and the door opened instantly. She looked down at a short, wizened old man with gossamer wisps of white hair combed across his head. His emaciated body was swathed in a blue jogging suit. The man glanced at Ansel and swatted at something behind him.

"No," he yelled. "I will get the muzzle. Do you want Papa to do that?" He twisted toward Ansel. "How do you do?"

"Hello. Are you Pete Becker?"

"Yes, I am."

A massive black nose poked out beside Becker's left elbow and a snuffled spray of mucus flew in all directions. Ansel took a step backward to protect her skirt and blouse. Did dog snot wash out of black cotton-polyester?

"My name is Ansel Phoenix. I got your address from a bulletin board at Rockheads in Butte. You advertised Baltic amber for sale."

Becker's vibrant, sapphire eyes dulled. "Did I advertise amber? Oh, I remember. Those pink pills the doctor gives me. They thin my blood and my brain cells. I put the ad up a long time ago. Come in, pretty lady. Make yourself at home." He stepped back and swung the door wider. "Doppelbock loves visitors."

Becker's living companion was a one hundred and seventy pound Harlequin Great Dane. Becker held Doppelbock's thick, leather collar, allowing the friendly black and white Dane to greet Ansel from a distance. The dog sniffed energetically with a tennis ball-sized nose, licked her hand with eight inches of red tongue, and slashed his tail back and forth like a bullwhip. Despite his enormous size, Doppelbock had a gentle spirit.

Becker smiled. "He likes you."

"He's beautiful. How old is he?"

"Three years. I bred Danes for protecting livestock. They are good ranch dogs."

"I didn't know that. My father owns an Angus ranch."

"Yes. Danes are very dependable and courageous," Becker said, patting Doppelbock's massive head. "Enough, Dop. You will drive our guest away. Back to the bedroom." Using his bony hip as leverage, he pushed the Dane's forequarters toward the foyer.

"Papa says," he coaxed, pointing a finger down the hallway. The Dane's eyes, one gold and one blue, stared right through Ansel. At last, the dog pranced down the hallway on saucer-sized feet and disappeared around a right-hand corner.

"Come sit down in the living room. You are thirsty?"

"No thank you. I wanted to discuss your amber, Mr. Becker."

"All right."

Becker's living room resembled a spread from *Architectural Digest*. Aside from the cream-colored walls and tongue-and-groove wood flooring, all the interior woodwork was made of light bird's-eye maple. The furniture's rounded, cherry edges and marble accents gave the home a formal feel. A large contemporary gas fireplace set into a slate fascia took up an entire wall.

Ansel took a seat on a wingback chair placed next to a picture window overlooking the backyard. It was lovely with its bright green grass and a huge rock garden. Koi flitted through the blue-green water in a garden pond with flowering lily pads and bronzed waterbird statuary.

Next to her chair she noticed a round table with fly-tying equipment. An unfinished lure still in the vise was being constructed with thread and brown feathers. Becker was a seasoned trout or bass fisherman, too.

He sat on a Queen Anne-style sofa. "Now we will talk about my amber. You want to buy some?"

"I must be honest, Mr. Becker. I haven't come to buy it. I've come to ask about a friend who might have purchased some last year. Nick Capos."

"Yes, Mr. Capos bought my amber. Why do you ask?"

"Nick was a good friend of mine. He was murdered. I suspect he was involved in a research project that got him killed. I'm trying to find out what it was. My legwork led me to you."

"Murder? Shouldn't the police ask me these questions?"

"The police are investigating other leads. Quite frankly, this theory isn't considered a top priority. Before his death, he sold a life-long collection of valuable fossils and began collecting and studying amber. I want to know why."

"I sold him one large piece of amber which I will tell you about."

Ansel sighed with relief. "Thank you. That would be very helpful."

"I inherited several pieces of amber from my father. He was an amber gatherer in Germany, like his father and grandfather before him. Always the Beckers of Palmnicken collected the mineral from the amber mines.

"My amber comes from the Blue-Earth mines. These gray-green clay sediments are from the ancient German lagoons. My father dug into the amber pits only thirty feet from the ocean and forty feet beneath sea level. Water was pumped out of the shafts so they could go into the mines and break apart Blue-Earth clods. Amber was tossed into a bucket of water, while leftover dirt was hoisted three levels onto a raised platform reached only by narrow ladders. At the top it was loaded into electric rail cars and taken away."

Becker took a deep breath and continued. "The pits grew deeper and wider, the mines constantly moving along the coastline as the big companies searched for new amber deposits. Later, big commercial operations made the skills of my ancestors obsolete. Now amber is exposed by diesel shovels with moving buckets, deposited on conveyors, and washed and sorted on sluices."

"When did Nick come to see you?"

"Let me think. I placed the ad on the board last June. I believe he came in July or August."

"Can I see some of the amber you were selling?"

Becker nodded. "Certainly. We must go to the garage."

Becker led her through an archway near the fireplace and down a wide hall. Ansel passed a kitchen filled with marble-top counters, glass-fronted cabinetry, Mission-style fixtures, and stainless steel appliances. They went through a maple door which led to a covered outdoor foot path, then directly into the detached garage.

The garage was converted into a woodworking shop filled with carpentry tools. Large lumber and sawdust piles hugged the walls. The smells of pine, cedar, cherry, and mahogany infused the air. The remainder of the room stored a cache of Becker's handmade furniture and whimsical wood sculptures of people and animals carved from logs.

Becker went to a corner and pulled out a grapefruit crate. "These are the pieces I showed Mr. Capos. There are only two left." He took out a chamois-covered object and unwrapped it. A four-inch-long lump fell into his knobby fingers. Ansel peered at the amber chunk, a bumpy, pear-shaped blob of stone-like material. The surface looked like rough, brown-black tree bark.

"It doesn't even look like amber," she said in amazement.

"This is pit amber," Becker replied, passing the resin to her. "Amber looks this way when it comes from the Blue-

Earth mines. Sea stone, or amber floating in the ocean, has already lost this outer crust and appears more polished. After this wrinkled layer is removed, you can tell the true quality of the resin. My samples are from the East Sea shores. My father said these were top grade, as golden as burnt honey."

Ansel's heart skipped a beat. Freddy's message from the spirits was, "Burnt honey keeps the bees warm."

"Could this amber have inclusions, Mr. Becker?"

"Yes. My father said he would sometimes find insects inside."

"Did he ever mention any larger fossil specimens?"

Becker shook his gnome-like head. "Not that I remember."

"Why was Nick buying the piece?"

"He only said that he wanted a large sample of fine amber. He mentioned nothing about inclusions. I told him if he wasn't happy with the quality to bring it back, and I would refund his money."

Ansel fondled the amber nodule. It fascinated her. The mineral was warm in her hand and extraordinarily light. "How big was the piece Nick bought?"

"He bought my largest piece. About two hundred and fifty millimeters in size."

"It looked like this?"

Becker nodded vigorously. "Just twice as big."

"How much did he pay?"

"Fifteen hundred dollars. A very good price for old Baltic amber."

It was a lot of money, Ansel ruminated, but if Nick was selling his collection and milking money from Leslie Maze, he could easily afford it. The question was: what did he want the amber for? She handed the chunk back.

"How did your father get these pieces?"

Becker wrapped the amber in its covering and replaced it inside the crate. "He stole them. Very slowly and very carefully over a period of years," Becker said bluntly. He stood. "He knew that the new commercial machines would leave him jobless and penniless so he took them and sold them to the jewelry makers. He wanted the money to leave Germany."

Ansel understood such desperate measures. Her reservation relatives knew the fear of hunger and homelessness every day of their lives, even if she didn't. "He planned ahead. He was a good father and husband."

"Yes. He was afraid for our future, and he took a great risk. Avoiding capture by the mine overseers who watched constantly for pilfering was a dangerous game. Workers were kept moving through the pits every minute and thoroughly searched when they left at the end of the day. Not even my mother knew how my father got them out of the mines, but he sold enough pieces to get our boat tickets to America. This is the last amber from my homeland. If no one buys them, I will leave them to my spoiled grandchildren."

They returned to the living room. "Thank you, Mr. Becker."

"It was my pleasure. I will give you one of my cards," he said, walking over to the fly-making table and opening a drawer. He pulled out a white card. "Come to visit anytime. Dop would love to see you again."

She dropped his card into her purse and handed him a Phoenix Studios card. "Just in case you think of anything you need to tell me."

Becker's smile was warm and wide. "Yes, thank you. I will show you out."

Moments later Ansel waved a final good-bye to the kindly old man before the heavy maple door closed. She hurried down the stone walkway just as a squirrel among the trees gave a startled cry and scuttled up a trunk.

Ansel turned toward the animal. An immense shadow moved in the corner of her left eye. Before she could turn, a cold metal object was jammed under her left breast and angled upward toward her heart. A face pressed against her head, familiar rough lips brushing her left ear.

"Keep walking and don't scream," ordered the cowboy. "We're going for a ride."

Chapter 26

"Indians chase the vision,
white men chase the dollar."

Lame Deer, Sioux

Ansel turned her head. There was no mistaking the black hat, leather jacket, and despoiled skin as belonging to anyone but the cowboy. The right side of his face was red, swollen, and badly scabbed by the muriatic acid she'd thrown at him.

The man pushed her forward with a firm, one-armed grip around the waist. Her gun was in the purse hanging from her right shoulder, but she couldn't reach it. She had little choice but to get hustled along like a rag doll. Her stomach cramped painfully. She felt like vomiting.

"Hurry it up, bitch."

Ansel prayed that Becker would see what was happening and let Dopplebock out the front door. As she was propelled further from the house her fleeting hopes of heroic canine rescue dissolved. The cowboy shoved her toward the street. Her truck and Becker's Bronco were on the drive behind her. There were no other vehicles in sight.

"Where are we going?"

"Shut up."

A black, vinyl-roofed Cadillac limousine sped down the street toward them. Twenty feet of clear-coated metal with ebony-tinted windows halted by the curb with a shuddering bounce. A double-door in the middle popped open.

"You're kidnapping me in a limousine?"

"Too bad it's not a coffin," the cowboy complained.

Anger displaced Ansel's fear. She dug her heels into the flagstones and sagged her body, becoming dead weight. "I'm not getting in that car."

The man shoved her into a white-leather bench seat so fast that Ansel's head spun. She landed face down. The cowboy yanked her purse away and slammed the door. An automatic door lock snapped down as the vehicle sped off.

"Good afternoon, Ansel." Another man sat on a leather bench facing her at a ninety-degree angle.

Ansel bolted upright. She made a lunge for the door handle and frantically tried to open it. She glanced toward the opposite side. There was no handle. The limo was covered by a full-length hardwood console with a stocked bar containing assorted stainless steel ice chests, glass service, Champagne chateau, and a small TV/VCP combo. Above the console, a picture window gave her a great view of the Helena city streets flashing by.

Ansel looked toward the windshield. A full-length glass divider separated them from a uniformed chauffeur. Beneath the impenetrable barrier, a customized panel displayed a huge *utchat*. The Eye of Apollo.

Ansel crossed her arms. "Let me out of here, Doctor Stouraitis. Now."

"You know who I am?" Stouraitis asked, grinning with extraordinarily large teeth. "Wonderful. That will speed things up."

"You've kidnapped me. I'll press charges."

Stouraitis brushed the sleeve of his double-breasted, gray silk suit, fussed with his gold silk tie, and situated his black leather loafers more comfortably on the white and gray carpeting before acknowledging her.

"You have nothing to fear. I just want to have a conversation."

"Nothing to fear? What do you call almost getting raped and shot by your goon with the acid wash on his face?"

Stouraitis ran a hand over his perfectly coiffed, thick silver hair. "I apologize. Milos is impetuous. I didn't send him to hurt you. I sent him to ask you some questions. It seems you handled him very well under the circumstances. You've scarred him for life. As for the events of the last few minutes, if I'd asked you to take a ride with me, would you?"

"Absolutely not."

"Exactly. Perhaps you want some refreshments. I have wine, beer, soda, or mineral water."

"I want out of this car," Ansel insisted.

"Some ouzo? It's a Greek drink considered an aperitif."

"No."

Stouraitis shrugged. He withdrew a short, crystal-cut glass from a console shelf, opened the bottle, and poured a bit of flavored liqueur into it. "I have appetizers as well. There is feta cheese, psomi bread, and fruit." He slid back a hidden panel and removed a gold-leafed dish with tastefully displayed munchies. He held it out.

"No thanks. I'm on a strychnine-free diet."

Stouraitis set the plate down beside him and selected some cheese. "You do me a great disservice. I didn't kill Nicholas or that woman."

"Her name was Evelyn Benchley, and I don't believe you, Doctor."

"Please, call me Athanasios. My master, Apollo, has told me so much about you that I feel I've known you for a long time."

Ansel shook her head. "You're crazy. You talk about a mythical Greek god as if he were a fishing buddy. Did Apollo mention that my father is Chase Phoenix and that when he finds out you're responsible for terrorizing me, he's going to make a tobacco pouch out of your scrotum?"

Stouraitis cringed. "Such disrespect. It's one of the things I find so vulgar about Americans." He dropped a cube of feta with distaste, wiped his face and hands with a lace-edged napkin, then set the dish on the console. "All right. We'll get to business." He gave her a piercing, brown-eyed gaze. "I want to know where the griffin is. And my money."

Ansel glanced out the picture window for a second, thinking about what to say. The limousine had left Helena, and dusk had fallen. They traveled south on Highway 15 toward Butte, passing dark, vast expanses of ranch land and prairie.

Ansel looked at the ornithologist. "I don't even know what the griffin is."

"I'm not in the mood for games," Stouraitis said with irritation. "You mentioned the griffin to Milos inside your home."

"Someone told me Nick used the word during a phone conversation. I threw it out in the heat of the moment."

Stouraitis pursed his full lips, then gulped down his ouzo. He reached for a refill, taking time to mix the liqueur with water. After the first sip, he grabbed a phone receiver on the wall behind him and punched a button. The chauffeur picked up a dash phone.

"Samos. *Stamahteesteh*," Stouraitis ordered.

In seconds the limousine slowed and veered toward the shoulder. Ansel tensed. "What are you doing?"

"Letting you out. Our conversation is finished."

"You're dumping me out here in the dark?"

"Your truck is behind us. Milos has been following."

Ansel turned. Through a tinted rear window, she could see the headlights of her truck a car length behind. That meant Milos had gone through her purse to get her truck keys. He had her gun. The limousine glided to a stop on an asphalt strip beside a sheep pasture. Milos pulled over with the Ford.

"What is the griffin, Dr. Stouraitis?"

"You must go now. You can't help me, and I can't have you going to the police about my private affairs." The door lock jumped up.

Ansel bit her lip. She should leave and never look back, but she was close to cracking the mystery of Nick's murder. She could feel it. Stouraitis wasn't afraid of the police. He'd baited her, dangling his knowledge about the griffin to convince her to stay and help him in some way. Dorbandt would be furious if she consorted with a delusional millionaire and his criminal lackey, but he'd never taken her seriously. Proving him wrong was incentive enough.

Ansel exhaled. "I won't go to the police, but I want to know what Nick and you were involved in. I'll guess it involved an *Archaeopteryx* and Baltic amber."

Stouraitis' face remained calm and thoughtful, his gaze steady. He picked up the phone. "*Pahrahkahlo*, Samos."

The chauffeur nodded, and the limousine pulled onto the highway. In seconds they accelerated back to a smooth-as-glass, sixty-five-mile-per-hour cruising speed. Milos, behind them, did the same.

"You see that vase?" Stouraitis pointed toward the console. A six-inch black ceramic flower vase filled with yellow tulips perched near the roof. "It is an artifact made in 550 B.C. and a splendid example of red-figure technique developed by Athenian craftsmen at the end of the sixth century. The design is very similar to the famous Vulci vase in the Metropolitan Museum. It illustrates Hercules using a sling to drive away swan-like birds which, according to Greek mythology, infested Lake Stymphalis. My hobby is collecting nice things relating to bird lore."

"Like fossil artifacts?"

A quirky smile appeared on Stouraitis' face. "I knew Nicholas from the day he was born. His father Isidoro and I were acquaintances long before the second world war. When Isidoro left to come to America, I stayed and fought. After the war, I went to college. I became interested in the true personal fulfillment and harmony associated with the Heroic Path, and I realized I have an intuitive gift for watching bird behavior. Sometimes I can actually understand the language of the birds. Since the time of Calchas, Melampus, and Tiresias, a chosen few have been able to develop abilities of augury. I am one of them. Nicholas knew of my powers, and he respected them. He was even a member of my group, the Avis Arcana. So you see, Ansel, Nicholas' death is a great personal loss for me."

"Okay. You're wealthy, artistic, and sensitive. Tell me about the griffin."

"Nicholas came to me in February and said he had found a piece of Baltic amber with something inside it. A broken egg with a fossil reptile-bird. He wanted me to see it and help verify its authenticity. He could not afford the many expensive scientific tests required. I agreed."

A shiver skittered up Ansel's spine. Could it be possible that Nick had stumbled onto the inclusion of all time inside Becker's crusty amber?

"Where did Nick get it?"

"From the man you just visited. Peter Becker." Stouraitis fixed her with a curious stare. "Nicholas had been looking for a large piece of Baltic amber for his collection. Finding the griffin inside the resin was an accident."

Stouraitis turned to stare at the Eye of Apollo. "The griffin was meant to come to me," he said in a trance-like voice. "It is my destiny to own it. You cannot imagine its beauty, Ansel. It is a creature from myth, half bird, half beast, captured within the hardened, golden tears of the Heliades."

Ansel leaned forward, excitement coursing through her. "What does the griffin look like?"

Stouraitis faced her. "Small. The egg is white, elongated and reptilian-like. Leathery. The griffin's head and one wing partially out of an opening in one end. It has a few gray downy feathers and featherless wings with little clawed hands. Reptilian eyes. The mouth is beak-like but has tiny teeth."

"What dinosaur species is it?"

"It has no name. It is similar to *Archaeopteryx*, but Nicholas said it was a new subspecies that lived about sixty million years ago."

"Have you had the amber tested?" Ansel asked.

Stouraitis chuckled. "For fakery? Of course. Do you think I would want it back so badly if I didn't know it was authentic? I paid handsomely for a world-class amber expert to evaluate it and keep its existence a secret. All the tests were done." He ticked off test parameters on his fingers. "Hardness, toughness, specific gravity, optical properties, polarized light, turbidity, structure, color, fluorescence, diaphaneity, heat, and electrical characteristics. I have the documentation to prove it, and I have a history of its provenance through Becker. The Baltic amber is real. The griffin is real. And it's mine."

"What are you going to do with it?"

"It will remain in my private collection. I paid Nicholas for it. I own it."

Ansel had no patience with such selfish greed, but she wouldn't argue now. She needed him just as much as he needed her. "How much did you pay Nick for the griffin?"

"Two million dollars."

Ansel blinked. No wonder Stouraitis had sent Milos looking for his money. Still, two million was a cheap price to pay for the world's only preserved dinosaur. "And you still don't have the griffin in your possession. What happened?"

"I don't know," Stouraitis said, throwing up his hands in anger. "I paid Nicholas June second. We agreed he'd bring the griffin to me the next day. He never showed up. He disappeared until you found his body. Since he'd spent time with you," Stouraitis said suggestively, "I assumed you knew about the griffin and the money."

"And that I'd killed Nick," Ansel finished.

"The thought crossed my mind," he admitted.

"Well, I didn't. Did you know that Evelyn Benchley had a six-month affair with Nick?"

"When did this happen?"

"From June to December of last year. After he bought Becker's amber and before he came to you. Evelyn never knew about the amber or the reptile inclusion."

"How can you be sure?"

"I know."

"Maybe somebody thought she knew and killed her."

"Maybe," Ansel agreed. She eyed the man across from her. "Who else hated Nick enough to poison him with strychnine?"

"I have no idea, but the name strychnine comes from the Greek word *Strychnos*. It means 'nightshade.' At one time death by strychnine was an ancient method of execution in my country. I was struck by this coincidence when I first heard that Nicholas had been poisoned with such a concoction. Someone else had to know about the griffin," Stouraitis said emphatically.

He glanced out the window. "Ah, we are nearing Butte. You will be leaving here." He gestured toward the glass divider, and the ever vigilant Samos nodded.

Ansel was more than ready to leave. She had to think about what Stouraitis had said and figure out what was the truth and what wasn't. She waited patiently as the limo pulled into a grocery parking lot, then reached for the door handle.

"I have recorded our conversation on video," said Stouraitis with a predatory smile. Just in case your father or the police would like to see it. Have a nice evening."

Ansel resisted the urge to tell Stouraitis where he could rewind his tape and exited the vehicle. Milos had parked her truck behind the limo. He swaggered toward her, and she made a point of giving him a wide berth. Milos sneered, then disappeared through the limo door. The car took off, leaving her alone.

Ansel opened the truck door and saw her black purse on the passenger's seat, along with the paper bag containing

Nick's orange pick. So far so good. Hopping into the cab, she closed the door, then noticed the faint odor of ammonia. She looked toward the ignition. Her keys weren't there. Next she glanced at her purse as the taint of urine got stronger in the closed confines. The fabric sides looked wet.

"No way," Ansel spat, hoping her suspicions were wrong, especially with her keys, wallet, and gun in there.

She cursed like a longshoreman as she twisted toward the backseat looking for a box of sterile, rubber gloves she always carried for digging up delicate fossils or making plaster castings. She needed them before she opened her handbag.

That sick creep had pissed in her purse like a dog marking its territory.

Chapter 27

*"If a man loses anything and goes back
and looks carefully for it, he will find it..."*

Sitting Bull, Sioux

On Friday morning, Dorbandt was happy for the first time in days. A fax on top of his IN basket listed all the manufacturers in India who exported strychnine to the United States, as well as Montana distributors, manufacturers, and medical supply houses that sold the poison.

Not quite ready to go into McKenzie's office to discuss what he'd discovered, Dorbandt picked up the phone. He'd wanted to make this call for days, but had resisted the urge to annoy the cantankerous Dr. Arlen Floyd.

"Serology/DNA," answered a female voice.

"I'm Detective Dorbandt. Lacrosse Sheriff's Department. Is Dr. Floyd there?"

"Just a minute."

"Yes, detective," Floyd's voice suddenly boomed.

"Have you completed testing on the Capos feather? Case 01-06-23-H-0007," he said, anticipating the doctor's demands.

"No."

"Why not? This is a high-profile homicide. It has priority."

"Wrong. Your feather is not a priority over bloodstains, saliva, and semen testing. All I'm going to be able to tell you is what family the bird sample comes from. Not the species."

"Explain what the word 'family' means," Dorbandt demanded.

"It means I can tell you if it comes from a goose, a vulture or a chicken, but not which type of goose, vulture or chicken. I don't have the resources for that sort of DNA comparison."

"Where can I get more detailed testing?"

"If you want to know specifics such as the species or family, you need a forensic zoologist. Try a wildlife forensics laboratory. I have to go."

Dorbandt scribbled a note. "Where is the closest wildlife lab?"

"Wait a minute." The receiver fell hard, and Floyd didn't return for a full minute. "Try the Clark R. Bavin National Fish and Wildlife Forensics Lab in Ashland, Oregon."

"Oregon? You're kidding me."

"I don't have time to joke."

"Arlen, throw me a bone. What's in state I can use?"

"Well, you could contact a national wildlife refuge and ask them to route you to a lab. Or try a university or private lab. In any case, the test results won't come cheap."

Dorbandt probed his brain for a name. Montana didn't lack for government refuges, fisheries, or field offices. The first place that came to mind was the Charles M. Russell National Wildlife Refuge in Jordan.

"Do you want me to test the feather or get it packed for a transfer?"

"Can you do your test first?"

"Not enough blood in the feather shaft. Make a decision. I don't have all day."

"I'll let you know what I'm going to do in a couple hours."

"I can hardly wait." The phone went dead.

Dorbandt replaced the receiver, picked up a folder, and walked over to Fiskar. The detective was hunkered over his desk, attention riveted to a ballistics report.

"Odie, I need you to chase down something."

Fiskar looked up. His somber, Paul Bunyan face transformed into an eager-to-please grin. "Sure, Reid."

"I need you to ask somebody at the Charles Russell Refuge in Jordan if there's a lab near here that can do DNA testing on the Capos feather. I need to know exactly what type of bird it comes from, and I mean everything: family, genus, species."

"Let me write that down." One of Fiskar's massive hands grabbed a notepad. "You still working on that Melba lead?"

Dorbandt shook his head. "I've got something hotter. I'll fill you in later."

Fiskar's eyes widened. "Sounds good. I'll see what I can do and get back to you."

"Thanks." Dorbandt thumbed toward McKenzie's glass-partitioned office. "I'm going into Count Dracula's crypt and make my blood offering."

Odie chuckled. "You need backup?"

Dorbandt smiled wickedly. "No. I had a garlic bagel for breakfast. I'll just fart if things turn ugly."

Odie sniggered as he headed for the office. Dorbandt's smile got smaller in direct proportion to his proximity to McKenzie's door. Bracing himself for battle, he walked into the small room. McKenzie sat behind his desk, sharpening a pencil in an electric machine whirring like a can opener. The urge to grab the pointed implement out of McKenzie's hand and stake the supervisor's heart appealed to him.

"Dorbandt," McKenzie growled. "Just the person I want to see."

You're not going to be able to dump on me this time, thought Dorbandt. "I've got a solid suspect on the strychnine case. Karen Capos' boyfriend in residence, Alexander King."

McKenzie pulled the pencil out of the sharpener, and the room became deathly quiet. "The stud? This better be good. I can't afford any screw-ups."

Dorbandt put the fax down on his desk. "Just got this list of twelve major pharmaceutical houses in India that export strychnine into the country. Got a list of their Montana distributors, too. Bombay Laboratories Limited sells strychnine to Universal Veterinary Supply in Billings. Universal's address is on Mariah Street. The location looked familiar, so I went through my files to find out why."

He placed a printout of King's employment records in front of McKenzie. "Eight years ago King managed a pet shop called Ancare Pets in Glasgow before opening his Bird Haven store. King's social security records listed his employer as Ancare Pets with the same Mariah Street address. Ancare Pets was a sister company of Universal Veterinary Supply, their attempt to move into the retail pet business. Ancare paychecks were issued by Universal. This connects King directly to a strychnine distributor."

McKenzie leaned back in his chair and chewed on the pencil eraser. "Why does Universal handle strychnine?"

"Vets use it as part of a medicinal tonic to stimulate digestion in horses and cattle. The tonic is administered orally and as a subcutaneous or intramuscular injection," Dorbandt explained. "Perfect for a dart gun."

McKenzie leaned back in his chair. "Eight years is a long time to keep poison."

Dorbandt shrugged. "Strychnine doesn't go bad. Universal still sells a one-ounce bottle of concentrate for fifty-four dollars. And UVS was also the sole supplier for Ancare inventory. Ancare carried equine supplies. King was a manager. He had easy access to strychnine. Now he's shacking up with Capos' wife. That gives him the means, motive, and opportunity."

"Why would he kill Benchley?"

"Let me bring him in for questioning, and I'll ask him. If there's any meat to this nut, maybe I can crack it open with the right leverage."

McKenzie nodded, a small smile appearing at the corners of his mouth. "I like it, Dorbandt. Problem is, you can bring

King in for questioning but unless he confesses, he walks right out. I want an arrest. You need to match this Universal strychnine with that used to kill Capos."

"I've got those wheels moving, but it will take time. What I really want is a search warrant for King's bird shop and Karen Capos' house. If there's strychnine in either place, we'll find it. To get a warrant, I'll need more evidence to convince a judge that King is a legitimate suspect. I might be able to do that, if you help me," Dorbandt said, staring at McKenzie.

"How?"

"There's some trace evidence that might link King to Capos. A small feather was found on Capos' body. It could be transfer evidence between the perp and the victim. The feather's at the state lab waiting for DNA testing. Could take up to six weeks. If King has the bird that feather belongs to in his store or at home, it means he was probably at the Capos crime scene."

McKenzie nodded. "I'll expedite things at the lab." He reached for the phone.

"There's a problem."

He withdrew his hand. "What now?"

"The lab isn't set up to give us the detailed DNA analysis we need. We've got to match that feather to the exact bird it came from. That requires a special lab."

McKenzie tapped the pencil against his front teeth. "What kind of lab?"

"A wildlife forensics lab or a research facility dealing with bird DNA. I'm trying to track one down right now. I'll have to hand carry the feather to the lab and hang around until the tests are completed in order to speed things up. It's going to require departmental funds."

"I can't commit to that." McKenzie threw the pencil down on his desk.

Dorbandt expected this response. "You want to cheap out on this, Captain? There's a crazy running around poisoning people with tranquilizer darts like they're animals."

McKenzie's face darkened. "Don't bulldoze me with my own conscience. You know I want this freak just as much as you. I've already got bite marks on my ass from the press."

Dorbandt reached down and picked the sheets off the desk. "Wonder how Sheriff Combs and the media will feel about your reluctance to close this case as fast as possible. We need to move on leads like this feather when they pop up." He turned and headed for the door.

"Hold it, Dorbandt," McKenzie sputtered. "You hit me cold with this idea of a trip. Money doesn't grow on hat trees around here. Can't you give a man time to think?"

You're not a man, you're an ambulatory turd, Dorbandt thought nastily. He stopped halfway through the door and pivoted on his heels. "Time is crucial. Can I go to another lab or not?"

"Come back and see me when you know where you're going," McKenzie acquiesced with a glare. "We'll discuss how to fund it then."

"Great."

"And Dorbandt," McKenzie added, "You'd better solve this case, or you'll be kicked out of Homicide so fast, *your* ass will break the sound barrier."

Dorbandt grinned. "You won't regret this. I promise."

Chapter 28

*"Tirawa, The One Above, sent certain animals
to tell men that he showed himself through the
beasts, and that from them...should man learn."*

Eagle Chief, Pawnee

Ansel dreamed of buzz saw blades. All around her hundreds
of serrated blades flew through the air like twirling Frisbees,
felling colossal redwoods and threatening to cut her. The trees
oozed and dripped with a viscous, golden sap, and every time
she jumped away from a deadly blade, her feet landed in
ankle-deep mires of amber syrup. A spinning blade approached.
She would be sliced in half, flattened by a tree trunk, or
drowned in the ever-rising pool of sticky goo. She screamed.

Ansel jerked awake as a moan of terror gurgled in her
throat. Disoriented, she didn't recognize her own trailer bedroom, expecting to see the Arrowhead furniture. Then she
remembered that she'd returned home the night before,
collapsing after a stressful twelve-hour day on the road. Only
Godzilla intruded into her personal space, not bloodthirsty,
serrated disks and suffocating resin.

The clock on the nightstand read eleven. She rubbed her
hands across her sweaty face and through her damp hair. God,
what a dream. Or was it? She still heard an incessant buzzing.

She looked toward the window. Yes, the sound was coming from outside.

Ansel rose and went to the sill. She pulled back the curtain, squinting through dusty glass. The noise droned louder. She didn't see anything unusual: gas grill, overgrown lawn, peach-tree willow. And then she saw the bees.

"What the hell?"

Wearing only a tee shirt and satin boxer shorts, Ansel plodded out of the room. She ached all over, and her stomach rumbled with hunger. That's what I get for being thrown into a limousine and not eating solid food for a day, she reasoned as she went to the front door. Blue sky and temperate breezes greeted her.

She bounded down the porch steps and toward the west side of the trailer, stopping abruptly when the angry hum became unnaturally loud. Ansel peeked around the corner. A two-foot-long, undulating mass of honeybees hung from a low, weight-burdened tree branch. Hundreds of other insects dive-bombed the area in excited loops. True to Feltus Pitt's prediction, her field colony had swarmed.

Ansel retreated to the front door. She had to call Pitt and solicit his beekeeping services. Once inside, she dialed his number, and he answered right away.

"Pitt's Pigs."

"Hello, Mister Pitt. This is Ansel Phoenix."

"Howdy, ma'am. You doing all right after all the hubbub here?"

"Yes. I'm sorry for what happened at your farm. I hope you won't let it interfere in your relationship with the Pangaea Society." She crossed her fingers.

"Don't worry. My business wasn't hurt. In fact, more people are coming out to buy pigs for barbecues than ever before just to get a gander at the ranch. And my pigs haven't complained. You can come out any time and look for big lizards. I'm sorry about that Capos fella though, him being a friend of yours and all."

"Thank you, Mr. Pitt. I called for another reason, too. My bees swarmed, and I don't know what to do."

"When did the brood split?"

"Huh?"

Pitt laughed, more cough then chuckle. "Guess I'd better talk English instead of bee-speak. When did the colony swarm?"

"I'm not sure. I've been gone and just found them in my willow tree."

"Bees usually swarm in the midmorning hours. The scouts are looking for a new nest. You've got to hurry and hive them before they take off again. You got a new apiary set up?"

"No. Just the old one in the field."

Pitt exhaled. "You'll need another apiary to move this swarm into. And you'll need to check the old hive. Some of the original colony is still in it."

"Can you set everything up for me? I'll pay you, Mr. Pitt."

"Sure. Always wanted to try my hand at hiving a feral swarm. A new apiary will cost around a hundred fifty dollars, plus my gas and time hiving them. Then I still have to check the old colony."

"No problem. Just take care of it for me," Ansel said with relief. She didn't like the idea of feral bees looking for a home outside her bedroom window.

"I'll be there in a bit. Got to get some things together. Don't go near them. Bees get testy when they've swarmed and haven't eaten."

"I'll keep my distance. Thanks, Mr. Pitt."

This task taken care of, Ansel went out to the back porch. Last night she had set towels on a folding card table and laid out the contents of her ruined black purse to dry. Dorbandt's business card was there. Taking the yellowed card with her, she went inside and dialed his number. With a missing amber inclusion containing a dinosaur fossil and two million dollars in cash unaccounted for, Dorbandt had to take Nick's involvement with Dr. Athanasios Stouraitis seriously.

The phone rang several times before a male voice responded. "Detective Division. Fiskar."

"Lieutenant Dorbandt, please."

"He's not here. Who's calling?"

Ansel frowned. She could never reach Dorbandt when she needed him. "This is Ansel Phoenix. I need to speak with him regarding the Capos case. When will he be back?"

"Is this an emergency?"

"No, but he'll find this information very helpful."

"Give me your number, and I'll pass the message on to him," Fiskar said politely.

She told him and added, "I need to speak with him regarding Dr. Anthanasios Stouraitis."

"Spell that name, please."

"When will he return?" she asked after complying.

"He's out of town for a few days. I assure you, I'll get this message to him, and he'll return your call, Miss Phoenix. Anything else I can help you with?"

"No. Thank you."

Ansel felt stymied. Why had Dorbandt gone out of town when the action was happening here?

She ate a bowl of cereal, wrote checks for her bills, and got them ready to mail. She spent almost another two hours cleaning out her truck cab, which had de-evolved from a place of transport into a rolling dirt museum. Months of fossil hunting and society functions had filled the cab with accumulated junk.

She placed fossil-hunting tools into the Delta truck box on the flatbed, including Nick's orange pick hammer. Papers went into the trailer. She disposed of trash and began vacuuming the interior to get the truck as presentable as possible for the Beastly Buffet. Next came the outside wash with soap and water. As she was polishing the truck with car wax, a dusty postal service truck sped up the drive and a young, blond-haired man got out. It was her postman, Barry.

"Hey, Miss Phoenix. Got a certified envelope for you. I need you to sign for it. He held up a small red, white and blue postal packet.

A sudden gust of wind almost snatched the mail from her grasp before she read the return address on the letter. *Science Quest.* The check for the Stegosaurus artwork. Barry passed her a postal receipt card and a pen. She scrawled her name with waxy fingers.

"Thanks, Barry."

The postman was shooting down the road in his SUV in less than a minute. Ansel tore open the top of the cardboard envelope and reached for the letter inside just as a pickup sputtered toward her house.

No time to read Rodgers' comments now, but she did notice the mustard yellow rectangle of paper between the paper folds as Feltus Pitt pulled up next to her truck. The check was there. She quickly turned and clipped the envelope to the sun visor above the driver's seat for safekeeping and closed the door.

Pitt hopped out of his mud-splattered truck. "Looks like a storm brewing," he said. "Radio's talking about a thunderhead coming in from the Rockies. I just brought my suit and one hive box with a rain cover. Won't have time to set up a whole apiary and check the old hive. Got to get these loose bees boxed and out of the rain."

Ansel noticed that to the west a bright summer sky had darkened into a gray, roiling mass of rain clouds. The temperature was dropping, and wind pummeled the trailer. The smell of rain permeated the air. Of course, she'd just washed and waxed the truck and now Mother Nature was going to ruin it all.

"Show me the swarm," Feltus said.

Ansel led Pitt around the trailer. Bees still clung to the tree branch, but the colony looked smaller.

"Yup, they're balling up," Pitt assessed. "They hate it when it rains and the temperature drops. Good sized swarm. About twenty-thousand."

Lightning flashed inside approaching thunderclouds. "Will you be able to move them?"

"Yes, ma'am, if I hurry. Go on inside. I don't know how the swarm's going to react."

Ansel did as he said. From the living-room window she watched Pitt unload equipment from the topper of his rusted Chevy. He pulled on white coveralls, a boxy mesh helmet and leather gloves, then picked up a hive box with a blue-handled tool on top. These he carried out of her range of vision.

Moving back to the bedroom window, Ansel observed as Pitt carefully constructed a concrete block base and set the hive box on top of it, along with a ramp of cardboard leading into the hive entrance. He placed the structure directly under the hanging swarm.

Pitt disappeared and returned carrying a metal can with a spout and bellows attached to the cannister's sides. Curls of smoke puffed from the container. Ansel's mind raced when she saw it. This was the same type of cannister she'd found in Nick's work room. She'd never gotten the chance to research the digital picture she'd taken.

Pitt took a hand saw and cut off the drooping branch just above the swarm, then firmly shook it two times over the cardboard platform. Most of the bees dropped onto the cardboard as a lethargic clump. Pitt gently laid the branch on top of the fallen bees and directed them toward the hive door with the billowing smoke.

As Ansel watched, fascinated, her mind still reeled over the discovery that Nick had a bee-keeping tool. Soon lightning flashed and a thunderous boom reverberated in the sky. She turned away, wincing at the storm's ferocity. A moment later, a knock sounded at the front door. Pitt was there, looking like a space man wearing a safari helmet who was trying not to be blown back to Mars.

"Gonna be a gully washer," the farmer said. "I've done all I can today, ma'am. Gonna take about half an hour for those bees to go into the box. I got the queen in so they'll follow. I'll come back tomorrow and finish up." Pitt looked up at the black clouds only a few miles away. "Do you mind, ma'am, if I leave my suit and a few supplies here?"

"Not at all. Bring everything into the trailer." Ansel helped Pitt store his few supplies in a living-room corner. "Mr. Pitt, what do you call the metal can with the bellows?"

"That's a smoker. Bees don't like the smell of smoke. Reminds them of a forest fire. Smoke makes them roost and start eating. Also makes them real docile. You can do hive work with bees using just a smoker if they're well fed beforehand. Don't even need a suit."

Pitt reassured her again that if the rains let up, he'd return in the morning, then put pedal to the metal going down her driveway as huge raindrops pattered on her trailer roof.

Ansel wasted no time going to a dinosaur calendar on the kitchen wall. She looked at the first week of the month. Sunday June third, the day Nick was supposed to bring the amber to Stouraitis. Nick had stayed with her Saturday night. *Burnt honey keeps the bees warm.*

Ansel's body trembled with anger. Nick had slept with her the day he'd received two million dollars. Had he drugged her wine, assuring she'd be pliable and sleep late the next morning? Had he gone out to her apiary while she slept, opened the hive, and hidden the money and the fossil find of the century?

But hide them from whom? And if he hid the money, did that mean he had no intention of giving the amber to Stouraitis the next day? How did Nick plan to get everything out of her hive without her knowing it? So many questions with no answers.

Ansel walked to the sofa and looked out the window. The rain fell in a torrent, and she could barely see the Langstroth hive in the field. She bit her lips, considering what to do very carefully. *I can't do it,* she thought. Bees are fine in their place, but I don't want to be close to thousands of them. Buzzing, flying, and stinging.

Ansel swallowed back the foul lump of fear in her throat. If ever she needed her lucky Iniskim around her neck, it was now. Too bad. She stared hard at Feltus Pitt's folded bee suit.

After the rain stopped, she'd take a look inside the apiary.

Chapter 29

*"I thought of dozens of ways to die,
but came to the conclusion that there
is no easy way to die. Dying is hard."*

Crying Wind, Kickapoo

Two hours later the thunderstorm had finally passed, dumping water so quickly that the ground couldn't drink it up fast enough. Ansel trekked across the last few feet in front of the fifty-inch-high hive, her shoes and pants soaked clear through. The few bees flying across the soppy field ignored her.

Ansel felt as though she was moving in slow motion inside the bee suit. It was baggy and hot. The Velcro straps pinched her ankles, and the vented, white helmet with a circular steel mesh veil was heavy and awkward. Her hands functioned like flippers inside the oversized leather gloves. Her right hand gripped a blue-handled, paint scraper-like tool with a hooked end.

Ansel licked her lips and stared at the pine board hive. The apiary resembled a square, towering insect condo with one entrance at the bottom. Her mouth had gone dry as she neared the bees. The rain-proof, galvanized metal cover had to be removed first. She carefully aligned the scraper edge into a crack between the cover and the box below it. A large, droning honeybee landed on the veil in front of her. Could bees smell fear?

Ansel froze. Her eyes crossed as she watched the insect and tried to deal emotionally with this new dilemma. She shut her eyes and held her breath. The bee's legs produced little clicking sounds as it walked across the mesh. This was worse. She opened her eyes. Resisting the urge to slap the bee into pulp, Ansel slowly raised her left hand and gently pushed it away. The insect hummed like a light aircraft engine and flew away. She exhaled her relief.

Jamming the scraper deeper into the box seam, Ansel pried up the cover edge. She pushed the scraper into a suit pocket, grabbed the two-inch-deep lid with both hands, and pulled up.

She expected a massive swarm to funnel out of the hive and chase her, but nothing happened. Beneath the cover was a solid board panel with an oval center hole. She set the cover frame on the ground, took the hive tool, and pried up the second barrier. More bees landed on her veil and upper body. They strutted along the suit a few paces, then flew away.

Under this inner board Ansel found a shallow hive box with a few bees inside. This wasn't right. Even she knew that the box should be filled with slide-in hive frames containing brood chambers. Instead she saw two small bundles tightly wrapped in black plastic and sealed with duct tape. Her pulse pounded.

Damn you, Nick. You used me.

The packages were stippled with a sticky, yellow-brown material smelling like decaying flowers. Rather than remove the messy packages, Ansel decided to take the useless hive box back to the trailer. Working the swollen wood joints apart bit by bit, she pried it off before pocketing the scraper.

As she lifted the hive box and walked away, more bees flitted through the air, landed on her suit and stayed. She was getting used to the noisy insects and went several steps before realizing she'd forgotten to replace the cover top needed to seal the apiary from the elements.

Ansel make an abrupt about-face. Her oversized helmet slid backward and only her hair pinned up inside stopped it from sliding completely off her head. As the veil slipped down her back, she heard a distant popping sound. Something struck her between the shoulder blades with a solid punch.

Ansel halted and turned. Lying by her toes, half-hidden in the tall, wet grass, was an orange object. She set the hive box on the ground, held on to her annoying, off-center helmet, and picked up the brightly colored tube with floppy-fingers.

Disbelief and horror gripped her. A plastic cylinder with a metal head and a needle dangled from her hand. Cloudy liquid dripped from the stainless steel point. A dart. If her hat and veil hadn't slipped, the syringe would have pierced her suit and her flesh. Strychnine.

Ansel dropped the dart as if it singed her gloves, then threw herself to the ground. As she lay flat on her stomach, terrifying thoughts whirled through her head. Had the dart punctured her suit anyway? She didn't feel anything except rampant fear. Who was shooting at her? They couldn't be far away. She was a prime target trapped in an open field and wearing a white bee suit.

Looking for someone with a gun, Ansel surveyed the land as best she could through the helmet veil and wet grass. She faced the trailer, some two hundred feet away. To her left at about three-hundred feet was the hangar. There was no sound except the song of a yellow warbler perched on the building's roof. From where had the dart been fired?

Had the shooter left, thinking she'd die a horrible death? Or was the person waiting for her to become paralyzed before approaching? Maybe the killer thought she'd simply been tending to her bees rather than searching for something in the hive. Well, she wasn't leaving the wrapped bundles for Nick and Evelyn's killer. Ansel grabbed the hive box and dragged it closer.

She quickly pulled the sticky packets over the rim and onto the ground, then rolled over on one hip and unzipped the coveralls. She stuffed both packages against her stomach. The elastic waistband would keep them from slipping down if she stood. Bees roamed over her suit, and she tried not to zip them inside. Adjusting the veil one more time, she re-assessed her position.

Ansel looked at the trailer and then the workshop. Which way to run? The shooter could be hiding near either. She turned back onto her stomach, facing the apiary. The dart lay in front of her. She wasn't going to leave it for the killer to destroy.

Ansel pulled off the right glove with her teeth and picked up the spent dart with her other gloved hand. She bent the needle backward toward the cylinder neck and shoved it point first into the thick leather glove so it wouldn't jab her. Then she unfastened one Velcro ankle strap and secured the glove beneath it. Now she could run without worrying about it.

She scrambled toward the hive on her stomach, then jumped to her feet and crouched behind the apiary. Her breath came in ragged gasps. The shooter knew she was alive and mobile now. She had nothing to protect herself with except the hive tool in her pocket. Not true. Inspiration struck and she grabbed the apiary cover lying on ground. The metal top would be a perfect shield for her chest. Where to go with it?

The workshop was locked, keys inside the trailer. Her truck was open, but the keys were in the trailer, too. The back porch was unlocked. Her gun was on the folding table where she'd dried it after emptying her ruined purse. She'd planned on thoroughly cleaning and oiling it later. Back porch, she decided.

Ansel looked around both corners of the hive. She saw nothing suspicious. Maybe the shooter had left. Bees moved around her in a thicker swarm. They landed on her suit, congregating on her shoulders and on the veil, buzzing louder. Their apiary top was gone, and they were agitated because their home was open to danger. She had to get out of here. Now.

Ansel didn't think. She simply bolted, making a dash for the rear porch. She held the metal top in front of her with both hands.

Suddenly her right foot stepped into a muddy gopher hole. She stumbled and fell flat on her stomach, the metal cover pinned beneath her. The bundles slammed into her abdomen. The helmet veil almost fell off. Keep going. She adjusted the mesh so she could see, jumped up again and ran, fear fueling her flight as she trundled awkwardly through the grass and beautiful meadow flowers. The porch seemed so far away.

She fell again. The damn helmet slid forward, blinding her. She wanted to toss it away, but she needed it. Cursing, she bolted madly forward on hands and knees, dragging the hive cover until she could get her feet under her and run. She concentrated on not falling a third time. She didn't think she could get up if she went down. Adrenalin pushed her, but she was tired and wet. Her right leg hurt. Only a few feet. The porch door waited for her.

Ansel yanked open the porch door with her gloveless hand. She tossed the metal cover to the ground, stumbled in, slammed the screen shut, and locked it. A quick look into the yard told her no one was behind her. She grabbed the pistol from the card table before running into the trailer and locking the second door.

In a flurry of motion, Ansel tossed the gun onto the sofa, pulled off the helmet and veil, and unzipped the bee suit. She pulled the bundles out, as well as the gloved dart in her ankle strap, throwing them beside the gun. Then she stripped off the coveralls and rushed to the bedroom's dresser mirror. She tore off her shirt and bra, frantically peering over her shoulder at the reflection of her naked back. There was no puncture mark. Not even a bruise.

Ansel pulled her shirt on, relief rolling over her in a torrent of gratitude to the higher powers that had saved her from a heinous death. Tears threatened, but she pushed back the emotional tsunami. She didn't have time. Some faceless coward had trespassed on her land and taken a potshot at her while her back was turned. Now what was she going to do? Call the police? Call her father?

Ansel took the box of cartridges from her night stand, returned to the living room, and reloaded the Colt pistol. Hot anger cemented her resolve. Nobody was running her off her land. She couldn't go home every time the world booted her in the rump. She'd give the packages to Dorbandt when she was damn good and ready.

"I am a force of nature to be reckoned with," Ansel said.

She picked up the stippled packages and set them on the pass-through. From a kitchen drawer she pulled out scissors. She cut through the duct tape on the smaller package first, peeling away the black plastic wrap from a hard, unyielding object. Her hands shook with excitement. There was a yellow chamois. Her heart thudded. The soft, leathery cloth fell away and a four-by-six-inch chunk of amber weighted her palm.

There was no crust. Nick had removed the ugly exterior, filed the resin into its oval dimensions, and polished the surface to a shiny, golden gloss. The interior wasn't completely clear but peppered with minute specks, black spots made up of plant and dirt debris trapped within. She wasn't an expert, but the fossilized resin looked natural and genuine. And it had already been tested by Stouraitis' expert. He had declared the chunk to be authentic Baltic amber.

Not only forest debris had been entombed. Ansel stared at the large inclusion with awe. An inch-and-a-half oblong egg rested near the nodule's outer edge. The rough-textured egg had crumpled rather than broken into shell fragments. From one end protruded the upper chest, one wing, neck and head of a blackish creature. It resembled a bird hatchling but had a tiny wing claw, a long reptilian snout, and tiny teeth.

Ansel rotated the amber in her hands, carefully studying the inclusion from all angles. The beast was a uniform, brown-black color typical of fossilized inclusions. She estimated its weight in life had been between seventeen and twenty-one grams. The skin was covered with tiny bumps like chicken skin. The body was featherless except for a sprout of black-brown down on the top of the head. The slightly parted mouth showed nothing of the tongue. Frozen, yellow reptilian eyes with horizontal pupils looked back at her.

The lower body remained hidden, nestled within the flattened egg so that the tail and feet remained a mystery. Around the hatchling's head, a cluster of trapped air bubbles glimmered like crystal beads, possibly made during the reptile's death struggles as it suffocated in tree sap.

Ansel assessed the basic morphological traits. The head looked reptilian: long black snout, sharp ratchet teeth. The neck was goose-like. Halfway up the wing an oversized, hand-like claw displaying three digits sprawled open. The middle finger was the longest of the three. By her reckoning, the overall physiology of the Cretaceous reptile appeared similar to *Archaeopteryx* of fossil limestones.

Ansel covered the amber with Becker's chamois and laid it on the counter. She cut through the second package. When she spread the plastic apart, she saw a five-by-seven cardboard box. Inside, surrounded by foam, were three clear plastic cases.

Each case contained a large gold coin imprinted with the figure of a long-haired woman wearing a toga. She held a staff in her right hand and a leafy branch in her left. Raised lettering with "Liberty" and "1927D" was stamped on the front. On the reverse, a left profile of a bald eagle, along with the words "Twenty Dollars," was inscribed. The coins had a cardboard insert that read "Saint-Gaudens Double Eagle."

Ansel stared at the inch-and-a-half-diameter coins. Where had the two million dollars gone? More unanswered questions. She placed the three cases on the counter beside the amber.

She'd do some Internet research. Then she'd find a place to hide everything so it would be safe until Dorbandt returned. Nothing would make her happier than to give it all to him.

Especially the loathsome dart used to try and kill her.

Chapter 30

*"When I shot any kind of bird, when
I killed, I saw that its life went out with
its blood...I came into this world to die."*

Toohoolhoolzote, Nez Perce

Dorbandt's mid-morning had been a blur of activity: filling
out departmental voucher requests, rushing to get packed,
making a hasty departure for Missoula. He had spent the
rest of the afternoon changing modes of transportation and
clock watching. Time doesn't fly, Dorbandt decided as he
navigated a rented Bronco along I-90 near Deer Lodge,
Montana. Time lurches with more fits and stops than a three-
legged horse.

Fiskar's assignment to find the closest facility that could
identify the feather had been a challenge. A Charles Russell
Refuge ranger told Odie to call the National Wildlife
Forensics Lab in Oregon. The staff there told him to contact
the University of Montana in Missoula, which ran a top-
notch DNA lab in the Montana Molecular Biology Department. From there, Fiskar had been directed to the Harrier
Institute in western Montana.

As a result, Dorbandt had driven north toward Wolf Point
to catch a twelve-ten departure flight on Big Sky Airlines.

Then he'd sat for over seven hours in a plane. From the Missoula airport he'd rented a Bronco and had gone to the state lab to pick up the feather from a forensic tech staying late just to hand it to him. Now he had almost completed the one-hour drive south of Missoula to Deer Lodge, where a genetics specialist would complete the feather analysis.

In spite of the exhausting day, Dorbandt's adrenalin pumped hard as he entered the town of Deer Lodge. He felt in his gut that this feather was the case breaker he needed. The only thing bothering him was his acid reflux. A day on the go without proper meals played havoc with his stomach.

Dorbandt reached for a tablet inside a foil packet sliding along the dash as he drove past the Grants-Kohrs Ranch. The fifteen-hundred-acre National Historic Site commemorating the western cattle industry of the 1850s had been established by Canadian fur trader John Grant. Later it was expanded by cattle baron Conrad Kohrs. The Harrier Institute was next to the ranch.

Dorbandt swallowed the medicine dry while making the final turn up a winding asphalt driveway surrounded by a copse of ponderosa pine. A long, single-story concrete block building came into view. Dorbandt looked at the dash clock. Precisely eleven o'clock. The lateness of the hour didn't matter. He was expected, and the building glowed with light. He parked, picked up the small, sealed box sitting on the seat, and exited the Bronco.

The air smelled of aromatic pine resin mixed with an intermittent odor of cow dung. A gravid, white moon hung high in the sky above the tree line and shone down on the distant, saw-toothed peaks of the Continental Divide. Dorbandt pushed an intercom button next to the door.

"Yes?" said a distorted speaker voice.

"Lieutenant Dorbandt. Lacrosse County Sheriff's Department."

"Just a moment."

A deadbolt clicked, and the large portal opened. Dorbandt stared at a short, large-bellied man wearing a lab smock. "Please come in. I'm Doctor Paul Fletcher. Pleasure to meet you."

Dorbandt stepped into a small waiting room, not unlike that of a doctor's office or a hospital. "I need to get this evidence identified tonight."

Fletcher smiled. "I'll be doing the tests. Is that the sample?"

"Yes." Dorbandt relinquished the box to the specialist. "What exactly do you do here?"

"This institute is an avian genome resource bank."

They moved past industrial-grade, cushioned chairs and sofa-lined walls. There were also the obligatory coffee tables and framed, scenic prints. The only thing missing were the entertainment magazines. Fletcher motioned Dorbandt to follow him through a rear door of the waiting room.

"You've lost me already, Dr. Fletcher. Pare that down so I can understand."

Fletcher chuckled. "We take blood and tissue samples from birds and study them for genetic information. The research not only maps their genetic makeup, but tells us how bird species are interrelated to one another. I'll be able to tell you exactly what species of bird we're dealing with here."

"Can you tell me the sex of it, too?"

"Definitely. Humans are sexed by their two X and Y chromosomes, but birds have a W and Z. Unlike humans, the male bird has the two copies of the same chromosome, ZZ, whereas female birds have Z and Y. I like to think of it as nature's way of adhering to the rules of fair play among the sexes."

"Women's Libbers would love it," Dorbandt agreed as he entered a humongous laboratory.

It resembled the one he'd seen at the Montana Cooperative, except that it was filled with birds rather than soil samples and plants.

Stuffed specimens roosted along the counters and shelving units. Intact feathered bird skins with cotton stuffed in the eye sockets were laid in rows upon huge trays. Bird limbs and internal organs floated in huge, sealed jars set along other flat surfaces. Dorbandt took in the bizarre tableau, then watched Fletcher open the box and remove the forensic bag with the brown and white feather. He held it up to the light.

"This is a pennaceous feather from an adult bird. Let me take a closer look at the morphology," Fletcher said, pulling on sterile gloves and removing the evidence with forceps. "Hopefully this feather was collected while still growing on the bird."

"Why?"

"A growing feather is fed by blood in the epidermis which remains if the rachis or shaft is suddenly removed. A molted feather is detached from the epidermis naturally and may not have any blood."

He held up the feather and stared at it. "Hmm. It's not a primary, what is often called a flight feather. That's the best to work with, but it is a contour feather with a planar vane. That's better than a downy sample. Now for the shaft under-structure."

Fletcher placed the feather on a large glass plate and used a scalpel to cut the feather into two halves. He dropped the thicker, lower half into a tiny vial, then capped and placed the tube in a vial stand. The other piece of shaft he split lengthwise and used forceps to place onto a glass slide, which he carefully positioned beneath a compound microscope.

"I'll see if I can determine what order this is."

Dorbandt held his breath while his esophagus burned. Could he know this quickly if he was on the right track with Alexander King?

"The rachis groove looks U-shaped, but it's questionable."

"What does that mean?"

"It means I need the blood work to make sure. However, I think we may be dealing with a member of the order Galliform. This is a medium-sized group comprising birds of three families, with pheasants, grouses, turkeys, partridges, guinea fowls, and quails."

Dorbandt was disappointed. Game birds. Not the type of birds sold as pets in retail stores. The only bell that rang was the name Theodore Melba. He'd lost his ranch to a flock of sage grouse. Where did that leave his theory about King and strychnine?

"What happens next?"

"I have to extract the blood from the feather shaft, amplify it through a polymerase chain reaction that synthetically generates DNA from the original sample, cut the strand at particular points with enzymes, and view the DNA chromosomes through electrophoresis. The whole procedure takes about six hours."

"Then what?"

Fletcher smiled. "I just compare the chromosome points with the institute's genome database to find the exact bird species it matches and the gender."

"How can you be sure this bird will match one of your samples?"

"That might be a problem with a U.S. Wildlife lab that has limited bird specimens against which to compare, but not here. There are over thirteen thousand species of birds in the world, and we have collected DNA from almost five thousand of them. We're the Library of Congress when it comes to bird genomics."

"I'll wait out front." He headed toward the waiting room.

"Detective, there's a room for lab personnel through this other door." Fletcher pointed to the right. "It has a small kitchen and a couple of sofas to sack out on. The fridge is always stocked. Have something to eat. I'll check in with you from time to time."

"Thanks, Doctor."

He left the geneticist to his research and entered a room with a small kitchen. The fridge had everything from lunch meats to frozen dinners, as well as liquid refreshments. Tons of snack food filled in the rest of the dietary gaps. Needing something for his stomach, Dorbandt was soon sitting at a polished walnut table eating a ham and cheese sandwich and drinking milk.

When he finished the midnight meal, he carefully cleaned the dishware in a double stainless steel sink, dried them, and put each piece away in the cabinets. Too keyed up to sleep, Dorbandt sat on a plush, brown corduroy sofa and pulled out his cell phone. There were three messages on his voice mail.

"Dorbandt. McKenzie. Check in with me."

"Reid, this is Odie. I just got a call from Miss Ansel Phoenix. Says she has info on Dr. Anthanasios Stouraitis pertinent to the Capos case. Call her back. That's it."

"Dorbandt. McKenzie again. Where the hell are you? Call me."

Dorbandt left the cell phone on and slipped it into his coat pocket. The messages must have come through while he was in the air over Montana. He hadn't even thought about checking in since then. He shook his head in amazement. McKenzie didn't quit.

And Phoenix didn't either. For a second he wondered what Ansel had seen in Capos. Capos had been a first-class jerk, and Ansel seemed too savvy to fall for such a con artist. He couldn't imagine them together, even for one night.

Dorbandt stretched out on the sofa, thinking about the test going on outside the door. His thoughts bounced back and forth between knowing he was on the right track with Alexander King and not being sure about his hunch at all.

The next thing Dorbandt knew, something shook him. He jumped up, his left hand reaching instinctively toward the shoulder holster. He relaxed when he recognized the smocked scientist.

"What's wrong?" Dorbandt demanded, half asleep and sure that some disaster had occurred because he'd let his guard down.

"Nothing," Fletcher grinned. "The test is done."

Dorbandt rubbed a hand across his gritty eyes. "What time is it?"

"Almost six in the morning. I'll show you what I've found. It's quite interesting."

Fletcher led him to a lab counter where he picked up an oversized photo negative. "This is a DNA amplification of the blood taken from the shaft. Those lighted bars on the numbered scale indicate the multiple chromosome markers that identify the bird species. I found a match, and I was right about it being a game bird. Your feather came from a female hoatzin."

"What's a hoatzin?"

Fletcher pulled a large book toward him and pointed to an open page with a color picture. "A monotypic bird species currently assigned to the order Galliformes, family Opistho-comidae, genus Opisthocomus, and species Opisthocomus Hoatzin. A hoatzin is a very odd, fourteen-inch-long bird with a large golden crest. Hoatzins live in backwater swamps of the Amazon and Orinoco basins of South America."

"South America?"

Fletcher nodded. "The hoatzin is a colorful, vegetarian bird with a foregut rather than a crop like other birds. The foregut ferments vegetable matter like a cow, sheep or deer. Most remarkable about the bird is that hatchling chicks have functional claws on the first and second digits of the forelimbs."

Dorbandt blinked. "Tell me about these claws."

"The claws are on the tips of each wing. After hatching, hoatzin chicks begin to wander around the branches near their nest. The hatchlings are weak, but the claws help to support them on the branches over the water. If they fall into the water, they swim to shore, climb the tree, and get back into their nest. As the wing feathers develop, these claws degenerate. They're fascinating birds with an antediluvian morphology sometimes compared to the proto-bird *Archae-opteryx*."

Suddenly Ansel Phoenix's obsession with ambers and feathered dinosaurs with clawed wings didn't sound so ridiculous. "Can you buy one of these hoatzins at a pet shop?"

Fletcher laughed. "You don't buy hoatzins, Detective Dorbandt. Though they are not a globally threatened species or considered endangered in their indigenous habitats, they don't survive in captivity. Attempts to start a breeding colony in the 1960s and the late 1980s by two zoological societies failed miserably."

"Could you get one if you had to?"

"If you were in South America, yes. Tribal people still collect the eggs for consumption. They'll also take adults for the feathers, medicinal purposes or just to use as fish bait." Fletcher shrugged. "Even if you got a live specimen in South America, you'd have a hell of a time getting it into this country unless it's smuggled in. And for what purpose? They eat special diets consisting mostly of Moko-moko plants, have a foul odor, and die in captivity. Not much there in the way of pet attraction, is there?"

Dorbandt didn't know the answer to that question. "Are you are saying that this feather had to come from a bird in South America?"

Fletcher nodded. "Absolutely. Whoever you got this feather from, had either a hoatzin, part of a hoatzin, or some feathers from a South American specimen, and this person either went to get it or had it brought into the United States."

Maybe both, Dorbandt considered. Could King smuggle a hoatzin in through his bird business? Would he have to go to South America or might someone have brought the bird to him? But why? Perhaps as part of his research on *Archaeopteryx*?

"Exactly where in South America do these hoatzins live?"

"Let me check on that." Fletcher went to a PC keyboard and began punching keys.

In a moment he said, "The species lives east of the Andes from Colombia to Venezuela and the Guianas, south to Ecuador and Peru, and in north and central Brazil and Bolivia."

Dorbandt stared at the screen. "Can you print that out?"

"Certainly."

"Thanks, Doctor Fletcher. Just get me an invoice for the test expenses and sign my chain of custody receipt, and I'm done here." He reached into a breast pocket to pull out the form.

Fletcher took it and moved off to gather his materials. "I'll also give you a copy of the DNA photo and a picture of a hoatzin to take back."

Dorbandt moved toward the front lobby. He pulled out his cell phone and dialed Fiskar's home phone.

"Fiskar residence," said a female voice after two rings.

"Is Odie there?"

"Who's calling?"

"Detective Dorbandt."

"Just a minute."

Odie came on a second later. "Reid, you're up early."

"Sorry to call the house, Odie, but this can't wait."

"It's okay. Did you get the feather analyzed?"

"Just. It's from a South American bird called a hoatzin. Listen, when you go into the office this morning, I need you to grab a red file on my desk. It has a list of every person involved in the Capos case. I want you to drop everything and see if anybody on it has taken a trip to South America during the past two years. Check everything commercial or rental. Planes, boats, and charters. Call me pronto if there's a hit. If I don't hear from you first, I'll check in during my layover at Billings. Got that?"

"Right. When will you be back?"

"Sometime in the afternoon. I still have to book a flight out of Missoula." Dorbandt grinned. "Tell McKenzie I'm on my way."

Chapter 31

*"If you see no reason to give
thanks, the fault lies in yourself."*

Tecumseh, Shawnee

Ansel arrived at the Arrowhead Ranch at noon the next day.
The Beastly Buffet had begun, and more than a hundred
vehicles were already parked in a mowed field next to the
horse pasture behind the main house.

She waved at the ranch hand directing attendees through
a cattle gate and onto a flat, tree-lined patch of land used as
a calving ground during the late summer months. Before
leaving the truck, she put on her hat and strapped on her
fanny pouch, the trusty Colt crammed inside.

The air smelled of barbecued meat, exhaust fumes, and
trampled grass. Ansel donned her sunglasses and looked up.
Thank goodness the weather was cooperating. A cloudless,
turquoise sky hung overhead, and the temperature had risen
into the lower eighties with a constant eight-mile-per-hour
breeze coming from the west.

As she walked toward the buffet, Ansel saw that Pearl had
spared no expense. Four huge tents were tethered on the grassy
turf, each situated next to pine trees for optimum shade.
Three served as buffet stations for appetizers, entrees, and

desserts. The fourth contained long tables and chairs where people could sit, eat, and drink.

Ansel tried to concentrate on enjoying the buffet, but her mind replayed her theories revolving around Nick, Evelyn, Stouraitis, and a dinosaur trapped in resin. She'd finally read Leslie's paper on caustobioliths and spent most of the night doing Internet research on amber, *Archaeopteryx*, and Double Eagle coins.

She'd discovered why Nick hadn't stashed two million dollars inside the bee hive. A Saint-Gaudens Double Eagle coin minted in 1927 by the Denver mint was the rarest U.S. coin in the world. More than one hundred eighty thousand of the coins had been produced, but, they were later collected and melted down by the government. For this reason and because undiscovered hoards of the coins were believed to be stashed in European banks to this day, a single coin in uncirculated condition could sell for $675,000 on the numismatic market.

With three coins in his possession, Nick could have gone anywhere in the world and sold them to recoup their two-million-dollar cash value. It was brilliant. The vintage coins were easy to transport and legal to have and sell as collectibles. As Nick's assets, they would have been practically untraceable.

Ansel had no doubt that Stouraitis had paid with the coins. The lovely, one Troy ounce of golden metal with an inscribed eagle and a woman in a toga-style gown would appeal to his taste for rare bird treasures. Stouraitis could have gotten the coins anywhere, including on the European black market.

She passed an eight-foot-long charcoal pit centered among the phalanx of tents. A huge metal rack set across the block pit supported half a split buffalo carcass, and a hired server continually sliced off juicy pieces. Nearby a high-volume, five-man country western band stood on a wooden platform and belted out a Garth Brooks tune. Next to the band was a large refreshment trailer that served as a full-service bar powered by a belching gas generator. A burly, cowboy bartender couldn't dispense the drinks over the counter fast enough.

Her stomach rumbled as every plate filled with exotic goodies passed by her. Her appetite had dwindled after she had nearly been poisoned by a maniac with a dart gun, but now it had returned with a vengeance.

Ansel walked through the surging crowd of dancing couples, running kids, and group huddles of all sizes and types. Everyone was decked out in their cowboy finest, from ten-gallon hats to alligator-hide boots, and she knew most of the people who made the joyful affair a colorful swirl of bright colors and gay voices.

Smiling, Pearl rushed from a crowd of partygoers and grabbed her arm. "Ansel, I was getting worried. Thought you'd be here earlier."

Ansel gave her stepmother a hug and a kiss. "I had to do some bee repairs," she said, thinking of her morning spent waiting as Feltus Pitt finished up the hive work.

Before sunset the day before, she'd returned to the apiary and replaced the missing hive box and metal cover. Pitt, God bless him, hadn't made a single comment about his bee suit having grass stains all over it, though she'd given them a quick toss into her washing machine.

"I'll tell you all about it later. Did the crow gut arrive?"

"It sure did. Jessie and Lucy are here somewhere. You look tired. I was going to drag you around to meet friends, but let's get something to eat first. Maybe we'll see your father."

They were both ravenous and decided to go directly into the entree tent. Heated stainless steel trays were set up on long tables with black tablecloths. Beside each entree, a numbered eight-by-ten sheet had been taped, describing the dish, its recipe, and lines for people to sign their names. Each name represented one vote toward selecting the item as the best appetizer, entree or dessert dish of the Beastly Buffet. Near the end of the party, the winners would be announced. Originality, taste, and gross-out factor figured in the voting process to varying degrees, and the lucky winners would get a special mystery prize to take home with them.

Ansel looked over the exotic fare. Most of the main dishes contained common domestic and wild meats. The challenge for the cooks was to prepare something edible from highly unusual body parts such as heads, snouts, eyes, ears, jowls, feet, udders, and tails. Ansel stopped at a tray holding Rocky Mountain Oysters and laughed. Somebody always made this infamous Montana recipe for deep-fried bull testicles.

Ansel noted some of the most unusual entrees: roast polar bear, Canadian lynx stew, curried kangaroo tail, savory seal hearts, french-fried skunk, woodchuck chili, fried beaver tail, muskrat burgers, rat kabobs, mice meatballs, fruit bat soup, jellied caribou snouts, stuffed camel, roast emu, swan gizzards, hoot owl pie, iguana soup, and lizard tongue macaroni and cheese.

She also saw weird seafood entrees like stuffed squid with chocolate sauce, octopus eye stew, whale Bobotee, and baked cod fish tongues. Giant land snail with mushroom sauce, slug fritters, and earthworm pasta made up a slimy contingent of dishes as well.

"What looks like the best of the worst to you?" asked Pearl as they circumnavigated the tables together, filling their plates very slowly.

Ansel winced. The insect recipes were the worst for her, and there was a great supply of creepy-crawly things. She eyed beetle biscuits, fried green tomato hornworms, meal-worm fried rice, sour cream locusts, bee grub scrambled eggs, french fried maggots, dragonfly gazpacho, ant brood tacos, crickets and beans salad, grasshopper pasta, cicada souffle, and broiled moth cakes. The most memorable dishes were the tarantula salad and the garlic wood louse bread sticks.

"I'd say the giant silk worm pupae quiche. Did you see the size of those things? They were bigger than mice." Ansel grimaced, placing a helping of crow casserole next to a previous dollop of curried kangaroo tail. Kangi beware, she thought, remembering the Red Rose scam artist.

Pearl giggled. "I'm voting for the seal brain fritters. Your crow gut is going fast."

"That's because it's made with ingredients that cowards like me will eat. Elk intestines turned inside out and stuffed with meat and vegetables looks tame around here."

While walking toward the dining tent, people stopped to say hello and chat. Ansel dutifully chuckled with the Big Toe mayor and his wife, the chief of police, and a couple of old family friends. Everyone wanted to discuss the strychnine murders, while Pearl wanted to discuss the news that Ansel was still single and available to the right man.

When they reached the dining tent, Pearl set her plate on the table and left for the beer wagon. Ansel sat and began eating, nodding and waving to everyone she knew at the same time. Suddenly, her father plopped into Pearl's empty seat.

"Hey, honey. I heard you were over here."

Her father looked good, all dressed up in a teal color-block shirt, black jeans, lizard-skin belt, concha-button boots, and a white Specialist hat.

"Hi, Daddy. I've missed you." She gave him a big hug, latching on as if she might not see him again. Her experience the day before had made her appreciate her family more than ever.

He patted her back. "You wouldn't miss me if you stayed at the ranch. I don't like the idea of you being at the trailer. We agreed you should stay home until these murders are solved."

Ansel pulled away. If he knew someone had tried to kill her with a poison dart, he'd be horrified. She wasn't going to ruin the party for him. "I know, but I'm a big girl now."

"Sure," Chase said, giving her a scrutinizing stare. "Is Detective Dorbandt coming?"

She picked at her food. "He's out of town. Chasing leads."

"I don't know, Sarcee. He might show up. I've seen the way he looks at you."

"Yeah, like a murder suspect. Speaking of suspicious behaviors, why were you two giving each other funny looks before you drove away from my trailer the other night?"

Chase used two fingers and grabbed a piece of kangaroo meat from her plate. "What is this? Tastes like spotted mule and piccalilli sauce."

"Don't change the subject."

Chase gave her a cagey smile. "Why don't you ask Dorbandt?"

"Never mind. He and I are oil and vinegar."

Chase laughed. "Which are you?"

Ansel made a face. "Very funny."

"Hey, I'm just curious who's at the top of the jug?"

"Me."

"Figures." Chase shook his head. "Smooth on the palate, but slicker than a wet noodle to get a bite hold on."

Ansel smirked. "I think Dorbandt's already found that out."

"Oh, I don't doubt that a bit. Well, remember that oil and vinegar can make one great vinaigrette," he said, waggling his eyebrows.

Ansel's features darkened. "Don't even think it, Daddy. I have absolutely no interest in Dorbandt."

"What are you two jaybirds squawking about now?" Pearl appeared, bearing two large plastic cups of beer.

Chase stood so Pearl could have the seat. "Salads."

Pearl sat down and passed a cup to Ansel. She looked up at Chase. "Are you going to eat with us?"

"No, I've got to patrol the fences. Nothing worse than city slickers going loco on firewater."

"You'd better eat or your blood sugar will go south on you," Pearl said.

"I had a slab of buffalo ribs. I'll catch up with you two in a bit."

"Talk to you later, Daddy."

"You bet," he said as he gave them a wave and departed.

Pearl and she quickly finished their meals, drank their beers, and gabbed for another fifteen minutes until Pearl said, "I've got to circulate. Want to come with me?"

Ansel shook her head. "I think I'll go to the dessert tent. Go have fun."

"Are you sure you're all right? You seem distracted. Anything you want to talk about?"

"I'm great. I'll catch up to you."

Pearl left reluctantly and Ansel wandered through the dessert tent. The chocolate-covered grasshoppers, jellied bug blox, candied cricket Spumoni sorbet, mealworm chocolate chip cookies, and maggot cake did nothing for her. She settled on the dubious choice of a cow udder eclair, only because it was smothered in chocolate syrup and whipped cream. As she walked out of the tent with her plate, Lydia Hodges appeared.

"Hi, Ms. Phoenix," she said. "I'm glad I found you."

Ansel was very surprised to see Lydia. "Hi. How are you doing?"

"All right. Especially since I'm out of school. How about you?"

"I'm fine. I'm just glad the funeral is over. I was really surprised to see you there."

"I wasn't really comfortable going, but I'm glad I went. Tim said it would be a catharsis for me to go. You know, so I wouldn't always think of Mr. Capos looking like we found him in that horrible grave. He was right," Lydia said. "He's here, too."

Ansel took a small taste of her salty, chocolate dessert. "Tim?"

"Uh huh. We met in the parking lot. He's at the bar getting us a drink."

"My, you two are becoming a pair, aren't you?" Ansel teased.

Lydia's cheeks flared crimson. "I wouldn't say that. We just have a few things in common, that's all."

"Like what?"

"Well, we both like to cook. Tim makes a wonderful roast suckling pig. It's fabulous. I think it's the orange juice the meat is soaked in before cooking that makes the meat so good. He says that orange juice is a deoxidizer that tenderizes meat."

Ansel wondered if Tim used California Valencia oranges for his gourmet meals just as she looked up to see him walking toward them. He was wearing his usual jeans, flowered Hawaiian shirt, boots, and white hat. His 35mm camera hung around his neck. He also carried two frosty cups of brew.

"Hi, Miss Phoenix," he said before passing a beer to Lydia. "Hope it's cold enough for you."

Lydia looked at Tim with unabashed adoration. "It's perfect."

"How are you, Tim?"

Tim turned toward her. His blue eyes darkened a bit. "Super. How about you?"

"No complaints," Ansel said. "How do you like the buffet so far?"

Tim sipped his beer. "I like it a lot. I thought it would be cool to see how exotic animal foods look and taste. And Lydia talked me into it." He gave the girl a glance, then turned back toward Ansel. "What are you eating?"

"Something called a cow udder eclair. I could live without it."

"Sounds disgusting," Lydia said.

Tim laughed. "Last summer when I was on a blackwater lake near Iquitos, South America, the local Yanomamo Indians showed me how to cut out the lean meat from fourteen-inch-long walking stick insects, roast it in a small cauldron, and add it to a boiled soup made with native greens and herbs. Of course, I had to eat some. To be polite."

Lydia scowled. "What did it taste like?"

"Not bad. The meat had a nutty flavor, but it wasn't crunchy."

"I don't mind bugs," Lydia said, "but eating them is another thing."

"You eat bugs every day. You just don't know it," Tim replied. "For instance, take that chocolate sauce you've got on your dessert, Miss Phoenix. For every one hundred grams of processed chocolate there are about eighty microscopic insect fragments in it."

Lydia shivered. "Gross."

Ansel swallowed revulsion and set her fork down. She had the distinct impression that Tim was enjoying the effect his perverse conversation was having on Lydia and her. He didn't stop.

"A lot of processed foods with grains, fruits, and vegetables have even more bugs. The worst is mushrooms. One can has up to twenty maggots processed with it."

"Enough, Tim. We get the point." Lydia stared at him.

Ansel went for a diversion tactic. "How interesting that you visited South America. The latest fossil discoveries in that country have been fascinating. I was going to discuss those during one of our seminars."

"I really enjoyed my stay in the Amazon. I went on a nine day student rainforest workshop sponsored by the National Zoo in Washington, D.C. Someone paid my way so it didn't cost me a thing."

Lydia moved closer to him. "So, you want to go see what's in this tent, Tim?"

Ansel looked at Lydia. "Why don't you go ahead. I want to ask Tim something. It will only take a second."

Lydia cast a woeful gaze in Tim's direction. "All right. Come find me."

When she left, Tim stared at Ansel, but said nothing.

"Tim, I'm curious about something that happened the day we found Nick Capos. When you saw him, you took some pictures. What did you do with those photos?"

"I didn't do anything with them," he said after taking a long sip of his beer. "The police confiscated the roll. I was lucky they didn't take my camera, too." He cocked his head sideways as if studying her critically.

Ansel shrugged. "I should have realized that. I was hoping that if you still had them, I could see them. I wanted to take another look at the area around Nick's body. Oh, before I forget, you got my email about the fossil seminar at my workshop tomorrow, right?"

"Sure. I also got your recommendation letter. Thanks for that. It should really help with my admission application."

"You're welcome. O.K. I'll see you tomorrow. Enjoy the party." She turned and started to walk away.

"Hey, Miss Phoenix," Tim called.

Ansel turned.

"Say bones." Tim raised his camera and snapped a picture. "Great shot. I'll bring you a copy tomorrow." In a second he disappeared into the tent.

Ansel stood paralyzed, watching as Tim Shanks went through the canopied opening. Goosebumps skittered up her arms, and the summer heat did nothing to warm her. She couldn't believe the revelation spinning through her head, but it all made such perfect sense.

Deinonychus, she remembered. An attractive-looking social animal, quick, strong, and very good with its hands. That's how she'd classified Tim's social behaviors to dinosaurian characteristics. He was all those things, from his blond good looks to the way he deftly manipulated his camera.

Just like he'd used the camera to take her picture in the Rockheads aisle. The clicking sound she'd heard had been his camera shutter, and she'd seen the flash of his bright red Hawaiian shirt as he'd scampered out of view. He'd followed her. Had he tried to dart her? Was he a killer?

Tim attended Bowie College. Had Nick been speaking to him on the pay phone? Nick could have met him there, but what did Tim have to do with the amber inclusion or the coins worth two million dollars?

Get Dorbandt, her conscience screamed as fear coursed through her. Go straight to the sheriff's office right now and tell Detective Fiskar everything. Ask him if Tim's film was confiscated or not. Tim's photographing of Nick's decomposed body *had* seemed grotesque at the time. Obscene.

But what good would it do talking to Fiskar? Dorbandt was out of town. No one would rush to question Tim unless she had proof of his involvement with Nick and Evelyn. She had to find evidence here and now while he was occupied with Lydia.

But how to prove Tim Shanks could be the killer, Ansel pondered frantically? She didn't know much about him: where he hung out, where he lived. And then she thought of one desperate way she might get proof.

Ansel hurried toward a metal barrel. She dumped her eclair into the trash and moved into a thick crowd of party-goers near the band stand, twining in and out of knotted groupings to make sure Tim couldn't follow her again.

She'd know his battered brown station wagon anywhere. Maybe he hadn't locked the vehicle, and she could get into it. Maybe there would be something linking him to Nick or Evelyn. Maybe a dart gun or a tranquilizer dart.

Maybe even some strychnine.

Chapter 32

*"Sing your death song and
die like a hero going home."*

Tecumseh, Shawnee

The parking area was deserted. The cowboy attendant had left, and all the guests had made their way to the buffet. Except for a few scattered pines, hiding places were minimal, so Ansel ducked behind cars as she searched the well-ordered rows. She found Shanks' car very quickly.

Up close the long, brown Chevy Impala five-door looked ancient. The paint had faded, the roof racks had rusted, and the dents and scratches from hood to rear door resembled battle wounds that had never healed.

Ansel crouched past the wagon bed. The driver's door was unlocked. She opened it, slid behind the steering wheel, and closed the door. She scrunched down further in the seat and placed her sunglasses on her lap.

The stifling car smelled like old hamburger meat, dust, and mildew. The balding cloth seats were well-abused, and the sun-faded dash looked cracked and brittle under the loose papers, napkins, maps, and gas receipts stuffed onto it.

Even the passenger seat was covered with spiral notebooks, plastic binders, a mountain of returned homework papers, and movie soundtrack CDs. A similar mound of material filled the dirt-encrusted floorboard beneath the passenger seat. Ansel quickly fingered through the dash debris and seat piles, making sure she didn't miss any incriminating evidence linking Tim to Nick or Evelyn. Nothing.

She opened the glove compartment. It bulged with accumulated debris from years of road travel. Among the mess the only things she saw of interest were two ratty paperback novels entitled *On Death and Dying* and *Death Be Not Proud*. Classroom assignments or a chilling glimpse into Shanks' psyche?

The rear seat seemed to be Tim's dumping ground for old take-out food containers and bagged lunches, which littered the seats and overflowed onto the floor. Sighing, Ansel got back out of the car, sunglasses in hand, and opened the backseat door. She pawed through the food trash. This proved useless. Next she peered over the backseat into the wagon bed. Only a grungy, khaki backpack rested on a stretch of dirty, moth-eaten carpet.

Ansel reached over the rear seat and grabbed the backpack. It was heavy. She undid the metal straps and dumped everything onto the trash-covered seat. Textbooks. More papers. And a hail of loose objects that had accumulated at the bottom of the sack.

When a clear, round object rolled to a stop by her right leg, Ansel's limbs froze. Nick's glass paperweight with two hearts. Evelyn had the collectible last, she realized. Tim must have gotten it the night Evelyn died. When he poisoned her.

"Oh, my God," she said, her heart beating a frenzied rhythm against her rib cage. *Get out of here.*

Ansel padded her hand with some notebook papers and picked up the small globe, wrapping the ends around the incriminating evidence. She dug into the trash on the floorboards and found a used plastic bag, then stuffed the paper bundle into it and sealed the top. She hurriedly pushed the bulky bag into a large front pocket of her carpenter jeans.

Ansel left the ransacked backpack, grabbed her sunglasses, and exited the Impala. She pulled out her truck keys from another pocket. As she shut the door, a pressure against her lower right abdomen made her glance down. A hand holding a black box was pressed against her blue twill blouse. In an instant, a buzzing crackle erupted against her kidneys, and her world turned into a fiery universe of pain and confusion.

Her body twitched out of control. She fell backward against the car, emitting a startled grunt as her legs, arms, head, and torso jerked in different directions. Her hat flew off, and she dropped her sunglasses and keys to the ground as an agony of vibrating, burning pain seized her. Her eyes rolled back in her head before something grabbed her under the left armpit. She felt no fear. Her short-circuited brain couldn't handle such a complicated emotion. Blurred images flicked by her open eyes, but she couldn't recognize any of them.

"I hit you with a stun gun. You shouldn't have nosed around my car."

Ansel gurgled a response. Her tongue didn't work. As her head lolled on a neck made of rubber, she was vaguely aware of the grass, and her boots dragging across ground. Other boots.

"We're going to your truck. Don't fight or scream. I'll zap you again. Gotta love these guns. Thirty bucks for a hundred thousand volts of power, and it only needs a nine-volt battery."

Suddenly they stopped, and Ansel's back sagged against hot metal. Her legs and arms had started tingling, but at least the pain had dissipated. She just couldn't move. Her body didn't seem connected to her brain. Then the person moved her again. Upward. Hot again. A loud, metallic bang focused her wandering gaze. A car door? Her drooping head was snapped around. A hand steadied her chin.

"Listen to me. Pay attention. Where is the two million dollars?"

"What?" Ansel managed to whisper, her eyes staring at an angry male face. It looked familiar. Tim? A bolt of instinctual fear struck her, something so primitive that even her discombobulated brain circuits couldn't jumble the message up. This was bad. The taste of blood filled her mouth. She'd bitten her lip or tongue but didn't remember doing it.

"I haven't got all day. Tell me, or I'll kill you right here." They were in her truck. She vaguely recognized the shiny, cleaned vinyl of the dash. "Don't know," Ansel said, louder.

"Lying whore." A second hand around her throat tightened. "The money is mine. I worked for it. I want it."

The feeling in Ansel's body returned in waves. She could move her hands a bit, but not her arms. She could also move her toes though her legs were numb. She didn't budge, afraid of letting Tim know that her limbs felt something. Cool air struck her face. The car idled and the air conditioning blasted full force. Why were they in her truck?

"Am-ber?" she muttered more coherently.

Tim's eyes widened. "Yeah, I'm talking about the amber. Where's the cash?"

Ansel shook her leaden head. "Don't know."

Tim hit her with his fist. Hard. She groaned as her head rocked against the seat, and pain enveloped her left cheek. She could do nothing. Her entire body tingled with returning feeling but wasn't under her control. He grabbed her arms and yanked her back up, shaking her like a mad dog with a helpless animal in its jaws.

"I don't give a damn about the fake amber. Do you hear me, you stupid half-breed?"

When Tim quit shaking her, Ansel slumped in his hands and pretended to be more incapacitated than she was. The throttling brought sensation flooding back into her body. He was stimulating her nervous system more than hurting her.

"Not fake," she insisted. "Real dinosaur."

Tim laughed. "Fooled you too, huh? It's just bird and reptile parts with rubber and resin molds. Your lover boy supervised my work, and then got it into the amber. Don't know how he did it, but he fooled that old Greek fag." His face became a twisted mask. "Nick stiffed me. I was supposed to get a million for helping. We'll just go somewhere else to discuss my money."

He let her go, put the truck into reverse, and backed out of the parking space. Ansel knew she couldn't let him leave with her. Her arms tingled, but felt weak. She couldn't get the zipper of her fanny pack open and retrieve the pistol. The gun was useless. She couldn't even open her door and get out. Her legs, however, had feeling.

Ansel tried lifting her left leg a bit so Tim wouldn't notice and found that she had some control over it. She had to make her move after Tim shifted the automatic transmission from Reverse into Drive. It was her only chance of drawing notice from party goers.

The truck reversed and faced a corridor between two rows of parked vehicles. The cattle fence exit onto the main ranch road was at the end of the row. Tim shifted the transmission into drive, and Ansel waited until he gave the truck gas. The Ford rolled forward.

Ansel lifted her left leg, guided it over the floor hump and on top of Tim's boot. She also dropped her body across the front seat toward him. Her surprise tactic caught him totally off guard, and his head whipped toward her.

"No," he screamed, but she stomped on his boot as hard as she could.

The truck accelerated like a bull out of a chute, gas feeding its V-6 engine in a rush of power. Tim tried to push her away with one hand while the other steered the suddenly speeding vehicle. Ansel used her weakened arms against him and managed to get one hand on the camera strap hanging around his neck, holding on to it so Tim couldn't shift her weight off the pedal.

The truck gunned down the parking row. Trying not to hit vehicles on either side, Tim opted to keep the truck going forward while pushing Ansel away from him. The end of the row loomed directly ahead. They had to turn or risk hitting the heavy pole fencing bordering the ranch road.

"Get off, bitch!" Tim's face contorted with killing rage. His right fist hit Ansel's head with repeated blows.

She screamed, pain exploding inside her skull. Her grip on the camera strap evaporated. Her foot came off the pedal. Ansel slumped on the seat, too dazed to move. Her great idea had failed.

The truck decelerated as Tim neared the turn toward the exit gate. A white sedan appeared at the end of the row, its turn signal indicating it was coming toward them. He was forced to go left or hit the car.

Tim took the turn like a racetrack driver on two churning wheels, sending grass clumps spinning into the air. He barely missed clipping the sedan's front end as the pickup sped onward, toward the barbed-wire fence separating the parking lot from the horse pasture.

Ansel pushed herself up into a sitting position just in time to see a wire fence rushing at them. Neither Tim nor she wore seatbelts. She used her weakened arms to brace herself as best she could against the dash. Anything to stop from being thrown into the windshield. Tim screamed as the Ford slammed into the barrier doing thirty miles an hour.

Headlights exploded. A tremendous screech of metal eclipsed all sound as anchored, three-inch diameter fence-posts jack-knifed over the grill and flew toward the windshield like missiles. Luckily, none of poles cracked the glass. A drag line of barbed wire scraped across the hood, then snapped, whip-tailing over the roof like a biting snake. Ansel closed her eyes just before her head slammed into the roof top when the truck bounced over a grass knoll. It landed in the horse pasture with a bone-jarring thud.

The piercing sound of a police siren wailed behind them. Ansel turned to look through the rear window. Incredulous, she watched as the white sedan gave chase through the shattered fencing. A single red siren lamp twirled on the roof above the driver's side. Dorbandt's unmarked police car. She'd never been so happy to see a cop in her life.

Ansel peered over at Tim. Once through the fence, he'd kept the truck speeding across the pasture. He looked in the rearview mirror, then shot a hateful glance at her. "Look what you've done. I'm going to fry you." His right hand reached for the stun gun, which bounced along the dash in front of the steering wheel.

Fear motivated Ansel despite her pounding head and dragging limbs. She pulled her arms toward her lap and fumbled with the fanny pack zipper. When it opened, she pawed at the Colt. Tim grabbed the stun gun with his right hand and hurriedly tried to get a proper grip on it while driving. Ansel leaned into the passenger door away from him and lugged the pistol out just as he turned to jab her with the device.

"You sick bastard," Ansel said, raising the gun toward Tim's head. She held her arms straight in front of her, both hands glued to the buffalo horn grip. It required all her strength to hold the pistol steady as she released the safety. "Drop it and stop the truck."

Tim flashed a feral smile. He tossed the stun gun to the floorboard, then screeched with a horrendous whoop of pleasure. He also punched the accelerator, and the truck zoomed past frightened and running horses. They headed straight for the ranch house.

"Yeah, show me what you've got, Missssss Phoenixxxx," he said, a mad glint in his eyes.

Ansel didn't risk looking at the speedometer, but it had to be up around sixty. Every fiber of her being concentrated on Tim and the gun in her hands. "Stop the truck."

The whoop of the siren faded, or seemed to. She couldn't tell. Everything was dead quiet, as if a bell jar had been dropped over the truck. She couldn't hear the truck's engine, the bouncing tires, or the air conditioning. Fear and adrenalin were shutting her auditory senses down. Everything focused only on her survival.

"You've got more guts than any of them," Tim said conversationally as the truck bolted across the field. "Nick cried while the strychnine goosed him. And Evelyn just screamed and screamed." He smiled. "It was great, but it was like shooting fish in a barrel. Not like you. You're different. A scrapper."

The truck raced on relentlessly. Time slowed. It seemed like hours had passed, though it was only seconds. Outside the front windshield, the ranch house drew closer. The twenty-three ounces of gun shook in her hands. Her arms felt like lead.

"I will kill you," Ansel said. She meant all four words with every fiber of her being.

Tim sneered and made a grab for the Colt with his right hand. Ansel adjusted her aim to avoid his hand and pulled the trigger. The sudden explosion of real sound deafened her as the bullet struck the taller man beneath the right armpit.

The hollow-point bullet entered his body with a whump. The shell casing ejected from the pistol chamber and struck the windshield in the blink of an eye while foul smoke curled from the gun barrel. An instant later Tim's lifeless body dropped over the right side of the steering wheel. Blood pumped from his open mouth. His dead, wide-open eyes locked directly upon her.

The truck made an abrupt right-hand turn as Tim's dead weight skewed the wheel. Ansel looked through the windshield. No, her mind screamed.

War Bonnet, her beloved horse, stood grazing in the truck's path. The old paint stallion lifted his head and looked toward her fearfully, ears flicking forward with startled alarm. The vehicle would never stop in time to avoid hitting him.

Ansel dropped the gun and lunged for control. She yanked the steering wheel harder right and the Ford jerked away from War Bonnet but lost traction. The vehicle left the ground, tilting dangerously to the right, then rolling over. She slammed into the passenger door. Tim's limp body, hurtled from behind the wheel, crushed against her as everything in her vision turned upside down.

The truck rolled again and again, momentum spinning it like a log. Ansel bounced inside the cab, slamming into everything: dash, seats, steering wheel. All the while, Tim's careening corpse pummeled her with flailing body parts: head, arms, legs. Everything became a topsy-turvy world of screeching and deafening sound. The roof crumpled inward. Doors buckled. Then the truck landed upside down with a jarring thump, rocking violently several times before finally settling.

A hazy darkness enveloped Ansel. She rested on her back, dazed and gasping. Her body was stretched parallel to the dash above her and humped over the caved-in roof liner in a tangled mass of limbs, hers and Tim's. Something incredibly cold crept along her shoulders and neck. She became aware of a tomb-like silence in the cab, disturbed only by creaking metal and the muted splashes and trickles of liquid. Water. A welter of unspeakable terror gripped her. Not again, her mind begged. The pond.

Feeling spent beyond all reserves of energy and her head throbbing, Ansel forced herself to move her right hand. She managed to touch the cold spot along her neck. She withdrew her fingers to stare at them. Not blood. Water. She whimpered and found the strength to turn her head and look out the windshield beside her. A murky brown soup filled her view, but she could see the black mud pushed up against the glass and the slimy, floating strands of green algae. A large black bass skittered by. The truck was underwater.

More water seeped into the cab every second. The closed windows had prevented a sudden onrush of water, but openings in the undercarriage or under the hood still remained. Not to mention the damaged roof, thought Ansel. Already the water beneath her had risen above her armpits. It would continue to rise until it covered her. She tried to move, but she couldn't. Had she hurt her back? Was she paralyzed?

Terror took root in her chest. A tremble started in her shoulder blades and spread through her body in a numbing embrace. Her thoughts flew to long-ago images of white ice and murky waters, but there was no one up there to snag her jacket with a fishing line and reel her to the surface. Trapped in this metal cubicle with a dead maniac, she would die by either suffocation or drowning.

A sudden thump on the windshield startled her. Ansel could barely move her head to gaze out into the airless world ready to devour her. Her teeth chattered. A ghost looked back. Large staring eyes and fine brown seaweed hair wavered in the mucky water. No. Not a ghost. A shoeless man, wearing a white shirt, tie, and dark pants.

Dorbandt knocked on the glass again, trying to get her full attention. Ansel couldn't respond with anything but a stare. He looked into the cab, took in her expressionless face and Tim's bloody body lying on top of her, then swam away.

Giving up, thought Ansel. I would, too. She had no idea how long it was before Dorbandt returned and tapped on the glass again. She had blacked out. Cold water splashed over her breasts now.

Dorbandt swam around to the passenger door by her head and reached for the handle. Before Ansel could try and yell for him not to touch the door and let the water in, he pulled on the outside lever. Nothing happened. The door wouldn't open. He looked surprised and disgusted. She was relieved, but wondered why it hadn't moved. Was it locked?

Ansel watched as Dorbandt swam frantically around the front of the truck and tried the driver's door. Again, nothing happened. He kept yanking at the door. Even braced his feet against the side of the cab, but it made no difference. He made a finger sign that he was going up for air and disappeared from Ansel's view.

Alone again, Ansel noticed that the water had risen over her chest, its color a vibrant red from Tim's blood. She was so cold. She lifted her chin above the water and closed her eyes, refusing to acknowledge that a dead man lay on her stomach. A man she'd killed, even if she'd done so in self defense.

Dorbandt rapped on the windshield. His cheeks bulged with a mouthful of air. He wanted her attention. He brandished something long and orange. Ansel's eyes widened with recognition. Nick's pick hammer. Somehow he'd gotten it out of the tool box on the flat bed.

The detective came very close to the glass, placing his left hand against it. He smiled encouragingly. Ansel placed her hand on the cold glass over his. She nodded her understanding.

Silly man, Ansel thought. He believed he could save her, but she knew she'd never get out again, no matter how good his intentions. She'd cheated this pond of her death once before. It wasn't going to happen again. Her only regret was that she couldn't die with her mother's Iniskim around her neck.

She turned away from Dorbandt and stared at the upsidedown seats and floorboards hanging above her. She began to sing in a whisper, chanting a Blackfoot prayer her mother had taught her.

Dorbandt struck the windshield twice with the pick, and the black pond waters raged inward. Ansel twitched as glass shards raked over her, and water thundered into the cab. A torrent of brackish filth swirled around her body, clawing at her life force with sharp, icy fingers she'd felt before. In only seconds, the truck's interior became the domain of primordial, underwater things.

Ansel lay in Tim Shanks' embrace, singing her death song until the stinking, bloody water poured into her mouth. Then Dorbandt pulled her into his arms.

Chapter 33

*"The outline of the stone is round,
having no end and no beginning:
like the power of the stone, it is endless."*

Chased-By-Bears, Santee-Yanktonai Sioux

Ansel's battered body hurt all over. A mild concussion, sprained wrist, bruised tail bone, spine and cheekbone, electric shock, and near drowning had taken its toll. She pulled tan jeans up over the shirttails of a white long-sleeved blouse, which was unbuttoned low enough to get attention. A horsehair belt and suede loafers were added last to the ensemble.

She peered into the dresser mirror. Some wounds nice clothes, makeup, and cleavage couldn't hide. Her face looked like something squashed on the floor of the Red Rose restroom. A glove-like wrist support covered her left hand. Her left cheek had a half-dollar-size blue bruise where Tim had hit her. Not to mention the large gauze patch taped to her right forehead, where something had hit her skull during the rollover into the pond.

The pond, Ansel thought, taking a deep breath to calm herself. She didn't remember too much. Just enough to feel anxious. She did remember Tim Shanks, and the emotional scars from killing him were going to last a long time.

And the truck. Totaled, her father had told her. Hauled out by a salvage wrecker, and impounded by the sheriff's department while she lay in the Big Toe hospital for three days. Her father had lent her a ranch pickup until she got an insurance settlement and bought another. The police had also taken her gun. Speaking of cops, she'd better get going.

Ansel found Dorbandt standing by the sofa. He stared out the rear window toward the two apiaries.

"Thanks for waiting."

Dorbandt turned his lean, muscled body. "How are you?"

"I feel like bruised fruit."

Dorbandt had interviewed her after she'd awakened in the emergency room. She'd been groggy, but had managed to tell him about the crystal paperweight in her jeans, which had been stripped off as triage techs stabilized her vital signs.

Later in her hospital room, Ansel had told him everything about Becker, Stouraitis, Milos, Nick, and Shanks. She also told him what she'd found in the bee hive. With her trailer key, he'd fetched the amber, coins, and tranquilizer dart she'd hidden in a ceiling panel over the kitchen sink. She hadn't seen him since he'd returned the key at the hospital.

"Well, you look a hell of a lot better than you did," he said, smiling sympathetically.

"Thanks to you. Pearl said you performed CPR on me. You saved my life."

Dorbandt rubbed nervously at his neck with one hand. "Don't thank me. Thank that orange hammer. I couldn't see a thing in that pond until the pick stood out against the bottom mud. Guess it was thrown from the flatbed when the truck tumbled."

Ansel sat down on the sofa. "It was a miracle. Have a seat."

Dorbandt sat next to her. "I stopped by to fill you in. We found a .22 caliber dart rifle and a Benjamin Sheridan air pistol in Shanks' apartment. We figure he used the pistol on Capos and Benchley. The rifle on you. The dart you gave me didn't have any prints, but it matches disposable darts we found in his bedroom drawer."

Ansel shivered. "Did you find the strychnine?"

"Yeah. Shanks stashed it in a cologne vial on his dresser."

"Where did he get it?"

Dorbandt shrugged. "I don't know, but he was damaged goods. We found pictures he'd taken of Capos and Benchley while they died. He'd blown them up into eight by tens. If we hadn't confiscated the roll of film in his camera and all the rolls in his car at the Capos crime scene, he'd probably have photos of Capos at the grave. Shanks also had thousands of pictures of dead pigs."

Ansel's eyes widened in horror. "Pigs?"

Dorbandt nodded. "Yeah, and I think Shanks' father is responsible for how his son turned out. William Shanks Sr. is an environmental scientist. Owns a couple hundred acres of empty land near Glendive and leases them out to a swine farrowing facility for pig composting. Pigs dying from natural and unnatural causes are trucked in by eighteen wheelers and shoveled with front-end loaders into twelve by thirty-four foot bins built on the property. Nasty business."

Ansel nodded. "I've heard about composting, but never seen it. Since they closed the state rendering plants, my father has to pay twelve dollars a carcass for the removal of any dead Angus in order to adhere to commercial livestock laws. Did Tim visit the pits?"

Dorbandt snorted. "Visited them and helped to work them during the summers. His father told me Tim had hung out there since he was eight years old. What kind of father takes a kid to a place like that? Nothing but afterbirths, piglets, and large breeder pigs that have to be split up the middle with a knife to compost. A lot of times the pigs and piglets aren't even dead. They bury them half alive in sawdust. No wonder Shanks took Capos out to Pitt's pig ranch to die. Probably seemed natural to him, and he knew the seminar was going to be there."

"That's horrible. I can't believe it. I liked Tim. I wrote a recommendation letter for his admission application to

Montana State just a few days ago, and he brought me some oranges from California."

Dorbandt noticed as Ansel's complexion went pasty. "Sorry. Sometimes I can't keep quiet."

"It's all right. What did you find out about the hoatzin?"

Dorbandt had already told her about finding the hoatzin feather on Nick's body and tracing Shanks' trip to South America via airplane tickets. Nick Capos had bought the tickets. Since Shanks' father had told Dorbandt that Tim was going to the Beastly Buffet with Lydia, he'd come looking for him.

"Shanks picked up the hoatzin parts for Capos. We found hoatzin feathers stuck into Tim's hatband. The Capos crime scene feather most likely came from it."

Ansel nodded. "Makes sense. Tim told me he faked the dinosaur inclusion with bird and reptile parts, rubber, and resin. I found Sil-Mold, Por-A-Kast, and Wonder Putty in Nick's work room. Those products are used to make fossil copies. The bee smoker was there, too."

"And we found the connection between Shanks and Capos at Bowie College," Dorbandt added. "Shanks helped Capos rent a small art department studio. According to a written request, Capos specifically wanted to use their hot glass glory hole oven and some propane tanks."

"A glory hole oven is used for glass blowing," Ansel replied. "Nick must have blown the hot amber around the fake inclusion and picked it up inside the resin the way ornamental paperweights are made. I bet he used Leslie's paper on caustobioliths and their breakdown by heat to figure out how to avoid destroying the amber's chemical structure so much that an expert would know he'd altered the resin. He knew that if the resin tested as genuine, the average fossil collector would never question the authenticity of the dinosaur inclusion."

Ansel thought of how she'd inadvertently missed Evelyn's funeral during her recuperation in the hospital. "Why did Tim kill Evelyn?"

"I'm guessing because of her relationship with Capos. Maybe even because she wore that necklace associated with Stouraitis' cult. Capos may have given it to her as a gift, but it made her a mark for Shanks' rage. Which brings us to Stouraitis. He'll get his coins back if he can prove he acquired them legally. Since the amber is a forgery, I can't charge him as guilty of anything except being gullible. Milos Elios is another story."

"You know his last name?"

"Through your sketch. Elios is a small-time bully with some aggravated assault arrests. He's into para-military politics and weapons. I need you to press charges against him for the two assaults, one here and the other at Becker's place."

"I'd be happy to," Ansel agreed, thinking of Milos peeing in her best black handbag.

"You'll have to go to court," he said carefully, "and testify."

"Good. I want Milos Elios out of circulation for a while."

"The papers are in my car. I'll go get them." He stood.

"Are you working undercover today? You're not wearing a suit."

When she'd first seen him, she'd hardly recognized him. He wore a red and blue plaid shirt, tight cinch jeans, and brown hiking shoes. And he looked very, very good.

"Today's my day off."

"Terrific. Come with me to the ranch for lunch. My parents are preparing a 'welcome home from the hospital' spread and inviting a few of my friends. It's the least I can do for the man who saved my life. You'll be my escort."

Uncertainty marred his face. "What about the papers on Elios?"

Ansel rose slowly from the couch. "We'll do those when you're on duty again. Come on, Dorbandt. Cut yourself some slack. We're having prime rib seasoned with onion and pepper, garlic new potatoes, corn on the cob, Caesar salad, and chocolate truffle torte."

Dorbandt's face brightened. "All right, but I can't stay too long."

"Let me grab my things, and I'll meet you outside."

"Hokay." Dorbandt opened the front door and disappeared into the sunshine.

Ansel moved her aching body over to the kitchen counter and grabbed a temporary leather purse. Pond water had ruined her fanny pack. A stack of four days' worth of mail fell off the counter onto the floor. She bent down with difficulty and retrieved the splayed envelopes and circulars. A nine-by-twelve-inch mailer had fallen right at her feet. It was from the law offices of Gabrielson and Zim. Preston Opel's attorneys.

Placing the other mail on the counter, Ansel opened the packet. Between her bandaged hand and her shaking limbs, it was slow going. She dreaded what might be waiting inside. Had Preston's sister filed a claim against the will bequeathing the Pangaea Society three hundred thousand dollars? Inside she found a thin stack of paper-clipped sheets. She read the top page.

Unbelievable. The law firm was notifying her that the memorial gift funds had been transferred to the Pangaea Society, Inc. banking account as per the terms of Preston Opel's last will and testament. All county, state and federal filings were completed. It was finally over. The POP Center could be built.

Ansel set down the package. She could hardly wait until the other members knew the good news. Suddenly an immense weight had been lifted off her shoulders. She quickly grabbed her father's truck keys. At the front door she punched a security code into a new alarm keypad before leaving. Dorbandt was leaning against the hood of his unmarked car, a flat brownish packet in his hands.

"Oh, no. We're not going to lunch in a cop car," Ansel said, marching toward an old black pickup. She tossed the keys to Dorbandt. "You drive. I'm injured, remember?" She held up her swaddled wrist.

"Like a pygmy rattler," Dorbandt mumbled, remembering McKenzie's statement about Phoenix bloodlines.

Ansel went to the borrowed Arrowhead truck and opened the passenger door. "What was that?"

"I wondered if this rattletrap will make it to the ranch?" Dorbandt replied, climbing behind the wheel. The inside smelled like sour hay and cigarette smoke.

Ansel donned her sunglasses. "What're you talking about? It's only got a hundred and fifty thousand miles on it. Where I come from, we don't ditch a truck unless it won't run long enough to cook brown salmon wrapped in foil on the engine block while we make the twenty-minute ride between towns."

"Terrific. Here, this is for you. The forensic techs are done with your car. This was clipped to a sun visor. Thought it might be important even if it is all muddied up."

Ansel took the wrinkled, discolored thing from his hands and realized that it was the postal envelope containing Rodgers' check. It felt stiff and thick. The inside looked almost black with dried scum. She'd assumed that she'd never see it again or that it would be totally ruined from a dowsing in the pond. She'd intended to request another payment from Folsom Publishing.

"It looks worthless," she said, disliking the very feel of the packet.

Dorbandt started the engine. It grated like a gas-powered tree clipper. "Do whatever you want with it."

Ansel forged ahead, pulling the gritty, smelly letter from the envelope and opening it slowly. The correspondence had been typewritten on good quality bond and was surprisingly legible. The check looked worse for wear, but she still might be able to deposit it even though it looked like it had been run through a washing machine, dyed black and eaten on by hungry mice.

Dear Ansel,

I have enclosed your second cash advance as per our contractual agreement. I look forward to working with you on future *Science Quest* projects. Your work is of outstanding quality and merit and is an asset to this publication. I have received several requests for your artwork by other distinguished contributors and would like to discuss available projects for you to consider taking on. Please contact me at your earliest convenience.

Best regards,
Phillip Rodgers
Editor, *Science Quest Magazine*

P.S. I have enclosed a small fossil which Dr. Andreasson believes is yours. The printer found it in your mailing box.

Her Iniskim. But how?

Ansel tossed the check and letter aside. At the bottom was a small, tissue-wrapped object. She scooped up the bundle and tore away the wrapping. The blue stone looked perfect. The star design on the fossil sea urchin's top shell was unbroken and unmarred.

This meant that the amulet had been inside the truck cab the entire time she and Tim had fought to the death. The charm had traveled across the country and returned to her just when she needed it to protect her from being shot or drowned.

"Everything all right?" Dorbandt scrutinized her carefully.

Only then did Ansel realize that he'd been sitting there watching her the whole time, the vehicle idling in the driveway. "I'm great. Let's get going."

Dorbandt shrugged, adjusted the air conditioning knobs, which had absolutely no effect on the air puffing weakly from the vents, and switched the manual gear into drive with a gut-wrenching squeal of transmission gears. Dorbandt shook his head.

"I'm telling you this pile of junk will never make it to the Arrowhead," he griped.

Ansel dug through her purse and noticed the envelope she'd addressed to Karen Capos. She'd tucked in the check from Gunther Osgoode and a brief note explaining that the money came from the last items sold from Nick's fossil collection. About fifty dollars. If Karen cashed it. The check had been saturated with urine. And it smelled. Somehow that made sending the money to Karen quite appropriate. She'd mail it on the way to the ranch.

"We'll get there. You worry too much, Dorbandt."

She pulled out her leather cord, threaded it through her Iniskim and hooked the clasp behind her neck. The stone fell into the crook of her throat. It felt wonderful. She grinned from ear to ear as the truck jolted down the drive.

"If we're going to lunch with your friends, I'd appreciate it if you'd call me Reid."

"Okay, I'll try, but I don't think of you as a Reid."

"Try real hard," Dorbandt said.

"Gee, I can't wait to introduce you to my friends." A sly grin covered her face.

Dorbandt glanced at her suspiciously. "I'm kind of curious about them myself."

"I have a really close friend that can't wait to meet you."

"Who's that?"

Ansel giggled. "Cute little devil. His name is Freddy Wing."

To receive a free catalog of other Poisoned Pen Press titles,
please contact us in one of the following ways:

Phone: 1-800-421-3976
Facsimile: 1-480-949-1707
Email: info@poisonedpenpress.com
Website: www.poisonedpenpress.com

Poisoned Pen Press
6962 E. First Ave. Ste 103
Scottsdale, AZ 85251